"A marvel, a fabulous trip . . . exciting, poignant, frightening and transcendent."
—Kate Wilhelm, Nebula and Hugo award–winning author

"Fascinating. . . . Antieau deftly weaves together stunning imagery and powerful concepts . . . very highly recommended."
—*House of Speculative Fiction*

"Erotic and profound."   —*Science Fiction Age*

"Bet on this book to be a winner."
—*Ann Arbor News*

"A powerful and impressive statement."
—*Kirkus Reviews*

"No doubt about it, *The Jigsaw Woman* belongs on your shelves."   —*Feminist Bookstore News*

"Kim Antieau writes beautifully."
—*Sentinel* (Waterville, Maine)

"Engaging and effective."   —*The Red Queen*

"Fabulous blending of the sensuous."
—*Waucoma Review*

"A writer with a certain amount of literary fearlessness."
—*New York Review of Science Fiction*

THE ROC FREQUENT READERS BOOK CLUB

BUY TWO ROC BOOKS AND GET ONE SF/FANTASY NOVEL FREE!

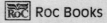

THE JIGSAW WOMAN

• ◆ • ◆ • ◆ • ◆ • ◆ • ◆ •

Kim Antieau

• ◆ • ◆ • ◆ • ◆ • ◆ • ◆ •

A ROC BOOK

ROC
Published by the Penguin Group
Penguin Books USA Inc., 375 Hudson Street,
New York, New York 10014, U.S.A.
Penguin Books Ltd, 27 Wrights Lane,
London W8 5TZ, England
Penguin Books Australia Ltd, Ringwood,
Victoria, Australia
Penguin Books Canada Ltd, 10 Alcorn Avenue,
Toronto, Ontario, Canada M4V 3B2
Penguin Books (N.Z.) Ltd, 182–190 Wairau Road,
Auckland 10, New Zealand

Penguin Books Ltd, Registered Offices:
Harmondsworth, Middlesex, England

First published by Roc, an imprint of Dutton Signet,
a division of Penguin Books USA Inc.
Previously published in a Roc trade paperback edition.

First Roc Mass Market Printing, June, 1997
10 9 8 7 6 5 4 3 2 1

 REGISTERED TRADEMARK—MARCA REGISTRADA

Printed in the United States of America

For my sisters,
Karen, Kathleen, Michelle, and Camille

Prologue

＊＊＊＊＊＊＊＊＊＊＊

Her story begins with me. I created her. I pieced together slabs of frozen flesh much in the way a seamstress stitches together pieces of cloth to make a magnificent gown. Sure, the seamstress might have had good material to work with, but if she had done a poor job of it, who would wear the gown?

He paid for it, Dr. Victor Beaufort, of course, by bribing the villagers for bodies. It is continually amazing to me what people will do for money. Especially in depressed or depressing times, eh? "I'll give you mounds of money, renovate your town, make life grand, just give me your gorgeous dead," he told them. Or words to that effect.

Look at me. A perfectly respectable scientist creating a woman. For money. Because *he* couldn't do it alone. I revel in that little tidbit.

He tried with Lilith. Poor little creature. But he is, at best, a good plastic surgeon. It required more, much more.

And I did it. She is the most exquisite creature God never had a hand in making. Blond, blue-eyed, breasts to die for, long-legged, tiny feet. She slept on the table, naked, while the color gradually returned to her shapely body. The sunlight lay across her hair like light across a treasure chest of jewels. As I watched her, I was overwhelmed with passion.

I leaned over her and kissed her blue lips. Her eyes fluttered open. She couldn't move because her arms and legs were strapped down. The crisscross scarring wreathed her neck and thighs prettily. I asked her if I could. She nodded. In a second I was on top of her, luxuriating in her flesh, her moans of passion. I'm certain she came a half-dozen times before I zipped up my lab trousers. It was glorious! I knew she was mine, then, and *he* could never have her! Certainly never the way I had had her . . .

. . . but enough of my fantasy life. I would not touch the poor wretched woman. Did not touch her. She needed to awaken on her own and discover all her bits and pieces—to find out what glue holds her together, or binds us all together. We are all jigsaw people, after all, aren't we? Scattered and shattered, perplexed and puzzled beyond hope or hopelessness. But she—she will surprise us all. She will remember what tore us apart. She will remember past knowing. I'm certain of it.

So I covered her up, careful not to brush a bit of her skin, and then I sat nearby, chewing my fingernails, and waited for her next coming.

PART 1

•••

DISMEMBERMENT

One

· · · · · · ·

N ear the beginning
I was born in a cross fire of hurricanes.
Or electrons, electrodes. Something. I don't remember much about the beginning. Fuzzies.
Flashes of stainless steel and white light. Was I
at a butcher's shop or a hospital? Moans. Some
scrawny guy sitting in a corner playing with
himself. The world spun. Fuzzed away. And I
shut my eyes.

"Cover those scars," someone said. "You know
I hate them ... reminds me ... you said they'd
be gone."

"You're the plastic surgeon." Another voice.
The scrawny guy?

"She's beautiful," first voice whispered.

I opened my eyes.

"Look at those eyes." First voice again.

Couldn't see his face. World out of focus. At least it didn't spin anymore.

"I've never seen such eyes," he said again, as if I weren't there staring up at him, trying to see him.

"Do you think she knows I'm here?" he asked.

"Ask her." Scrawny guy.

"Keelie?" he whispered.

Tea leaf? Did he call me tea leaf? What a peculiar world I had been born into.

I closed my eyes again.

A high-pitched laugh. Man. Turn it off. Opened my eyes. A disheveled head nodded at me. Grinned. Lopsided.

"Hi, little sister," she whispered. The whispered words turned into hisses. She had pretty black eyes. Pretty black eyes.

Her fingers touched my hand.

"He better not catch you in here," the scrawny guy said.

The head bobbed away. I tried to call to her, but no sound came out.

Scrawny guy looked down at me, smiling, stupid grin. I had seen that look a million times before. I blinked. Impossible. Hadn't I just been born? Born a grown woman. Missed all the stages in-between. The terrible twos. The titless teens. Wasn't I an all-grown-up w-o-m-a-n?

"I'm Dr. Griffin," the scrawny guy said. "How are you?"

I tried to say something again.

He smiled. "Don't worry. We had a little problem with your vocal cords. But they'll heal." He turned his head. "Lilith, I told you to leave. She doesn't want to see you. Get!" As if he were talking to a dog. Funny.

"Don't try to talk," he said as he turned back to me, the scowl becoming the lovesick smile. "There'll be time for that later."

Sleep again.

I opened my eyes to a white light, round, with distinct gray landscapes. The light was warm and cold at the same time and I wondered what it was until a bit more of the fog lifted its little cat feet and I knew I was looking at the moon.

I turned my head. I was no longer on the butcher/operating table. The mattress was soft beneath me, the covers warm. Slowly I sat up. The room spun for a moment, a sickening dance, which slowed after a moment. I had to stand. I had to walk to the window, which sloped up to become part of the ceiling. I had to look out at the moon. It was my first moon. My millionth moon?

I must have moaned. Cried. The lights came on. The moon disappeared. The scrawny man rose from his chair by the door, rubbing his eyes confusedly. Two cats, sitting side by side, each wearing the wrong body for its head, meowed and yawned from their perch on the canopy above my bed. No, not yawns. Smiles. Cheshire smiles. Cheshire cats. I stared at them. Were they speaking to me? Laughing? Snickering at me?

"Keelie," Griffin spoke, "you mustn't."

A pile on the floor near the window seat moved and I put my hand out, afraid the room was spinning again, but it was the bundle of hair and the crooked smile I had seen before. She rose to her full height, which wasn't tall. Her pretty black eyes on that distorted face. I couldn't quite tell what was wrong with her. Nothing seemed to be on right. Her back was slightly bent, her nose off center, her mouth, too. Most disconcerting. I didn't want to stare, but I didn't want to turn away either, because the sight of her nauseated me—and she knew it.

"Lilith," Griffin said, "get the hell out of here."

"Shut up," she said. Her voice was childlike. "She's not like you. She's like me. I know what she's going through. We're kindred creations. She'll let me stay." She smiled at me. Her pretty black eyes were perfect, filled with black tears.

I opened my mouth, pushed air, and no sound came out, except the slight hoarse sound of air escaping lungs.

"Don't try to talk yet," Griffin said. "You'll just damage yourself. Everything else is working perfectly."

He came toward me, arms outstretched. I backed up slightly, toward Lilith. She smiled and stuck out her tongue at the scrawny man. He looked hurt, and I felt bad. I wasn't certain why I backed away. But I felt slightly trapped. Why was I here? Who had brought me back? Brought me back from where?

All in good time, my sweet.

I looked up. The cats blinked at me.

"They're one of my earlier experiments," Griffin said, moving a bit closer to me. "They're an odd pair, don't you think? But they add to the atmosphere of Havenhurst."

I looked at him. Havenhurst?

"That's where you live, dear girl," Griffin said. "It's where we all live. Dr. Victor Lee Beaufort, proprietor."

"He's out of town," Lilith said. "He'll be upset he missed your awakening. Maybe we'll have to stage another for him, eh, Griff?"

"Don't you have anything to do, you little mess of flesh?" Dr. Griffin said.

I wished he would quit yelling at her.

I wished I could speak, too.

It's overrated. They can talk and look at them.

I glanced at the cats again. Each had one eye open, peering down at me.

"Come here, luv," Lilith said, tugging on my hand.

"Lilith, you cow. She's never walked before. She'll need weeks of therapy. You twit, if you keep pulling on her, she'll fall."

With Lilith's hand in mine, I walked slowly across the pale blue carpet. The feel of the piling against my bare feet felt new and wonderful, as if thousands of tiny fingers were tickling my soles. I smiled and followed the mass of hair to a huge walk-in closet. She let go of my hand, switched on the light, and then stood away from me.

The closet was filled with rows and rows of dresses, blouses, and sweaters. Most of them shimmering in the light, glittering, as if each were a party outfit. Each day a party?

"They were all custom-made for your particular body," she said.

My particular body. That sounded funny: my body. I suddenly realized I had no idea what I looked like. I knew I hadn't been brought into this world in the customary fashion. But I didn't know what fashion. And I didn't know what I looked like.

Lilith walked, limped, waddled, whatever she did, to the end of the closet where a gold beaded gown was hanging. She reached up for it and took it down, exposing a full-length mirror. And there I stood. Lilith on one side of me. The four-poster canopied bed behind me with the Cheshire cats sleeping on it. Dr. Griffin walking slowly toward me.

Me. I walked closer to the mirror.

A silk nightgown hugged my shapely body. My legs went up to the ceiling, which my breasts were pointing at. My long blond hair was just curly enough, and my eyes were bluer than blue.

I shook my head. My, my. Where did I come from?

A silk scarf covered my neck. I gently pulled it away. Small red and black scabs crisscrossed my neck.

"They'll go away," Dr. Griffin said. "I promise."

I looked at him in the mirror. So that was it. I was Bride of Frankenstein. Who was my Frankie?

I was suddenly exhausted. I wanted to feel the moon across my face again. Griffin looked as though he wanted to feel me up, so I swooned in Lilith's direction.

"She's still recovering," Griffin said.

The room was spinning. I wasn't certain who was holding what part of me.

"We better get her back to bed before she falls apart," Griffin said.

"You don't mean literally, do you?" Lilith asked.

The room went black, foggy with cat prints all over my face.

Two
•••••••

"**P**retend." A whisper. "Pretend this is the first time you've awakened."

I opened my eyes to semidarkness. Griffin's head moved away quickly, and *he* was bending over me.

"Hello," he said quietly. Light gleamed off his pearly whites as he smiled. His black hair was combed away from his chiseled features, his baby blues. He was prettier than . . . me.

Was this my Frankie?

He took my hand in his. A spark flashed between us.

"Oh my."

"I am Dr. Victor Beaufort," he said. "You are safe in my mansion. We have brought you back to life."

I tried to say thank you. Words still would not flow. I put my hand on my throat.

Griffin leaned over. "It's all right. You're healing. Don't try to talk."

Victor patted my hand and then gently stroked my cheek. I wanted to fall into that hand, into his arms. I didn't know who I was or how I had come into being but I knew I had looked for someone like Victor for an eternity, give or take a day or two.

"You have nothing to fear," he continued. The sound of his voice resonated deep inside of me. I was ready. What was the point of waiting? He was the bridegroom and I was the bride.

"I'm so glad you're awake. Do you feel all right?"

I smiled and nodded.

"What a beautiful smile!" Victor said. He glanced at Griffin. "She is all I hoped for, isn't she?"

"And more," Griffin said.

"You need to rest now," Victor said. "I didn't mean to wake you but I couldn't wait to see you any longer. I have to go out of town for a day or two, again. Dr. Griffin will be here to help with your convalescence."

I squeezed his hand. I didn't want him to go. He gently pulled away his hand and then kissed the top of my head.

"Like silk," he said to Griffin. "Soft as silk."

Then he was gone. The room seemed dark and empty.

Not for long.

I looked at my feet. The Cheshire cats were curled at the end of the bed, grinning at me.

Suddenly, the curtains opened. Sunlight flooded the room. A ball on the floor unfurled to become Lilith. She leaped onto the window seat and used the drapery cord as her swing.

"Me Tarzan! You Jane!" She pummeled her chest.

"You little idiot!" Griffin cried. "You'll scare her to death!"

I grabbed Griffin's arm as he jumped up. He looked at me, and I shook my head.

"See!" Lilith cried. "We're two of a kind. She understands."

"Victor could have seen you," Griffin said.

"I'm shaking?" she said and giggled. She was trembling, however, and her eyes glazed over slightly. Then she scurried out of the room like a giant black hamster. A moment later she returned balancing a breakfast tray.

I sat up, and she put the tray on my lap. A huge bowl of chicken noodle soup steamed my face.

"Dr. Beaufort can afford all sorts of fancy chefs, but he prefers me. Ain't I grand? This soup is sure to cure anything. Well, almost anything. I've tried it. And I'm just the same." She cackled.

"Ignore her," Griffin said. "She loves showing off."

"Showing off?" Lilith said. "Showing off what? Oh yes, I'm not really this grotesquely ugly thing you see. This is just a role. With the right makeup, you can become anyone. Even me." As she grinned, her nose seemed to ride her left cheekbone.

"Too many operations. Fools!" Griffin said quietly. Then halfheartedly he said, "Do shut up, Lilith. Now, Keelie, do you remember anything about your life before?"

I cocked an eyebrow. Like what? I knew I was on planet Earth. Morons were still running the country. A species went extinct every fourteen minutes. What else? Hmmm. I could not recall a single personal memory before waking up on the butcher's table.

I shook my head. No, I didn't remember anything of import.

"Essentially you died and I brought you back to life."

His chest—what little there was—puffed out slightly.

I put down the spoon and carefully pulled away the scarf from my neck. Then I hiked up my nightgown and exposed the crisscross scars on my thighs. I pointed to my neck and thighs. Griffin drooled.

I snapped my fingers and pointed to my scars.

"Oh. Sorry. Yes. Well. I think Victor would prefer to tell you what those scars are all about."

I tried to pull a pathetic face.

Charming. The cats yawned.

"Well." Griffin licked his lips.

"Come on, Griff," Lilith said, kicking the bed. "We're growing old waiting."

"All right! Obviously you're made from the parts of three women. I don't know anything about them, except they were all about thirty years old, and they died of natural causes."

Great. So I was pieced together from the body parts of three dead broads.

"I know something about the women," Lilith said. She dropped into a heap on the floor. Griff glared at her.

I pushed away my food and looked down at her. Well?

Now hear this.

"The first one, your head," Lilith said, "now she, my little darlin', was very refined. The second one was a woman of many many charms. And all I know about the third is that they called her Legs."

Legs?

"Lilith, that's enough."

Legs?

Did they call my head "the head" and my middle "torso"?

Legs?

Which part of me was Victor going to marry? Or bop. Cop. Roll around with.

The silent one, baby. The silent one.

I made them go away and I slept. A wonderful response to life. When I awakened I was still alone. I slowly got out of bed. The vertigo was apparently gone. Everything stayed in place. Including my body parts.

I went to the closet, slipped off my nightgown, and gently put on a loose-fitting dress—not an easy thing to find in this closet filled with Barbie doll dresses.

Then I left the room and began exploring my new home.

It was huge. The C-cats followed me through a few corridors, making smart-ass remarks, but apparently got bored and soon disappeared. Huge sweeping staircases. Vaulted ceilings. Stone fireplaces. French windows looked upon sloping manicured grounds where marble fawns gamboled. Danced. Trolloped. Stood in stone.

This was my home?

I felt all warm and gooey just thinking about it. I stood on the tips of my toes and twirled around.

Life, as it were, was grand.

After a while, as I wandered, I became weak and weary. I was lost. Frankenstein's lair was too much for me. I felt stupid. Not able to find my way back. Lost in some labyrinth of my mind. My making? Maybe one of my pieces was from someone who had the brain capacity of a gnat. Or the sense of direction of a beached whale. I beached myself on a window seat along a dark hallway. Below, the sun was spinning the green grass to gold. I closed my eyes and slept.

I awakened to Mozart.

I rubbed my eyes and sat up in the graying light. My fingers tickled my itchy neck. I liked the music. Perhaps Mozart could help me find my way back to my room.

I tiptoed down the hall. The music circled me, fondled my bare feet, prodded me toward the wavering light of a fireplace inside a room which was empty except for a piano, a bench, and a man. His hands moved furiously up and down the keys, his black hair shaking.

Victor.

Victor who told me he had gone away for a few days and now was hiding out here playing piano.

Suddenly, his fingers ceased their dancing, midair, stopping the solo abruptly, like a musical guillotine. My heart raced. Here was my Frankie and I was alone with him. What would I do? What would I say?

Nothing, you little idiot, you're mute.

Victor turned. Momentarily his eyes looked mad, crazy with something I knew nothing about. Then he truly saw me and his face re-laxed. He smiled and held his hand out to me.

"How nice to see you again," he said.

I went to him. His fingers touched mine. I wanted to drop into his arms. Yes, this was the reason for my existence. Him. It had to be.

I smiled. Pieced together to be a love machine for this gorgeous hunk of man.

I was ready.

"Sit with me," he said, gently pulling me down next to him. "Are you becoming comfortable in this brave new world of ours?"

I nodded. He squeezed my hand.

Enough foreplay. Let's just do it.

"I'm sorry I told you I was going away on business," he said. "It's just that I had to get away. It's best that you don't tell anyone you saw me. And you shouldn't come back up here. It might be dangerous."

He stopped.

Well? There must be more to the story.

He patted my hand.

"I won't bore you with my problems," he said. "At least not yet!" He laughed. "We have a lifetime to learn about each other." He stood. "I think you should get back now, before you're missed. You must be tired."

He squeezed my fingers again and then re-leased them.

I was getting the brush-off.

I glanced down at myself. This guy had picked out the parts, and now he didn't want to use them? I didn't understand.

Victor took me down the hall and a few staircases until I knew where I was. His lips brushed my cheek, and then he was gone, and I was alone in the dimly lit corridor leading to my room.

Not alone. The Cheshire cats rubbed my legs and smiled up at me. *There's three of you, remember?*

Three

••••••••

I awakened to Griff and Lilith bending over me.

"It's the scars," Griff said, moving out of my line of vision. Why was it I kept waking up with people bending over me, as if I were on an operating table, or a dissecting slab?

Lilith grinned her crooked grin before bobbing away.

I sat up and croaked. Still no voice.

I grabbed Griffin's notebook and pencil from his pocket.

"What about my scars?" I wrote.

"They aren't going away, luv. Ol' Griff here bet his life your scars would go away." She giggled. "As you can and cannot see, mine never went away. It pains our dear Victor greatly."

"Is that why he doesn't want me?" I scribbled.

"What?" Griffin asked. "What nonsense. Of

course he does. How could he not? He's just taking things slowly. Giving you a chance to get used to things."

"Like your new legs. You wanna dance?" Lilith.

"Shut up." Griffin patted the air above my hand. Why didn't he ever touch me? "In fact," he continued, "Dr. Beaufort has invited a Mr. Hart to stay with us." His lips curled slightly. "He's going to help with your adjustment period."

"What about you and Lilith?" I wrote.

Lilith hopped on the bed and laid her head against my shoulder. "We'll be here, dear, never fear."

"Hart's a psychologist," Griffin said. "Of sorts."

"Of sorts," Lilith mimicked. "He was disbarred. Or dismembered. Something. But ask him anything—he knows the gossip on and the whereabouts of anyone in these parts—"

"Shut up, shut up, shut up!" Griff cried. "I wish we'd severed your vocal cords!"

Severed vocal cords? I touched my throat.

"No, no," Griff said, his anger gone. "Your cords are fine. Just healing. You'll be able to speak any minute. Any day."

"I don't need a psychologist," I wrote. "Sounds like I need a good makeup job." I pulled the perennial scarf from my neck. The crisscrossing was hard with scabs.

"This Hart guy is kind of cute," Lilith whispered. "You'll like him."

"I could just strangle you sometimes," Griff said, his face bright with anger.

"Quit fighting," I wrote.

Lilith stuck out her tongue at him.

"Hart is downstairs now if you'd like to have breakfast with him," Griff said. He bowed and then quickly left the room.

"Griff's jealous," Lilith said, pulling on my hand to get me out of bed. "In a snit. He argued with Victor about Hart. Thought he was doing just fine on his own." We went to the closet. Lilith picked out a red sequined dress for me. "Here. This is suitable for breaky, isn't it?"

By the time Lilith was finished with me, I looked and felt like the whore of Babylon, whoever she was. The red dress was very low cut and very tight. I liked it.

Lilith took me to the kitchen where Griff sat with a man I took to be Hart. He was slightly built—not as scrawny as Griff—but small, with thinning red hair, blue eyes. Nice-looking. Pleasant smile, except for the drool. Both Griff's and Hart's mouths had dropped open when they saw me.

Lilith giggled and they snapped out of it.

"Lilith, Dr. Beaufort would have a fit if he

saw her in an evening dress at breakfast!"
Griffin.

"Well, that's why Mr. Hart is here. To lead
her astray. Or away."

Hart stood and held a chair out for me. I sat.
Lilith brought croissants, jam, and orange juice
to the table. Then she scrambled up onto the
counter and chewed on a roll. I winked at her;
she grinned bread crumbs. I sliced open a crois-
sant and spread butter and strawberry jam
across it. Pieces of it flaked onto my sequins as
I bit into it.

"She's really sewn together?" Hart finally
said.

I pulled the scarf away and my dress up.

"Home sewn," Lilith said, "home grown."

Hart blinked several times. "How are you ad-
justing?" he asked when I dropped my dress
down again. His eyes were all gooey, just like
Griff's. How come Victor didn't look at me
like that?

I took Griff's notebook from his pocket again
and asked Hart, "What are you doing here?"

"Didn't they tell you? I'm here to help you,"
he said. "You must have questions. Or memories. So much is new and strange for you. You
are the first of your kind, as far as we know."

I glanced at Lilith and then I wrote, "Do you
know who I was?"

"You mean the three women?" He swallowed

hard. He was probably imagining the women being sliced into pieces. Ick. How had they done that?

I nodded. "Yes. Who were they?"

"I—I don't know." He looked at his hands. All three of them looked at their hands. What incompetent liars they were.

After breakfast, Hart took me to a dark room with a fireplace and lots of books. I sat in an easy chair. Griff and Lilith listened outside the door. I could hear them jostling each other for the best position. I couldn't talk, yet Hart insisted on asking questions. I smiled politely and stroked the cats who sat on my lap.

He just wants your body like all the rest.

Not all. Victor doesn't. He's different.

Different all right. All night.

"Do you have any memories of your past lives?" Hart asked.

I shook my head.

"Feelings of affection for people you can't quite recall?"

I squinted. Frowned. No.

"Do you remember having children?"

I stared at him. Children?

"Just a thought," he said. "Any dreams?"

Nope.

"Crying spells?"

No sir.

"Any feelings of euphoria?"

Huh?

"Mania?"

I'm a maniac?

"Any feelings at all?"

I reached for his pen and scribbled on top of his pad, "I feel horny all of the time."

I gave back his pen, and he stared at his paper. I laughed, or rather, some semblance of a laugh came from my butchered throat.

His embarrassment gave way to a smile.

"Finally," he said, "a genuine expression of something, albeit laughter at my expense! You probably don't know it, but you walk around like someone out of *Night of the Living Dead*. Granted, you're better looking and better dressed."

I croaked again. I liked this guy. He reached for my hand, and I let him have it. "I'll be staying here for a while. If I can help in any way, let me know. We can meet once a day and talk if you like that idea."

Sure.

Okay.

We ate in the dining room that night, Lilith, Griff, Hart, and myself. Lilith darted in and out. Up and down. She had dessert on the chandelier. Griff and Hart eyed one another warily across the table. I supposed I was the prize. I tired early. Still no stamina. My stitches itched.

Lilith put me to bed. I dreamed I was making love to Mozart. Not to the music. To Mozart the man. Fast little guy but very pleasurable. Before he left me to go direct some opera, I whispered in his ear, "I want to come back as a dancer."

The following day, Hart and I went outside. Griff walked behind us, scampering forward every time I tipped a bit. The air was fragrant with spring. Wild poppies seemed to grow everywhere. I danced around the fountain where a marble fairy bent to take a sip.

"You're feeling better today?" Hart asked.

Wet dreams will do that.

I tried a whisper. It worked. Kind of. "I dreamed I wanted to be a dancer."

I twirled.

"Dr. Beaufort will be very upset if she gets hurt!" Griff called to us.

I smiled and waved at him. I was certain Victor was watching us from some part of the house. Hart and I sat at the edge of the fountain.

"Do you know what you want to do when you're stronger?" Hart asked.

I took the proffered pen and paper.

"Live here. Be with Victor. Isn't that why I was brought here? Created?"

"What about *you?* What do you want? Do you really want to be stuck in that mausoleum called a house being the bride of Frankenstein?"

"Sounds good to me," I wrote. I grinned.

"But you're just finding out about yourself. You're a unique being—you shouldn't shut yourself up here."

"You're a unique being, too, and you're here. Griff, Lilith. We're all a kind of family, right?"

He stared at me. Then he said quietly, "Just be careful. All is not what it seems."

No shit, Sherlock.

We walked back to the house to one of the huge raised porches looking out across the grounds. Piled on a stone table were several thick books. Hart motioned me to a stone chair, and I sat, carefully draping my dress about the chair. Griff sat at the table with us.

I looked from one man to the other.

"Victor thought it would be good for you to read up on things," Hart said, opening one of the books. "Like social science, history."

"Dr. Beaufort is particularly keen on history," Griff said.

"Probably because he doesn't remember his own history," Hart mumbled.

"Hart!" Griff snapped. "You needn't tell her that."

I cocked my head. I wondered if I looked like a dog. Should I wag my tail, too?

"It's not a secret," Hart said. He looked at me. "Victor remembers very little of his own childhood, so he's interested in other people's stories."

"Not so," Griff said. "He's interested in *history*."

"What do you think hissss-story is anyway?" Lilith was there suddenly, her grin in her belly. I blinked. She straightened somewhat. She was like an oil painting out in the rain. She quickly pushed the books away and sat on the table. "If you want some her-story instead of hissss-story, talk to me. I've got the scoop."

Griff angrily reached for her. I put my arm up to stop him.

Lilith smiled sweetly. "It's lunch. I'll let you guess whose soup I poisoned today." Then she was gone again, floating away like a tumbleweed blown by the wind.

Hart stood and held his arm out for me.

I asked on paper, "Victor wants me to read these books?"

"He suggested you might be interested," Hart said.

"Then I'll lunch out here and take a look," I wrote.

Griff smiled. "I'll have your lunch brought out."

Kiss ass, the cats meowed.

I looked through the books until the sun went down. The Cheshires sat on either side of me, quiet after I told them several times to get out of my mind. *You're already out of your mind*, they countered before shutting up. History was as boring as I remembered: compilations of dates of inventions and wars, a countdown of casualties, dead and dying. Why would Victor want me to know such things? It all made me weary and depressed.

I took dinner in my room, shooing them all away from me. When I crawled under my sheets, I found more books. I heard Lilith giggle somewhere in the house as I pulled the books out from underneath the covers. One book was red and had a one-word title: *Inanna*.

I pushed the books out of the bed. I was not in the mood. I switched off the light and closed my eyes. All I wanted was to get laid by the man of my dreams—or get laid by the man who thought I was the woman of his dreams.

Some hours later, I awakened with a headache. I sat up and pushed the covers off of me. A red spotlight shined down on a heap in the middle of my floor.

"Lilith?" I whispered.

Shhhhh.

The heap rose. Lilith smiled, almost symmetrical.

"Inanna," she said, her hands moving theatrically in the air, "was the Queen of heaven and Earth. She was the source of the life blood of the Earth." Lilith swayed, and the colored scarfs draped around her neck moved with her. I clapped once. Oh goodie, a show! "One day, Inanna heard the beat of the underworld." Lilith pounded the floor with her hands. Da-da. Da-da. Da-da. "She had everything, all of heaven and Earth, and a loving husband." Hand to her ear, Lilith said, "But she heeded the call to the underworld to visit Eriskegal, the great Earth Goddess who was more than her older sister.

"At the gates of the underworld, Inanna was stripped of all that she had and all that she was. Seven gates—the number seven represented wholeness to the Sumerians." The drumbeat continued. Lilith slowly drew off one scarf and let it float to the floor, and then another and another, until all the scarfs lay at her feet, their colors bleeding shades of red under the spot. "As Inanna went through each gate, she had to surrender her roles as queen, holy priestess, lover. She was stripped of all until she knelt naked, shivering, bent and broken, before the Queen of the underworld, who gnashed her nasty teeth and roared at Inanna with fetid breath." Lilith roared until the bed shook. "Then Eriskegal struck Inanna. How dare Inanna suppose she could visit the underworld on a lark! Eriskegal killed her and hung her corpse on a hook on the wall behind her throne."

Lilith twirled around. "Three days passed.

Her servant went to all the gods for help but everyone said Inanna deserved what she got. They were men, after all." She hissed. "Finally one sent some tiny creatures made from the stuff under his fingernails down to the underworld. They found Eriskegal groaning, 'Oh my insides! Oh my outsides!' So they groaned with her. They showed compassion. This caught the Goddess's attention. She said, 'I will grant your wish.' They asked for Inanna's corpse, and she gave it to them. They sprinkled dust on the Inanna corpse, which came alive; Inanna returned to the great above going through the seven gates again. She was alive, but she wasn't the same. No one ever is once they've been to the underworld. Demons clung to her. In a rage, she went all over the countryside looking for her husband, who had not searched for her while she was gone and who had actually taken over her empire! He would pay for this betrayal with his own trip to the underworld. You see, none can leave the underworld unless they find someone to take their place.

"Inanna's husband ran from her in fear. His sister begged Inanna for compassion. She relented and said he only had to live in the underworld for six months of the year. His sister, who had volunteered, would live there the other half of the year.

"All were satisfied with this outcome, though

to tell the truth Inanna was never quite the same. That is all I know."

Lilith bowed. I clapped.

She whirled around once. The spot went out. She jumped on my bed. The bed bounced up and down.

"Did you like?" she asked, stroking my hand.

I clapped again.

"It's a very old Sumerian myth," Lilith said. "One of the oldest. I used to teach mythology. Can you believe it? More fun than that crap Hart gave you. More meaningful. I've been to the underworld, don't you know, but I can't find my way out." She laughed, slurping as she did so. She leaned closer. "I knew so much before I was like this. I knew but this happened anyway, this heap of trash you see."

"Lilith!" I croaked.

Shhhh.

"There was a time before this world," she whispered, "when people lived in peace for thousands of years. Really! It's documented and all that, but they never told us about it, did they? Present day is like in Inanna's story when the Goddess went underground. She was only gone for a short while, but her husband took over: that's this world now. But she was only gone three days—it should end any time now, the time of the husband, the father—and then the world will be as it was, peaceful, only different."

I stared at her in the semidarkness. She laughed. "It'll make sense one day. You are Queen of heaven and Earth here, aren't you? The question is: are you on your way into hell or out of it?" She whispered again, "If you're on your way out, will you take me, too?"

I nodded.

The bed bounced again and Lilith scurried away. I lay down again, my headache gone, and went to sleep.

I slept through most of the next day. Before dinner, Lilith awakened me to say Victor was back, and he'd be dining with me.

I put on a beautiful white lace gown that pressed against every attractive curve and crevice I had. A scarf glittering with diamonds covered my throat. I looked so good I wanted to make love to myself.

Victor and Hart, dressed in tuxedos, stood when I entered the dining room. Victor took my hand and kissed it. Then he helped me with my seat.

"How have you been?" Victor asked.

I nodded.

"Good! Hart tells me you're progressing rapidly. Coming out of the fog? I'm so glad."

I smiled.

He poured wine for himself and Hart.

"None for you, dear. It's too soon. You look lovely. Doesn't she, Hart?"

"Beautiful," he answered.

I smiled. My face was killing me from all this smiling. Maybe I should try my voice. But what if I made that awful croaking noise? So I smiled.

Victor talked. I listened. Sometimes Hart talked. Victor took my hand midmeal and kissed it. He looked so happy. Content.

After dinner, Hart stayed inside while Victor and I went outside. We stared up at the almost full moon. Or was it full and a cloud was covering it? I leaned against Victor. I knew he wanted me. I knew it would happen soon. I turned and looked up at him. He gazed at the stars.

"What are you thinking?" I asked, my voice clear and melodious. Yes! I was in working order now.

He looked down at me. "Nothing," he answered.

I could finally talk and that was all he had to say?

"I have to go now," he said suddenly. "Don't stay out too late. I'll see you in a few days. Good night."

Then he was gone. I stared toward the house. What had happened? What had gone wrong?

You can talk now, baby. A walking, talking living doll. We told you he wanted silence.

* * *

I awakened screaming. Silently. I opened my eyes. One of the Cheshire cats sat on my chest, its eyes shining fluorescent green in the darkness.

All is not what it seems.

"Shut up," I said.

I pushed the cat away and got out of bed. Something was howling in the distance. In the house? Another Lilith performance? I went to the window. The full moon was dropping into dawn. It looked different—just a few hours ago it hadn't seemed quite full. Now?

I rubbed my eyes and turned away. I had dreamed of table saws.

I lay down again and pulled the covers up around me. I felt alone and frightened. Hart would be glad. I was feeling something and I knew what it was. Loneliness. Fear. Something else tickled the edges of my feeble little brain. But I didn't want to see it, feel it, remember it. I just wanted to fall asleep again.

I closed my eyes.

Something growled.

Inside my room.

"Chessy?" I whispered.

Not us, baby. Hasta la vista.

I opened my eyes. Across the room two eyes glowed. Blue. Baby blue.

"Victor?"

At last?

"It is I," he whispered. "Close your eyes."

Okay. I'll play. I held my arms out to him, eyes closed, and he came to me. I put my arms around him; he felt like a huge hairy beast. He growled again, "Keep your eyes closed."

"It's dark, Victor. I can't see anything."

"Regardless—"

"Okay, okay!" I couldn't see but I could feel. And he felt very different.

Was this Victor's deep dark secret—the reason he fled to some dark corner of the castle for days at a time? He turned into a beast before having sex?

I threw open the covers.

"Honey," I said. "I don't care. We'll just change the tale. Bride of Frankenstein to Beauty and the Beast."

I lifted my nightgown over my head, put my arms around him, and pressed his hairy body against mine. Every hair on my bod stood on end as he pushed into me. Together, we howled our ecstasy to Momma Moon.

Four
·······

I awakened just before dawn, and I was alone.
I fell back to sleep and wouldn't let anyone
get me up before lunch.

When I finally awakened and went down to
eat, I saw Victor outside, his hands behind his
back, surveying all that was his.

I came up and hugged him from behind.
"Hiya, sexy."

He whirled around to face me.

"Keelie?" He held my arms and stepped away
from my embrace.

I moved forward and kissed his cheek, so
smooth. I couldn't pull on his hair like I had the
night before.

"Keelie?" He was frowning.

"Victor?"

"We must take this slow, Keelie," he said,
smiling uncomfortably. "You are still recovering."

"After last night you want to take it slow?"
I asked.

He put his arm around me and turned so we were looking out at the lawn and the gardens beyond.

"Especially after last night," he said. "I wanted you so much."

And you had me. You can have me again.

"I think we should wait until we're married," he said.

I looked up at him. Was he from another planet?

"What are you talking about?"

"I want it to be right," he said. "I've made mistakes before. I want our life to be perfect."

He wants you to be perfect.

"I'm very confused," I said.

"I know," he said, squeezing me close to him. "That's one of the reasons I want to wait."

I pulled away from him.

"I think I'll take a walk," I said. I hurried down the stone path to the flower gardens. They wove themselves into a maze that ended with a bench. I sat on it.

Last night had been an orgiastic joy. All my fear and loathing had left me. I had felt only the pleasure of my body with the beast's body. No thought. Just pleasure. And now?

Hart stepped out of the maze.

"Hello, there," he said. "May I?" He indicated the space next to me.

I shrugged. "I won't be much company."

"What's wrong?"

I leaned against the bench. Birds twittered in the trees and bushes beyond.

"I'm so confused," I said.

"Life is confusing," he said.

"Could we skip the platitudes?" I said. "I've got a real problem."

He smiled. "I'm sorry. What is it?"

"It's Victor. If I tell you something you have to promise not to tell anyone."

"Of course. I am your therapist."

"Last night, Victor finally came to me. It was wonderful. Now today he doesn't want to talk about it. Doesn't want anything to do with me."

"It was a passionate encounter?" he asked.

"Yes! Aren't you listening? We tripped the light fandango. We rolled around in the hay. We humped, bumped, and jumped each other until dawn."

Hart scratched his chin. "I hate to speak ill of my benefactor, but Victor is a strange bird. I think he has a virgin-whore thing."

"What?"

"You know, he wants to be married to the virgin, but he wants to fuck the whore."

"And I'm supposed to be both?"

"It's the way many men are."

"I don't believe that's the way all men are!"

Hart shook his head. "You are so different from what I expected. I think you're different from what Victor expected."

"What do you mean?"

He looked quickly around and moved closer to me and said in a whispered voice, "Your top part, your head, her name was Anna. She was very quiet, cultured, refined. The perfect little aristocratic wife. You aren't like that."

"What are you saying? I'm an unrefined, uncultured, loud-mouthed whore?"

"You're getting upset."

I stood. "You're damn right, I'm upset. I just had the most pleasurable night of my life and I can't share it with the man I love. Granted, I haven't had many nights, so maybe this is no big deal. But look at the facts. I was created by Victor and Griffin, to be with Victor. Right? I thought I knew what my purpose in life was. Now I don't." I sat down again

Hart leaned over and kissed my cheek. His lips were so soft.

"You need to find yourself," he said.

"Find myself? My guess is the rest of me is decomposing in some nearby graveyard," I said. "I'll never find myself."

Hart kissed me again. This time my lips. My stomach issued forth butterflies, and then Hart was gone.

And Victor was there.

"Where'd you come from?" I asked, standing up, startled, wondering if he had seen or heard everything or anything.

"There's another entrance," Victor said. "Sit. I'm sorry. I didn't mean to frighten you. I actually came to apologize."

"Oh?" He sat next to me. I tried to conjure up the memory of my late self Anna, the refined one.

"I've been far away, I know," he said. "Much has been troubling me and I'm sorry it's affecting you. I would very much like to marry you. Would that be acceptable?"

I felt myself going all gooey-eyed.

"Victor," I said, breathless. He opened his hand. A silver ring with a huge diamond on it lay in his palm.

"Go ahead, take it."

I picked it up and put it on my left second finger. A perfect fit.

I put my arms around him, and this time he kissed me, softly, gently, slowly, for a long glorious time. Things suddenly seemed hunky dory once again.

"We'll have a party tomorrow," he said when we finally parted. "To celebrate. I'll invite everyone. You don't have to do a thing. I'll take care of it."

"So soon? I'm not certain I have the energy."

He hugged me. "Of course you do."

I scratched my scars. He frowned slightly.

"Don't worry," he said. "We won't tell them how you came into being. And they won't ask. You're so gorgeous you'll knock them out. Lilith can help you dress."

I smiled. "It'll be fun."

He kissed me quickly and stood. "We'll have a great life together. I'll see you later, sweetheart."

And then he was gone, too. I stared down at the huge rock on my finger. I hadn't even had a chance to tell him my answer.

Victor wasn't there for dinner, so the four of us ate and giggled and threw food at one another. Later, alone in bed in the darkness, the beast came. I opened the covers for him, let him tickle every part of my body with his hair, made love with him all over the room. When we finally finished and he lay against me, breathing heavily, I whispered, "Of course, I will marry you."

I fell to sleep. When I awakened, it was morning and he was gone.

Lilith was there.

"Today is the day," Lilith cried, throwing the covers off my naked bod.

"Lordy, you are a spectacular view," she said.

"Lilith," I sighed and pulled the covers back on.

Griff knocked and then stepped into the room.

"I told him it was too soon," Griff said. "Said you weren't 100 percent yet, but he insisted. I don't know why. He wants to announce your engagement."

"Look at that rock," Lilith said. She blew on the diamond and then rubbed my hand and the ring on the covers. "Wow."

"You won't get married for a while, of course," Griff said. "Not until—"

"My scars go away. I know. I know. What are we going to do about them?"

"I'll think of something. Eat. Get dressed. The party starts in a couple of hours."

"What!"

"You've slept through another day, sugar," Lilith said. "Now get out, Griff. We have to figure out what we'll wear."

Griff grunted, but he left. Lilith brought a tray of food and then sat on the bed and watched me eat.

"It's a costume party," Lilith said.

"Victor didn't tell me."

"He decided late last night. Won't it be fun? I've got the perfect costume for you."

"How can he get anyone to attend on such short notice?"

Lilith laughed. "Victor is a powerful man. They'll come. Now let me tell you about your costume. Victor is going as Frankenstein's crea-

ture. So what do you think you should go as?"
She clapped her hands gleefully.

"Bride of Frankenstein?"

"Yes! Remember that movie, *Bride of Frankenstein*? Elsa Lanchester with her big hair, wavy,
a foot off her head, with a white streak through
it like a lightning bolt. That's how we'll dress
you!"

"And we won't have to make up the scars.
I've already got them."

"Exactly."

"Who will you go as, Lilith?"

"Igor, of course."

Lilith and I had such fun dressing. It took the
longest time to get my pretty blond hair to wave
and stand on end. The streak of white was rela-
tively easy after that. Griffith tried to come in
several times, but we wouldn't let him. Lilith
found a long hospital gown for my dress. She
blackened my eyes and told me that Elsa Lanchester didn't talk, she only hissed.

Eight o'clock drew near, and I could hardly
wait to make my grand entrance into the ballroom on the third floor.

"What are you going to do for your costume?" I asked Lilith just before we left my
bedroom.

"I am my costume," she said.

She leaned her head out the door and made

a signal for the all clear. Giggling, she took me to the back stairs of the ballroom. I felt like a schoolgirl on her first date, whatever that felt like. I wondered what Hart and Griff were going to wear. As we neared the closed back door, I could hear voices, music.

"Ready?" Lilith asked.

"Let's go."

Lilith threw open the door. I lurched into the ballroom, my arms raised, hissing. The music stopped. Someone screamed. I looked around.

Everyone was dressed in tuxedos and evening gowns. Victor stood in the middle of the room, drink in hand, staring at me openmouthed.

People started laughing. Victor's face clouded with anger. I backed up. I was aghast. Agog. Ashamed. Embarrassed. Pissed off.

Victor started toward me. I turned and ran, not tripping over Lilith. She was long gone, the halls echoing with her laughter. I ran and ran. Stumbled. Ran. I didn't know where I was going. Maybe to kill Lilith. Maybe to hide in my room. If I had a better sense of humor, it would be funny. Maybe in a year or two. I should have known Victor wouldn't have had a costume party. Wasn't his style. Of course, it wasn't really his style to be a hairy beast making love to his woman, but he'd done that two nights in a row.

I stopped to catch my breath. I heard no footsteps. No one followed. As I glanced around, I realized I was in the part of the house where I had found Victor a few days ago alone playing the piano. I wandered toward the piano room. Inside, it was almost dark. I hadn't noticed a door on the other side of the room before. I went to it and turned the knob. The door opened easily, and I went inside.

Small white candles illuminated the room; candle wax dripped onto the parquet floors. A life-size picture of a woman rested against the cold fireplace. She was dressed in riding clothes, one boot forward, a riding crop in one hand, her hat in the other. She was laughing; the wind blew through her auburn hair. She was stunningly beautiful. All around the room were photographs of this woman; with her, in most of them, was a younger, smiling Victor.

"This was his first wife."

I turned around. Lilith leaned in the doorway. She wiped the drool from her mouth and smiled.

"How could you be so cruel?" I asked her. "We've been friends! You tricked me. You knew it wasn't a costume ball."

She shrugged, kind of. "Yes. But we had so much fun, didn't we?"

She waddled over to the picture and put her hand on the woman's face.

"They were very much in love," Lilith said. "The perfect couple."

"What happened to her?" I asked.

She smiled. "Why, honey, can't you see? You're looking at her. She is me and I is her."

I stared. "No," I said, shaking my head. "I don't see it."

This couldn't be true. Couldn't be.

Lilith sighed.

"Don't feel bad, I can't see the resemblance either."

"She's really you?" I asked. I had to sit down. How could they be the same person? "What happened?"

"Victor is a plastic surgeon, you know. We were happily married, and I thought he loved me the way I was. But one day he mentioned that one of my breasts was larger than the other and offered to correct that. I loved him, so I let him. Then he noticed some wrinkles. Then I began noticing imperfections. Not all of Victor's surgeries were successful. And then there were the surgeries to fix the surgeries. Those were the worst. Poor Victor. He was going to make me over into this raving beauty."

"But you already were a raving beauty," I said, looking at the life-size photograph. "I assume this is a before picture?"

"Yes." She sighed a sob. "And this body is an after."

"My god, Lilith. When were you divorced?"

She laughed. "We were never divorced. He is still my husband. I suppose when I heard about your engagement the ghost of my former self raised her beautiful head and tried to defend my place in this house. Unfortunately I took it out on the wrong person."

"Why this room? This shrine?"

Lilith shrugged. "Maybe it's a guilty conscience. Maybe it's because he only wants what he can't have. I don't really know."

"He asked me to marry him. How was that going to happen if you two were already married?"

"He probably just would have been married to both of us," she said. "He doesn't really care. I learned that far too late."

"Why do you stay?"

"Where would I go? Besides, luv, I own half of all this. And he'd probably kill me if I tried to leave. He's like that." She came to me and took my hand. "There's more."

I followed her through another door, down several stairs, down another hall. I was stunned. I paid little attention to where we were going until everything seemed too bright and shiny, stainless steel everywhere. My birthplace.

"This is where I was brought back to life," I said. "I remember."

"Do you remember anything else?" Lilith asked.

I shook my head. She shuffled to one end of the room where she opened a steel door, leading into what looked like some kind of cooler. She motioned me to her. I felt sick. I wanted to go to sleep.

Inside was cold. I immediately began shaking. I was terrified, my body trembling, shaking, as if from some memory I didn't have. Mist eddied about us, moving in and around three glass coffins. Two were filled.

"Look," Lilith insisted.

I peered at the naked women. They each had crisscross scars in the same places I did. Neither had legs as long as mine, and their breasts were smaller.

"This one is Legs. The head part is Legs, I mean. You got her legs."

She was pretty. Her hair black, wispy, and curly. She did not smile in her sleep. Her death.

"This one is Belle."

Her hair was bright red, dyed red, I imagined. Her face appeared older than mine or Legs'. She looked tired.

"Are they dead?" I whispered.

Lilith nodded. "They were the first. If you don't count me. He always wanted you. The other two were experiments, to make certain you lived. They didn't live very long."

"Why are they still here?"

Lilith moved slowly out of the cooler. I followed.

"Our dear Victor likes dead things, things that don't talk back. He finds that stimulating, if you know what I mean."

She slammed the door behind me as I stepped out. I shook my head.

"No, I don't know what you mean!"

"Those ladies in there sexually stimulate him more than you ever will."

"This is crazy. Are you telling me Victor only fucks corpses? Then who has been coming into my bedroom for the past couple of nights?"

Lilith sat in a chair near the operating table.

"It wasn't Victor. He was with me. I'm almost dead, I don't talk much, and the orifices are still in the right places."

"You're disgusting! I knew Victor had problems, but I thought it was because he turned into a werewolf during the full moon."

Lilith howled. "What? Honey, someone's been yankin' your chain. I don't know who you had in your bed, but it wasn't Victor."

I started shaking again. What the fuck was going on? What the fuck was going on? The room started spinning.

"If this is all true," I said, grabbing on to the operating table for balance, "why on Earth would he go to all the trouble of creating me? Of bringing me back to life?"

"You're asking the wrong person. Maybe it has to do with power. He's like a god to you. He gave you life, and he can take it away." She snapped her fingers. "Just like that."

"Lilith!" Griff was there. I ran to him, the dizziness gone. I clung to him. None of it made sense. I had felt sorry for Lilith. Now I was terrified of her.

"What have you told her?" Griff asked.

"Everything."

"Griff," I said, shaking him. "Tell me none of it is true. Tell me she's lying."

"He'll kill you, Lilith," Griff said.

"He already has," she said quietly.

Hart ran into the room, out of breath. Was Victor right behind him? I couldn't see him. Couldn't face him. Ever. Again.

"I've been looking everywhere for you," Hart said. "What's going on here? Keelie, are you all right?"

I laughed, and the sound was just like the croak I'd made before I'd gotten my voice. "You told me to find myself. I have. Just look in that cooler, freezer, whatever it is."

Hart went to the door and jerked it open. I started shaking again. Hart went inside and then came out again.

"What's going on?" Hart asked.

"Lilith! Keelie!" Victor's voice came down the corridor.

I ran to Hart.

"Take me away from here, before he sees me."

"He'll come after you," Griff said.

"I don't care. I've got to go."

Hart took my hand, and we began running.

"I'm sorry, Keelie." Lilith.

You'll never do it. Yes, you will. Yes, you will.

We slammed through the back door, slid down a corridor, and finally into the misty night. I was sobbing, sobbing. Hart patted his pockets and pulled out keys.

We ran to the garage. Hart's car was parked outside. "Get in."

I opened the door and jumped in. He started the car, and we roared away. I put my head in my hands and did not look back.

Five

•••••••

I awakened to a neon sign blinking on and off behind a closed curtain. Still night. I rubbed away the dream. A lost child crying for her mother. Sobbing for an eternity.

"Keelie?" Hart whispered.

"I'm all right," I said. "Where are we?"

"Away from Victor. I hid the car and used a fake name to register."

I scratched my head. My hair was stiff: still the Bride of Frankenstein.

I stood and stretched. Hart came to me in the darkness.

"You're safe," Hart said. "I promise to take care of you."

"No promises or reassurances, please. I've had enough of that. I'm taking a shower."

I stripped in the tiny bathroom, and then stood under the stream of hot water until it washed away the mousse, hair spray, and dark circles under my eyes.

When I felt clean, I turned off the water, stepped out, and stared at myself in the mirror.

Those fucking scars. I pulled away the scabs. When would the scars go away? Griff had promised.

Victor had promised.

I cradled my breasts.

Everyone had made promises. And now here I was. On the run from the man I loved.

Had loved?

Did love?

I shook my head. Stupid child. I knew nothing about the world. But I would learn. I wrapped a towel around myself and then opened the door.

"I want you to take me to their families."

"Whose?" Hart asked.

"Anna's. Belle's. Legs'. My families."

"I can't," Hart said.

"I'll do it with or without you. You can make it easier on me because you know everyone in town; you can find things out quicker."

He nodded. Sighed. Gave in. "Okay."

In the morning, I made Hart go out and buy me a pair of jeans and a couple of shirts, plus a scarf and sunglasses to disguise my face. Once I was dressed, Hart drove us into the country. To Anna's house.

Maples lined the road. Buds beginning to

break out into leaves, like arthritic fingers loosening into green. Colors flashed through my exhausted brain. Leaves? Shadow and light. I closed my eyes. I fingered the upholstery of Hart's wreck of a car. I was here. In his car. Now. I heard him sigh. With desire? Disgust? Longing? The car smelled moldy. Repulsive. I knew that smell from somewhere else. I hated it.

I hated everything.

And everyone.

Except Anna. I opened my eyes. The flashes of color returned.

Anna. Something about color.

"Victor might figure out where you're going," Hart said.

"I don't care."

"He can be dangerous."

The road curved. The trees thinned, opening into yellowing fields dotted with tree stumps.

"Victor doesn't scare me," I said. "Man, this country suddenly got ugly."

Hart slowed the car and turned down a paved drive. My heart skipped into my throat. Did this seem familiar? Or not. A large white house. Out of place on the treeless acres.

We stopped, and I got out. A lone birch leaned away from the house. From the tree, a crow caw-cawed. Or was it a vulture?

I went up the steps and used the knocker.

The door squeaked open. A tiny girl child with golden hair and blue eyes looked up at me.

I adjusted my sunglasses and scarf, hoping the child's huge blue eyes wouldn't see her mother's face.

Her mother's face?

This was Anna's child.

She reached a hand up to me. I clasped her wee fingers in mine and let her lead me into the house. We walked silently across the tile floor to the open back door. Once outside, we stood on the top step. The backyard was beautifully enclosed by young trees, shrubs, and flowers of every color. Irises. Tulips. Poppies. Lilacs. Johnny-jump-ups. Violets. Sweet peas. Mums. Must have been a warm winter. Everything seemed to be blooming at once.

I knew all this stuff? Sweet pea? What the hell was sweet pea?

I looked down at the little girl. She was. I crouched next to her.

"Where's your daddy, sweet pea?" I asked.

The girl pointed. Under a small weeping willow were chairs and a table. A man sat reading to a small boy on his lap.

Sweet pea let go of my hand and ran to her father. He looked up at me.

"Daddy! She called me sweet pea. Just Like Mommie."

The man set the boy down and stood. The three of them held hands and looked at me.

I went down the steps toward them. I heard Hart behind me.

"May I help you?" the man asked.

"I'm sorry to barge in on you and your family," Keelie said. "I—I was a friend of Anna's."

The children shook themselves loose from Dad and ran to me. Each one wrapped themselves around a leg.

I laughed and put a hand on each of the children.

These were my children. Out of my womb.

No. Scratch that. Anna's womb was not attached to my body.

"The man with me is Mr. Hart," I said. I liked the feel of the children crushed up against me. Anna's husband frowned. I moved forward slowly, letting the children hang on tightly to Legs.

"Keelie? I don't remember a Keelie."

"It was long ago. If this is a bad time, I can leave."

His eyes were tired. He glanced at my human leggings.

"Apparently the kids like you. Why don't you sit down."

As soon as I was in the chair, the boy and girl climbed onto my lap. Hart pulled out a chair opposite Anna's husband. Jim. His name was Jim.

"You know Anna died?" Anna's husband Jim asked.

I nodded. "That's why I came."

"This is her garden. She died last summer, but her garden still bloomed. Even the annuals."

"Mommie's here," Sweet pea said, looking at me.

Her father smiled. "Yes, she is."

Sweet pea was a bit brighter than her *père*.

The boy smiled at me. Then he laid his head against my chest.

"Your heart's different," he whispered.

"Shhh," Sweet pea said.

"What do you remember about Anna?" the husband Jim asked.

"Not a lot," I said. "She liked color?"

"There were so many things she wanted to do," he said. "We wanted to do." He smiled. "She should have been sitting on the banks of the Seine, painting. Not stuck in this wasteland."

"Wasteland of our own making."

"That's what she used to say," the husband said.

I was feeling a little closed in. Even in the great outdoors. Or would it be the lesser than great outdoors since humans had added and detracted quite a bit? How had I known his name? The child's nickname.

"May I ask how she died?"

Jim hesitated and then said, "She drowned. Accidentally. There was a party at my parents'. She was swimming in the pool alone. Nothing could be done to save her."

The children clung to me tightly, taking my breath away. I kissed the tops of their heads.

I felt dizzy.

"Perhaps this wasn't such a good idea," I said. Slowly my children—they *were* my children—climbed down and went to their father. He would take care of them. Anna's death had snapped him into life.

"I'm sorry I bothered you," I said.

They watched me. Something about their eyes.

Suddenly I couldn't breathe. My lungs were burning. Hands pulling me down. Everything was spinning. I didn't want the kids to see me. Not like this.

Someone was pulling me. I couldn't see anything. Except water blue. Turquoise. Couldn't breathe.

Everything went black. Star-studded black.

I dreamed I was dancing and drowning. Victor pulled me toward the drain. He pulled and pulled until my legs snapped off one by one.

Six

•••••

I awakened in another motel. On the way to Belle's place. I felt sick and disgusted. Dirty. Drowning in myself.

Victor, Lilith, and Griff seemed so far away. I missed the Chessies. I missed my ignorance. I missed my matching body parts.

I missed my entire body.

The door opened, a shaft of light fell across my body, and then the door closed.

"No sign of Victor," Hart said. "Maybe he's given up."

I sat up. I didn't really care. "Quit worrying about him. He can't hurt me."

Hart sat on his bed and looked around the room. I followed his gaze. It was a pigsty. Half-eaten boxes of Chinese food. Cold pizza. Empty cans of beer and pop. The room smelled, too.

Smelled of me. I certainly was no longer that ravishingly beautiful woman Hart had known only a few days ago.

Only days? Life was so sudden.

I rubbed my face. When I closed my eyes, I saw too much: the kids, the pool. Or I felt hands pulling me down.

"You have a beautiful face," Victor had said to Anna, emphasizing the word "face." He put his hand on her chin, my chin. "A lovely face. May I have it?"

Anna laughed. The sound echoed in my empty brain. "You've already bought and paid for my dead body, Victor. Remember?" She laughed. She didn't realize. I didn't see. Him. Watching.

But I feel him, pulling me. Pulling me. Anna's lungs fill with water and we drown.

"I'm beginning to remember things from my past lives," I said.

"How is that possible?"

"I don't know!" I snapped. I wanted to scream. "I want to see where Belle lived."

"You're not going to like it. She didn't have much. She left home early. Her parents were alcoholics." He started picking up the clutter.

"Are you going to take me or not?"

"You used to be nice."

"I used to be fucking stupid," I said.

*   *   *

71

We walked up the wooden steps to the apartment above the bar. Before we got to the door, I heard a man yelling and a child screaming.

I pounded on the door.

The man was big, had spent a lot of time on his biceps and hair. His face was distorted with anger. Until he saw me. Then he relaxed. I had cleaned up nice.

"What can I do for you, babe?"

"I'm not your babe," I said, pushing past him into the apartment.

"Hey, what's going on?" he said.

My stomach hurt. I recognized this cesspool. Darkness. Smell of beer. Moldy carpet. Smoke from the bar below. Bruises.

My body ached with bruises.

"I'm a friend of Belle's."

"That bitch is dead."

A child whimpered.

I touched my throat. Blood poured through my fingers and stained the carpet. I gasped and pulled my fingers away.

I looked at them. Nothing. No blood.

"Pearl?" I called. The child was Pearl, and she had come from this womb of mine.

A whimper.

I hurried into another room. A girl, about five or six, lay curled in a corner, naked, blood on her face and thighs.

"It's okay, Pearl," I said. "It's okay."

"What are you doing?" the man called.

I heard the click of a gun. The room fell silent. Hart had him in hand. I got some clothes from the dresser. Pearl cried quietly as I helped her dress. Then I picked her up. She wrapped her legs around me and buried her face in my hair. We went into the other room.

Hart held a gun on the man. I wondered where he had gotten that little toy. I didn't ask.

The man smiled. "You can have the kid for a couple hundred. She's not mine. That stupid bitch left her."

Without thinking about anything, including the poor child I held, I reached out and hit the man, hard, across the face.

"Is that what Victor Beaufort paid you to slit Belle's throat? A couple hundred bucks."

He wanted to hit me back. He had hit me many times, when all of me was Belle. She had been unable to leave him or this place until she saw the way he looked at Pearl. Then she had packed our bags. She had almost been out the door when he fell on her. Pearl had screamed and run away. I hope she hadn't seen him slice Belle's throat.

"He didn't have to pay me. I would have done that job for free. Just for the pleasure."

I wanted to kill him. I wanted him to grovel and scream. I wanted to cut off his penis. Gouge out his eyes. That was his way, I supposed. The way of this world.

Instead I held the child against me and left the apartment. I could feel Pearl's breath and tears on my neck. I opened the car door and tried to lay her in the backseat, but she wouldn't let go of me. I got in the front with her. A moment later, Hart got in and drove us away from Victor's town. Pearl laid her head against my breasts and fell to sleep.

Near dusk, we came to a small house set just outside a forest that blackened into the distance. The house was white with green shutters. The lawn was cluttered with a wagon, a broken fountain, and rosebushes. A gray-haired woman was bent over one of the bushes, stroking it. A teenaged boy stood next to her. When we turned into the gravel drive, they both looked up. This had been Legs' home.

Hart stopped the car and leaned on the steering wheel, exhausted into silence. Pearl now slept in the backseat. I got out and strode to the couple. The woman held out her hands. I grasped them.

"I want to come back as a dancer," I whispered.

The woman embraced me.

"She always thought Victor could do it," the woman said. Grace. That was her name. "And now you're here. Proof of it. What are you called?"

"They named me Keelie."

"It's pretty."

I shrugged. "I was named by a murderer and his minion, so I really don't attach much significance to it. You're Grace. And this is Ben, your son."

Ben looked totally perplexed. Grace patted his arm.

"Let's all go inside," Grace said. "I'll make us something to eat." Grace, the doctor.

"First I need help with a little girl."

We went to the car and opened the door. I slid my arms under the sleeping child and lifted her up. She sucked her thumb and slept on.

"Hart? Are you coming?"

The house was warm, cheerful, and comfortable. Hart dropped onto a couch and fell to sleep. Ben went into the kitchen, and I heard him getting out dishes. I followed Grace through the house and into her examining room. Pearl whimpered awake.

"Pearl, sweetheart, this is Grace. She's just going to check you over and make certain you're all right. She won't hurt you."

Pearl's brown eyes filled with tears, but she nodded. I stayed close while Grace listened, touched, and checked.

When she was finished, Grace took me aside.

"It looks like he tried penetration but stopped.
I'm sure once she starts talking, we'll find out
what he actually did. Or close to it."

"Mommie," Pearl whispered.

"I'm right here, sugar." I held her in my arms.
"You need to sleep now. We'll all be here when
you wake up." I carried the child into what had
been Legs' room. We tucked Pearl in, kissed her
good night, and left a night-light on. We stood
in the door watching while she went to sleep.

"I don't remember Legs' real name," I said.
"I remember other things, but not her name."

"Her name was Lee," Grace said.

"What happened to her?"

"One day she took too many pills, and I
couldn't save her. She'd fallen to pieces years
before and no matter how she tried, she couldn't
put herself back together again."

We closed the door partway and then went
into Grace's room.

"And you're certain she killed herself?"

Grace nodded. "She'd tried many times." She
opened her top dresser drawer and pulled out
a folded sheet of paper and handed it to me.

I opened it. "Dear Grace Under Pressure: I
just cannot bear it. Please forgive. I hope I come
back as a dancer."

"She loved you so much," I whispered,
remembering.

"I know. But it wasn't enough."

Grace fed us soup, salad, bread, pasta, fruit. I ate until the color returned to Hart's face. I ate until I pulled off the scarf and showed my scars. Ben watched me with interest, without lechery. He did his momma proud. Gradually, happily, I slipped into bed next to Pearl. I curled myself around her, becoming the mother-of-pearl that sheltered her from all.

Victor didn't follow us. Pearl began to speak and play. She told us where the man had put his thing. She took her anger out on dolls. I tried to explain to Pearl that I wasn't exactly her mother, but she didn't care. She called Grace Guppie, Lee's nickname for Grace Under Pressure. Grace took Pearl to a therapist in a nearby town. I spent time with Grace, too, in the garden out back. Hart stood on the edges of it all, watching, arms folded.

Grace tsked over a wilted sage bush. I squatted next to her. The moist spring earth smelled of birth, of rich humus.

"Why did Lee kill herself?" I asked.

Grace squinted at me. "Lee had a terrible childhood. She didn't like talking about it." She shrugged. Beyond her, Hart looked as though he wanted to bolt forward, jealous of our physical closeness. What was wrong with him?

"She didn't remember a lot actually," Grace

said, "but she felt a great deal. She felt atrocities in her body."

"What?"

Grace stood and stretched and then walked to a rosemary bush, three feet high; the air around it was fragrant with the plant's oil. "Lee thought she'd been a Jewish holocaust victim in another life and someone from the Burning Times—she'd dream of it. Those memories kept her from connecting in this place and time, I think."

"The burning times?"

She put her arm across my shoulders and squeezed. "The Burning Times were a terrible part of history that people don't talk about, but we remember it in our bodies—a kind of racial memory or something. Some say as many as nine million women were tortured and killed over a three-hundred-year period. That time period was a branding iron on our souls, a final, indelible reminder that we—women could be hunted down and killed again for any reason."

"And Lee remembered all that?"

"On some level," Grace said. "She couldn't get beyond the horror of that lifetime or this one." Grace kissed my cheek and then let me go. "There is more to remember. Life can be wonderful." She dug around the rosemary bush.

"Why were the women killed back then?" I asked.

"The church believed women were evil." She

sat back on her heels. "The pope put out a handbook on how evil we were and how to torture and kill us." Grace shuddered. "If you want to read something evil, read it. *The Malleus Maleficarum.* They killed women because the women remembered a time when god wasn't in heaven and women and nature were sacred. They killed them because they were old, single, widowed, rich, ugly, beautiful, poor. Because they braided or unbraided their hair. Because they were healers. Because they spoke out. Because they performed abortions and got abortions."

"What do you mean they remembered a different time?"

"A time when things were peaceful."

I thought of Lilith's tale of Inanna: the Goddess was merely in the underworld for a spell; all would be bliss and peacefulness once she returned. "I don't believe there was such a time," I said. The few memories I had told me only horror existed. "I'm not sure I even believe life can be wonderful here and now."

Grace looked at me. "Lee didn't believe it either."

And look what happened to her.

Days went by. I began to feel more and more anxious. About to explode. Almost remembering. Visions crowded my periphery. Phantom hands reached out and grabbed me. I heard screaming. Doors squeaking. My body ached.

And all was not as it seemed with Hart. He watched me and grew morose.

"Do you miss the old mansion?" I asked one night. "Is that why you pout all the time?"

His face shot with red. "No, I don't miss it. And I'm not pouting. I'm just wondering. What are we doing? Are we staying here? And how do I fit in? We never talk."

"I don't have time to talk," I said. "I'm trying to get myself together, so to speak."

"Well, it doesn't seem to be working."

He came and sat next to me. He took my hand and put it in his. "I want you. I want you so much it makes me ill."

I took my hand away and pointed toward the bathroom. "If you need to puke, that's the way. If you need to whack off, that's the way, too."

"You can't treat me like this." He started to get up, but I grabbed his arm and pulled him down.

"I'm sorry," I said. "I appreciate everything you've done. I just feel lost, bombarded, split apart."

He stared at me. He didn't care. He had saved me from the monster Victor, and he wanted payment. I rubbed my eyes and moved away from him. I was tired. Soon I would have to deal with him. But not yet. Not yet. I wanted some peace. From the memories that were pushing forward through time threatening to shatter me.

I think I knew what was going to happen next. It seemed inevitable.

Grace, Ben, and Pearl went to the circus. I wanted to go. To hear music, laughter. Eat cotton candy. To scream with delight.

But phantom limbs kept after me. Pulling me apart.

I slid a knife under my pillow and went to sleep. The moon was full. Her influence felt. An excuse men used to go berserk.

The beast came into my room. It wasn't Victor. Never had been. Had only masqueraded as him to get what he wanted: his cock in my body. This time I didn't open the covers and invite him in.

"What's wrong, Hart? Your testosterone in overdrive?"

"You wanted it before," he said.

"I don't want it now."

I won't give you the gory details. Suffice to say when he held me down, I had a million flashbacks of a million men doing the same to my bodies and others like them forever, through all of history it seemed. This time, this time, in spite of his brutal strength, because of the million times before I grasped the knife and plunged it into his back before his dick pushed its way to its final destination. He screamed and shivered into nothing. I regretted hurting him with his own weapon.

Wish

There

Could

Have

Been

Another

Way.

Another day.

Things slowed. Grace came in. Couldn't hear. Except maybe Hart still breathing. Could barely see. My mouth and breasts were speckled with blood where he had bitten me. I pulled off bloody clothes. Put on clean.

I couldn't get them to stop.

The flashbacks.

I was burning, twisting, dying on the rope.

"Pearl, love. Stay with Grace. She'll take care of you."

I stumbled into darkness, howling, tripping into the forest, crashing past trees, deeper and deeper into darkness until the howling stopped and my head cracked open.

Seven

◆◆◆◆◆◆◆◆

The room was dark gold with flame. Crackling wood. Warmth. Deep into the womb.
She spoon-fed me broth.

"Fattening me up before you push me into the oven, eh?" I murmured. "My name isn't Gretel, you know."

"What is your name?"

I wanted to see her face, lost in the raven blackness beyond the gold.

"Rumpelstiltskin," I answered. "And I've stomped myself all the way to hell."

The gold embraced me. Swept me into dreams.

First they pulled my legs and arms apart. Off of my body. Then they roasted me. Not with jokes. The flames licked my feet and I screamed myself awake.

I opened my eyes.

The gold had shifted to silvery morning light. Plants hung from the rafters. A huge black bird watched me. Glass eyes became human. Black hair streaking to gray. Raven.

"Hello, Rumpelstiltskin," she said.

"Call me Rumpled for short." My head throbbed. I touched the spot where it hurt. Clotted with blood.

The flashbacks had receded to the back of my consciousness. For now.

"Where am I?"

"In the forest."

"I thought I had died."

"Didn't you?"

"Time and time again."

Raven moved away from me, to the fireplace where she stirred the contents of a cauldron which hung over the fire. A sweet aroma filled the cottage.

I sat up. "Are you a good witch or a bad witch?"

Raven turned from the bubbling brew. "What do you think?"

"I think you answer my questions with questions."

She dropped a scoop of the concoction into a bowl and brought it to me. It was heavy with vegetables and rich with herbs.

"This will make you feel better."

Then my body hurt. I felt dizzy. My head pounded.

"You're remembering," she whispered.

"I'm hurting."

The phantom hands reached for me. Pushed various things into my orifices. Threw me into closets. Opened me up. Burned me at the stake. Kept me from. Kept me from.

I put my head in my hands. "How can I come from such suffering and survive? They didn't. We didn't. These pieces that are me. Two were murdered, I think. The other killed herself because she was killed when she was a child. There's too much fucking pain."

I lay down again and pulled the covers over my head.

I dreamed I was dancing.

Raven was outside feeding the birds. A veritable Cinderella: birds eating out of her hand. No. Not Cinderella. No cinched waist for her. Her cape lay across her shoulders, pouches hung from the belt that loosely held her purple dress in place. She turned and waved to me.

I got out of bed and wandered about until I found the toilet outside, enclosed by wood. A moon-shaped mirror hung on the door. I stared at myself. My gold hair was growing out, changing to dark brown or black. My hair was dyed? That bastard had even dyed my hair? I ran back into the house, found a sharp knife, and went outside again. There I stood in camisole and underpants in the great outdoors under an old redwood hacking away my goldilocks. As my hair fell to the ground, birds flew down and carried away the curls. Soon black hair tinged with gold stood out all over my head. Nice against my scars. Wouldn't those fucking scars ever go away?

"Guess I'll find out if blondes really do have more fun."

I watched Raven from afar, standing with my back against a redwood, my toes digging beneath the leaves and needles. Sometimes I climbed an oak. Other times I hugged a birch and watched.

Watched. As she talked to the animals. Earth. Air. Fire. Water. Clouds. She whistled and birds encircled her. She raised her arms to the sky and colors enfolded her.

When I wasn't watching her, she fed me. Tucked me in at night as we both waited for the nightly onslaught of memories.

One morning I awakened digging at my sides. "It's my eggs. I've figured it out, Raven. These fucking eggs are repositories of all the atrocities my ancestors have endured."

Raven just nodded. She was dressed in meadow green.

"There's so much pain," I said, drawing the blankets up around my knees.

"Is that all?"

"That's all I remember."

Raven went to the counter, reached into several jars, and then dropped the contents of her hand into a bowl. She scattered a bit from her hands onto the tile floor before turning back to me.

"You need to eat," she said, handing me a bowl filled with birdseed and pieces of fruit.

"I need to remember." I popped a raspberry into my mouth.

Raven nodded again. Was her hair gray or black? Raven black? I smiled. The raven changed colors, too.

"I need to know these women who are me, so that I can be whole. I need to remember. But I don't know how to do it."

"Yes, you do. You said it yourself. It's in your eggs. Your body. Your body remembers. And you can remember it."

"You make it sound so easy."

"It won't be. It'll be strange. Each place and time will be different. You'll be different."

"What are you talking about?"

"I'm talking about you finding your place in the world. Your home."

"And how do I do that?"

Raven placed her hand between my breasts, where my heart pounded beneath.

"There's no place like home," she whispered.

"Should I close my eyes, click my heels together three times, and say, 'There's no place like home, there's no place like home'?"

Raven laughed. "Okay."

I stood. I leaned across the space and time that separated us and kissed Raven's lips gently. Then I closed my eyes, clicked my heels together, and sang, "There's no place like home, there's no place like home." Raven's hand was warm against my chest.

She began singing, too, pulling time through to me or me through to time. I opened my eyes. Darkness swirled. Twirled. Pirouetted. Someone played "In-A-Gadda-Da-Vida" on my skull.

"Raven!" I cried, reaching for her.

She was gone.

Light snapped on. I was looking into turquoise. Tiny waves of turquoise. Anna sat alone by the pool. Long-legged, tanned, brown hair braided behind her. Her eyes were the color of the pool she stared into.

Behind her, on the veranda of a white house, people talked. I could barely hear them. It was as if they and the house were moving away almost imperceptibly. Anna sat still while they moved. Or darkness fell.

"Anna," I whispered. My toes were bare on the grass. Cool. "Anna?" I leaned toward her.

She didn't blink.

Victor stepped off of the dusk-colored veranda. Spotlighted. White suit. Sky-colored eyes. Black hair.

A party. Pool. Victor. Was it dying time again?

"Don't touch her, you bastard," I said.

He strode past me. Not seeing me. I did not exist. He knelt next to Anna and took her hand in his, looking every bit like a Southern gentleman about to ask the fair lady for her hand in marriage. What did that mean anyway: her hand in marriage? She only pledged her hand? The rest of her body was hers only?

Ha!

"Anna," I said, "don't talk to him."

"Anna," Victor whispered. "Why are you here all alone?"

"I'm not alone," she said.

"Hear that, you corpse-fucking bastard? She's not alone. Go away!"

He was a murderer, a pervert, and any number of other things, but he looked great in white, especially next to Anna. They looked like the perfect couple.

"Are you all right?" Victor asked.

"Do you mean have I taken my medication?" Anna said. "Have I slain the wicked demons that plague me? Yes, Father Victor, you are all victorious. They are slayed. Slain. Gone. I am well. I don't feel a thing."

"We only want you to be well." He sounded so sincere. But I had seen this act before.

"Watch it, Anna, sister; he's sly."

I knelt next to them and looked into Victor's baby blues. Geez. He actually looked frightened for her.

"Come up to the house. The guests miss you."

"Victor, dear, I've told you before. You can have me when I'm gone. Until then, bugger off."

"Thatta girl!" I cried.

Victor kissed her hand and then stood and walked back into the darkness. Turquoise and Anna's white dress were the only colors in the night.

Anna slowly looked away from the pool until she was gazing into my eyes.

"I lied," she whispered. "I didn't slay them all. You're still here. But not for long. I took enough tranks, antidepressants, and alcohol to clear the universe of demons."

"What? Anna! You'll die!" I started to run toward the house.

She giggled slightly. A slurred giggle. "You are a hopeless romantic," she said, her voice stopping me. "How many times have I told you? I've been in a box for as long as I can remember. I've just run out of air. Good-bye, Keelie. Tea leaf.''

She folded into the pool. Without a sound. As though the air had been let out of her. I dove in after her. I reached for her.

Touched her. And then I was her. My heart? Where was my heartbeat? My soul. Mind. She— we—I had lost it long ago. Scattered between this thought and another. Strung along the memories of my children. Clothespinned. Couldn't breathe. Couldn't breathe. I wanted to breathe. Live again. My arms wouldn't move.

I heard distant splashes. Continents away. A white suit, arms reached for me, pulled me. Pulled me. I. Could not. Breathe.

I floated, above it all. The pressure was gone. Anna and I held hands as Victor dripped on us, pushed air into our lifeless body, sobbed. He pushed his sobs into us. So he hadn't tried to drown her—us; I had been wrong about that. Our husband Jim watched. Tried to help. People dressed in pastels gathered. Champagne bubbles tickled my nose.

"It doesn't hurt anymore," Anna said. "Does it?"

Victor screamed. Someone pulled him away.

"I look like a fish," Anna said, gazing at her corpse. "Maybe I should have dyed my hair? A good hair day can take the edge off most any depression."

She giggled and squeezed my hand.

"He's so sad," I whispered. "I thought he was the devil incarnate."

"Victor? He's just a man."

"Where are you going now?" I asked her. We slowly floated away from the crowd.

"I'm going with you," she said.

She disappeared, and I felt her hand on my chest. A sob hiccuped out of my mouth. I closed my eyes, clicked my ethereal heels together three times, and whispered, "There's no place like home. There's no place like home. There's no place like home."

Snow covered the porch and Anna's garden beyond. She stood in the midst of the winter splendor, dressed in white, her arms wrapped around herself. Her cheeks were red with cold. Everything was still. Quiet. Did she always surround herself in such silence?

The Snow Queen.

She was so beautiful. Was that really the same face I saw every morning when I looked in the mirror?

"Keelie? Come out of the shadow, my little tea leaf. I haven't seen you in a long while."

The door behind me opened. "Who are you talking to?" Her husband Jim stood next to me. He seemed smaller than he had by the pool. Not as tired. Dressed in black pants, white shirt, and black tie.

"Just talking to myself, dear," she answered.

"You're sure you don't want to come to church with us?"

"Yes, I'm certain. Thank you." *I have played that role long enough. Time for a new one.*

She smiled at me. *Don't you remember, Keelie? We could read each other's minds. We're the same, you and I.*

Jim sighed. "The family will miss you."

Why? I've never really been there. Can't you all see the out-to-lunch sign I've hung around my life?

Jim turned abruptly and went inside. I heard the kids calling good-bye, tiny precious voices. I wanted to run after them. Maybe they could save her.

"Save me from what?" Anna said aloud. "Besides, they're kids. They shouldn't have to worry about anything."

I followed her inside the house. She dropped her coat in front of the fireplace. The heat curled the fake fur. She smoothed her hands across the long black dress she wore and then sat on the flowered couch. On the glass table in front of her lay the bible. She followed my gaze.

"I was raised on it," she said. "Remember? I did feel comforted by god's love at one time, I think, and terrified of his anger. Now—"

"And now you don't believe?"

"I look out beyond this house, Keelie, and see only destruction. They have cut down the forest, just as I feared. I can't look at it. The stumps remind me of amputated fingers. Cutting off the Earth's own fingers and leaving bloody stumps. Dominion over nature." She leaned forward. "That means dominion over us, too, in case you didn't catch that particular continental drift."

I shrugged and sat on her coat and warmed my hands. "I don't believe in god," I said, without thinking, because in my short life I had not cogitated upon this particular subject. "Or the devil."

"Then you're foolish. They surround us in the forms of men. Gods and devils. There's no difference. They're all the same."

"That's what I love about you." I turned. Victor strode across the room. "Your mind. Who you talking to?"

"Myself," she said, reaching up to him. "Have you come for my body?"

He scooped her up and carried her over to the fireplace, next to me. She reached for me, touched my fingers. Before I could pull away, we were one.

Does this help? I asked. Sex with Dr. Frankenstein himself.

Sometimes.

He lifted Anna's dress and kissed her pubic

hair. I sank into her body, slipping her on like a pair of gloves. She adjusted herself to me.

We aren't quite the same, you and I, she said. The idea made her shiver, aroused us. Victor moved slowly but we pulled him down into us, quickly. It was exquisite. Anna was exquisite. He was tender. Hard. Kissing her ear, whispering to her. I wanted to feel her tongue in my mouth, her fingers on my breasts. Victor sucked on our nipples, pulling Anna closer to me, us closer together. She opened to me. Opened. Until I felt Anna against me. Anna's mouth. Anna's breasts.

This is life, I whispered. Can't you seize it? Hold it?

You are a demon.

"God," Victor gasped. "Who are you? What's happening?"

She bit his lip. I felt myself spiraling away. With her.

"Come," she whispered.

Victor moved faster. Three bodies one. All mixed up. I held her closer. Closer. Her orgasm exploded through me, a palette of colors caressing, stroking, until Victor's undulated with hers and then mine, orgasms cascading across and through each other.

We held one another tightly for a long while. Finally Victor fell away from her. I stayed a moment longer before she let me go, too.

"That was nice," Victor said.

"That was the understatement of the century," I said.

Anna looked away.

"Anna?" I said.

"It changes nothing."

"How can you say that?" Victor and I asked.

"You don't understand."

"I don't understand?" Victor. "I said I'd marry you, take you away from this dreary backwater town."

"The dreariness would follow me," Anna said. She sat up, and I felt the semen draining out of her. "You aren't the solution."

"What is? Won't you do anything to help yourself?" Victor asked.

"Shut up, you fuck," I said.

"Why don't you let me stay here?" Anna whispered. "In the underworld. It's a temporary thing. I might find the answers. I need to go deep. Deep. I need to wallow in it. A pig in slop. A woman in darkness. I need to be here."

"You're depressed. You need medication."

Anna sighed. "I weary of this."

"Anna?" Had she forgotten me?

They are stronger than I am. The abyss is frightening and inviting. I can't tell if they're pulling me toward it or away from it. And what's best?

Don't die.

She laughed. Victor watched her.

Tea leaf, how will you ever be born if I don't?

You have more than I do. I was just his sick idea of a walking talking Barbie doll.

You're more. Much more. You'll see. Go now. And know that I never forgot and I never will.

"Anna?" Victor.

She pressed her hand against my chest. I closed my eyes, clicked my heels together, and said, "There's no place like home. There's no place like home."

"Where'd you come from?"

I opened my eyes. I was standing in a forest. A dirty-blond girl stood in front of me. She smiled and said, "This is my forest! I am fairy princess. Queen of all!" She laughed. "You can call me Anna or Annie. I like Annie better. It sounds more natural, doesn't it?"

"Hello, Annie," I said. "I'm Keelie."

"Tea leaf? What kind of name is that? Come on! Race you to the creek."

"Keelie! My name is Keelie," I called as I ran after her. A child's run. I glanced down. My breasts were nearly nonexistent. My legs much shorter than they had been a moment ago.

I was a girl again. Or a girl for the first time.

I raced to catch up with Anna. Her hair flew behind her. The sun showed me the color of gold it had been and the brown it was becoming.

We stopped together, gasping for breath on

the black muddy banks of a slow-moving stream.

"Wow! You're fast," she said. "Hey, look, we're almost twins."

We dropped to the ground. Mud oozed around our bare knees. We leaned over the water until we could see our faces.

We looked almost identical.

"That's amazing," Anna said. "Keelie. That's a funny name. What's it mean?"

I shrugged. "Tea leaf, I guess."

She laughed.

"I'm supposed to be at church but it was such a beautiful day," she said. "God won't mind, will he?"

"Be kind of stingy of him, wouldn't it?"

She plopped down on the grass and then took off her shoes and socks. I did the same. We squished our toes in the cool mud.

"I'll pull off your leeches if you pull off mine," she said.

"Not a chance," I said, quickly pulling my feet out. The mud made a sucking noise. I looked for leeches. Nothing. The hair on my legs was golden. I petted it. How little I was. My legs powerful with childhood.

"I call this creek Titania's Creek. She's the fairy queen from Shakespeare's *Midsummer Night's Dream*."

"I thought you only got to read the bible."

"How'd you know that?" The sun came through the oak and pine trees above us and dappled Anna's face, making huge freckles. Behind us, robins and meadowlarks sang. A red-winged blackbird watched us from a cattail that swayed slightly with the currents. Frogs ribbited.

"I know everything," I said.

"I won't be coming here much longer," she said. "Mom and Dad have pretty much had it with me. They'll probably cut down the trees just to keep me home." She laughed. "Not really."

We helped each other up and stood in the cool, clear creek. The water loosened the mud and then took it downstream. When our feet were clean, we picked up our shoes and socks and walked away from the river.

"I love it here. I've got names for all the trees," Anna said. "Well, most of them."

"They probably have names for you, too. Queen Titania, perhaps?" I bowed before her.

"Shhh! She'll hear you!" She pushed against me. We melted into each other for a moment and then were two again. "That was weird," Anna said. "Let's stop here. This is one of my favorite spots."

We dropped to our bellies and lay on a patch of moss. I ran my hand across it.

"Just like velvet," I said, "only better."

Tiny white flowers grew out of the moss. Ants busily went around the flowers and grass and over the moss.

"Like a blanket for the Earth," Anna said. "Momma-Earth."

We turned over and rested our heads on the moss. Overhead, clouds passed slowly by. We pointed out shapes to each other.

We giggled and held hands.

Then we closed our eyes and slept.

I heard birds call my name. The wind brushed my hair and stroked my face with warm fingers. I felt deeply rested.

"I've never had a friend like you," Anna said as the shadows lengthened.

"Me neither."

"Anna!" Someone called from far off.

Anna grabbed my hand. We melted.

"Do you ever feel scared?"

"Often," I answered.

"I feel like they're trying to put me in a box. And I'm afraid I'll never get out. Do you know what I mean?"

I nodded.

"Anna!" The voice was closer and not happy.

Anna let go of my hand.

"Thanks for being with me. I'll never forget you. Or this day."

"I'll see you again," she said.

She got up and ran away. A fairy sprite, lost in dusk.

I dug my fingers into the dirt.

"Don't forget yourself, Annie."

I knew she would forget. But I wouldn't.

When the meadowlark stopped singing, I put my hand on my chest, closed my eyes, and clicked my heels together.

Eight

* * * * * * * * *

My feet were burning up. I opened my eyes to desert light and danced on the scorched earth. No place to stand. No relief. Besides that, I was stark naked and extremely white. The sun didn't blink. Or even wink.

Suddenly a '57 Chevy drove up. Guys with greasy hair waved at me.

"Need a ride?"

"Hardly," I said. "How about some shoes?"

"Here they come!" One of them hurled something at me and then they roared away, throwing up rocks and dust. I caught a pair of ruby slippers. Shiny and new. Just my size. I put them on, feeling quite incongruous with this particular fashion statement. At least my feet were cool.

I sat on my haunches. Red thread appeared and began winding its way around my left arm, up across my shoulders and down my other arm.

A coyote walked out of a heat mirage, tongue lolling.

"And Toto, too?" I said.

"Quite an outfit," Coyote said.

The fabric hadn't quite reached my pubic hair yet.

"It's evolving," I said.

"Yeah, like I haven't heard that before. Can I help you with something?"

"I'm not sure. Are we related?"

Coyote laughed. "Don't be insulting."

The dress tickled my thighs and fell to my ankles.

"I'm remembering you so you must be a part of me."

"Maybe on my Aunt Jam's side. But that's iffy. In any case, it would be a very distant relation."

"I could use some food."

"Shall I run and break some poor unsuspecting stupid rabbit's neck for you. They're pretty tasty this time of day."

"Thanks but no thanks. Perhaps I best be on my way."

"Where?"

"Home."

"Home? Honey, ain't this home?"

A sign appeared around Coyote's neck: HOME, SWEET HOME.

I shook my head. "I think you're just here for comic relief."

"Are you relieved?"

I put my hand on my heart, closed my eyes, and did my little dance.

"You'll be sorry," Coyote whispered.

My hands were sticky. I opened my eyes. With blood. Soaking into Belle's carpet. Her life seeping into that fucking carpet. Mingling with mine as I fingered her blood. Stilled my heart. Gurgled in my cut throat.

"You motherfucker!" I screamed, grabbing the man's neck, the bastard with the knife, with the gleam in his eyes. He couldn't see me. But. He. Could. Feel. me. He started to choke. Cough. Then he shook me off and I couldn't get his attention. I pounded on his back. He flicked me away as if I were a fly. A gnat.

Pearl. Where was Pearl?

Everything smelled like blood. The man was swearing. Calling someone on the phone. "You come and piece her together. If you don't get her out of here and make sure nobody knows I did it, I'll hack her into little pieces and you won't have any of her. Don't yell at me, you cock-sucking bastard! She came after me. It was self-defense." He threw the phone across the room.

Pearl? I couldn't leave the living room. My ruby slippers were planted in Belle's blood.

Belle. Her face was contorted. Her body twisted. The bastard. I would kill him someday. Someday.

"Pearl!" I screamed.

"You can't change what happened," Belle spoke from my bloody fingertips. They were hers, too, weren't they? "It's not time to save Pearl."

"Then what the fuck am I doing here if I can't change anything!" I screamed.

I closed my eyes and clicked my heels together.

Country music blasted my ears. Smoke. Sweat.

"Girl, sit down before one of those assholes gets after you."

I opened my eyes. Had to be a bar. I had some ancient primal disgusting memory of one. Or many. I coughed. Did they really breathe this shit?

"Honey?"

Sitting in a red vinyl booth, red hair piled on top of her head, a cigarette in her hand, was Belle. Alive and well. She patted the space next to her.

I sat where she patted. She smelled like lavender. She smiled, and I wished she were my momma. If I could just lay my head on her bosom and tell her my troubles. Being bounced from memory to memory like a pinball was starting to get to me.

Beyond us, I could discern little except bodies bumping against other bodies. Posi-traction. Too noisy. People.

Death.

I stared at Belle's neck, remembering what I had seen only minutes ago.

"I like your dress," she said. "Yellow? Kind of sun-colored. Where'd you get it?"

I looked down and shrugged. "The desert." It had been red. I spread my fingers out in front of me. Just like my fingers had been red with your blood. Now. Just white tones. Beige.

"I'm Belle," she said, holding out a hand that ended in long painted fingernails.

I grasped her hand lightly. We melted. Her life flashed before me. Too quickly for comprehension.

She let go of me. "Honey, I don't want to be that close to anyone. How'd you do that? I bet you'd be great in bed. Not that I'm interested." She looked across the bar. "I'm only sexually attracted to men. It's a defect, I know. They're such assholes. I'm looking for Mr. Right and I keep finding Mr. Leftover."

I felt woozy. Wobbly.

"Sister, you need a drink?"

"I need something."

"Charlie! Bring the girl some of that chicken soup!"

Her shouts produced a shadow proffering a bowl of soup and bread. She took it and set it in front of me.

"Yeah, chicken soup in a bar. What can I tell you? My grandmother on my father's side was Jewish. Said chicken soup cured everything, so I showed Charlie how to make it. Something different. Most bars have chili and burgers. We got soup."

"Do you own this place?"

"Eat! No, I work here."

I picked up the spoon and was surprised I could hold it, amazed I could eat. The soup warmed me to my cockles, spreading across my body like a magic potion. The dizziness started to pass. The jukebox took a break.

"Tonight's my night off," she said, "so I'm just hanging out." She watched the patrons like a queen looking over her subjects. This was her domain. "Hiya, Pete," she said to some guy leaning over her shoulder. "Yeah, I'll be home tomorrow. Seven? Sure. See ya." She turned to me. "What's your name? You're getting some color back."

"How can you tell?"

She laughed and stubbed out her cigarette.

"My name's Keelie," I said.

"Keelie?"

"Yeah, and I have no idea what it means."

"It means beautiful. My Irish grandmother, on my mother's side, had the same name. I don't remember much about her except she was so nice to me—always telling me stories, hugging me. I think my mother must have been a foundling. She was such a bitch that I can't imagine her coming from Grandma Keelie. Small world. What a coincidence."

I don't think so.

"Hey, Bill, you shit, where were you last Saturday?" Another man whispered in Belle's ear. She slugged his arm and laughed.

"Do you know everyone?" I asked.

"Only the men, honey. I'm the town whore, I'm sure you guessed. Or one of them. Fucking assholes keeps me alive. Waitressing keeps me honest. You still look like shit. Why don't you come upstairs and clear your head."

"Anything to get out of here."

Belle waved to someone or everyone as she got up. I followed her into the night and breathed the clear air gratefully.

"What'd you come to Charlie's for if you hate it so much? Lordy, girl, you are beautiful. Except the hair. It's pretty bad." She started to touch my head and then stopped. She smiled.

"Do you do that—that melting merging thing every time you touch someone?"

"Depends on the someone."

"Yeah, well, come on." She went up the stairs next to the bar. I remembered climbing them before, with Hart, when we'd taken Pearl away from that man. That man who would one day murder Belle.

When?

What did it matter? I couldn't change it. Fix it.

Belle opened the door, and we went inside. Smelled of cigarettes and moldy carpet. At least the stench of blood was gone. Or had not yet come.

"Maria?" Belle whispered. "We take turns taking care of each other's kids," she said to me. A woman came out of the back room. They whispered in Spanish to each other. I knew I could understand if I wanted to, but I didn't. I sank onto the couch and closed my eyes.

Like Snow White. I drifted.

"Keelie? Here's some ginger ale. Maybe that'll help. You're positively green."

I opened my eyes and took the drink. Belle had turned on a table lamp. Maria was gone. The place was still dark and dank. Belle sat in an old recliner and put up her feet.

"Yeah, it's a dive," she said. "But it's a lot better than other places have been. And it's cheap. I'm saving my money—to find another place for me and Pearl."

"Pearl?" Feigned ignorance.

"My baby girl." Her voice grew momentarily soft. "You wouldn't believe I could produce someone like her. But I did. I almost died doing it. Had toxemia or something. While I lay there dying, I remembered all the crap from when I was a kid—my dad beat the shit out of me almost from day one—and I thought, with the toxemia and everything, that this would be a good time to check out. Cross over. You know, buy the big one. But Pearl kept calling to me. So I took her hand and pulled her into this world." She started to light a cigarette and then stopped. "Her daddy is very rich. But he doesn't know Pearl's his." She laughed. "I don't trust men much."

"I remember. Mr. Leftover." I grimaced. "But if this one is so rich, couldn't he help?"

"I don't need any help. Her daddy is Victor Beaufort. Ever heard of him?"

Victor? Gee, what a surprise. "No," I said.

"I loved him. Once. But he has some problems."

No shit.

"He was great in bed. He can stay hard for a month of Tuesdays. Most men come before they say hello. Not Victor." She laughed. "One day we got carried away and conceived Pearl. Now

I'm mother of shiny iridescent pearl." She smiled. "Do you want to spend the night? I've got extra blankets."

"Sure." Why not? I hadn't anywhere else to go, except back to another memory, and I was tired of being the pinball wizard of memories.

Belle got up and left the room. A moment later she returned, unfolded a blanket, and laid it across me. I pulled it up to my chin.

"Thanks."

She smiled. She looked younger than she had in the bar. Kind of sweet.

"You're not real, are you?" she asked. "I just told you all that stuff, and I don't know why. And none of those boys downstairs even glanced at you, and honey, I'm a dog next to you. Not a glance. What are you?"

"An alien."

"That's why you're able to do that melting thing, eh?" She put her hands on her hips. I could see my shape. My breasts, waist, hips. The pussy that had birthed little Pearl beneath tight red slacks. She had the prettiest green eyes. "Do aliens eat eggs and toast in the morning?"

"Sure, if I'm here."

She started to leave the room again. She stopped. "Should I tell him? I mean that Pearl is his?"

"Pearl isn't his," I said. "Pearl is her own little person."

"Yeah, all right then, should I tell him that he is her biological father?"

How the fuck should I know the answer to that question?

"Would he ever hurt you? I mean physically?"

She shook her head, thought for a moment, and then said, "They all have the potential, don't they? To be good guys or bad. My vagina is a radar for the bad ones, so yeah, I guess he could hurt me. Does it matter?"

"It would matter to me."

"Well, you ain't me, are you?" she said and then walked out of the room.

"Don't be too sure," I murmured.

I pulled the blanket up over my head. I wanted out of here. "I don't want to go back to Belle's fucking childhood either. Do you hear me, Raven, or the fates, or whoever is orchestrating this miserable trip down memory lane? I want some happy memories. I want some fun!" I wanted to sleep. So I did.

Dawn colored the dirty carpet in rose when I woke up. I stretched away the couch lumps. I heard the baby murmur and walked toward the sound.

They lay together on Belle's bed. Flowered sheets askew. Mother and child. Belle's face was freckled, her hair frizzy, red. Little Pearl sucked on her momma's left breast. Her hands caressed Belle's skin in jerky movements as she sighed and sucked, sighed and sucked. She and Belle seemed protected and precious, together always in this moment.

I had never seen anything quite so beautiful.

I put my hand on my chest, felt my own breasts, Belle's breasts, and remembered the tug of Pearl's mouth on my body. I closed my eyes, clicked my heels together, and whispered, "There's no place like home."

Nine

✦✦✦✦✦✦

I opened my eyes and guess where I was? Frankie's estate. Home of Dr. Frankenstein himself and his ghoulish sidekicks: Lilith, his deformed wife; Griffin, his witless surgeon; Hart, his dickless traitorous mercenary shrink. Or rather, my shrink.

Seemed so long ago.

I was in the garden where first Hart and then Victor had kissed me. People walked to and fro, talking of Michelangelo. Servants floated trays from guest to guest.

Haven't you had enough. Come back for a blast from the past?

I looked up. The Cheshire cats smiled down at me from the top of a bonsai. A precarious perch.

"Hi, kids. So what part of my past is this?"

Before us, oh our triadness. We just came to enjoy the sport.

Bushes resolved into chairs. White flowers everywhere. Either a funeral or a wedding was about to conspire. Or perspire. I wore orange.

My ruby slippers clashed.

"Dearly beloved," the guy in black began. Victor stood next to him, dressed in black, too, only younger, his face almost unlined with worry or memory of things to come. Next to him stood Lilith. Unbent.

I walked around the gaping masses. Birds fluttered away, but no one else noticed me. I stood next to the bride and groom. This was how he had intended it anyway, hadn't he? That Lilith and I should both be his wives?

Lilith's hair was pushed away from her face by two pearl combs laced with baby's breath. Her skin was radiant. Her smile all love. Her eyes were so bright and intelligent.

She was almost unrecognizable to me, and then I remembered the pictures she had shown me of herself before Victor had gotten his knife into her. Now their hands were clasped. Victor was certain of himself, the victor, and she of him, the victorious.

I felt fuzzy as I listened and watched. As if it were all a dream. Everything was fairy-tale beautiful. The smells. Sounds. The two of them. I had never seen two people look so radiantly happy and so much in love. Though, as I've pointed out before, my life experience wasn't much.

They looked happy. But I knew what would happen to them.

And to me.

"Why am I here with you, Vic ol' boy?" I fingered his sleeve.

Mistake.

I stumbled. Tumbled forward in time. Lights flashed.

Ruby slippers and all.

Griffin was crying. I pushed myself up off the floor where I had fallen. Candlelight flickered off Lilith's "before" pictures. Off Griffin's tear-soaked face. Off Lilith, who twisted above us on a rope, her body distorted, her neck broken.

"Lilith?" I whispered. She had been a bride only a moment ago.

See what happened when you left.

The Chessies licked their paws.

"This has nothing to do with me," I said. "Their problems started long before I even existed."

"Help us," Griffin cried.

"I'll find someone," I said.

I went through the piano room and then out into the huge hall. How long ago had I run down this hall in embarrassment. Dressed as the bride of Frankie? A lifetime. Lifetimes.

If I'd only stayed the Barbie doll. Wore the clothes. Danced the dance.

If only you'd never learned to talk.

"Shut up!" I hurried down the stairs.

If only she had learned to dance!

Victor stood in his library, looking out across the garden. I wondered if he was remembering his wedding? Or our kiss. I had wanted him so badly then. Now he looked worn. Out.

His face was too white.

Hart sat near to him, his arm in a sling.

"Lilith told Keelie that you—" Hart cleared his throat.

I stopped. Keelie? When was this? Hart's arm in a sling, his shoulders hunched, Hadn't I killed the bastard? No, only keeled him. Keelied him.

Stop it.

Sorry.

"Lilith told Keelie what?" Victor asked. His voice was stern. Angry.

"Lilith told her that the other two, the ones in the freezer . . ."

"Yes? What about them?" He turned from the window and gazed at Hart. Hart couldn't look at him.

"That you were sleeping with them."

"Sleeping with them? You mean fucking them?" That word sounded wrong coming out of Victor's mouth. "That's obscene. Why didn't you tell her it wasn't true?"

"Well," Hart said, clearing his throat, "it is kind of odd that they're still there."

"Just because you can't get an erection unless you turn into some kind of madman, doesn't mean all men are sexual perverts."

"Mine is an inherited malady—"

"Why'd Keelie try to kill you, Hart? Did you try to rape her? I can't believe I ever trusted her with you."

"We were talking about Lilith and Keelie," Hart said.

"We were talking about whatever I wanted to talk about! Leave Lilith out of this! What she did was inexcusable. She would have said anything to Keelie to get rid of her. Lilith has always blamed me for the plastic surgeries—she has this elaborate fantasy worked out that I did all the surgeries. I did one little nip and tuck at her request. I shouldn't have, but I did! I've had enough. I've called the lawyer and told Lilith I want a divorce."

The straw that broke the camel's back. Or Lilith's neck. "Too late," I said. "Lilith saved you the lawyer's fee. She's dead."

Victor looked toward me, through me. "Did you hear something?" he asked.

"Probably Griff and Lilith playing."

"Why is Keelie running away from me? I just wanted to protect her. I just wanted to create a world where she wouldn't be hurt. Where none of them would be hurt."

"Wake up, Victor," I said. "Life doesn't work that way. Listen. Go upstairs and help Griffin. And then let me go. Everything seems to revolve around you, after all. You must be the key. It's so typical. The entire fucking world revolves around men. Even my past! This was supposed to be about me."

"I heard a fly buzz," Victor said.

"When Lilith died," I murmured.

I closed my eyes and touched my chest. I wanted to go home.

I heard Brahms' Lullaby. Or was it Brahms himself rocking me to sleep? I opened my eyes. I stood in a school gymnasium. Afternoon light streamed in through the high windows that wrapped the building. On the butterscotch-colored floors, a woman stood. Danced. Her feet and legs were covered in lavender tights; a light pink, almost white dress covered the rest of her body, brushing her knees and back of her legs as she gracefully twirled across the floor. Her brown hair was tied in a ribbon. Her hands seemed almost separate from her, moving like reeds in a stream. Her eyes were closed, her face glowing as she moved. Danced. Her long legs stepping, twirling, carrying her to unknown places.

My legs. Lee. I had finally found Lee. Perhaps this then was near the end of my journey.

Someone else watched Lee. He was a shadow under the entrance. He sighed and whispered her name.

She must have sensed him because she folded onto the floor, stopping her dance. He moved out of the shadows and walked across the floor, his footsteps ringing in the huge emptiness which could hold only these two people and my ghost.

"Hiya, Legs." He knelt at her side and held out his hand. His face turned slightly so I could see him. Victor. I wasn't surprised. It seemed inevitable.

Lee lifted her head slowly. She was radiant. Her eyes bright blue.

"Hello, Victor," she said, taking his proffered hand. He lifted her up. They hesitated and then embraced deeply, falling into one another, as if this were the most natural place for them to be, the only place for them to be. In each other's arms.

I followed them out into the parking lot and into Victor's car. The day was bright with spring. The two of them said little as the car wove away from the school and into the country. I felt sleepy. Nothing bad was going to happen. These two liked one another too much. If nothing else, I'd be witness to another episode of Victor's sex life of the rich and perverted. The car pulled into Grace's driveway. Beyond the house, the forest loomed. I wondered for a moment if I could escape into it now, find my way back to Raven's cottage and then back out to Grace and Ben and Pearl again. In my own time. But I didn't have the energy. I wanted to follow Lee and Victor.

"Grace and Ben are away for a few days," Lee said. They held hands as they walked toward the house. Lee took off her shoes and walked barefoot on the spring-muddied lawn.

"Feels nice," she said. "You should try it."

Victor laughed. "You have been trying to get me into the mud since we were kids."

"And you always ran around in white," Lee said. "Without a speck of dirt."

They hesitated on the porch and then went inside. I followed, walking through the walls like an honest-to-goodness ghost. Which maybe I was. Maybe that's what this was all about. Me realizing I was dead.

"Place looks nice," Victor said, looking around. I followed his gaze. The house seemed almost the same as when I left it. Flowers everywhere. Books and papers. Wood. Comfy flowery chairs. Lived in.

They sat in the living room. Her on one chair, him in the other. It seemed unnatural them being apart. As if they strained to stay away from each other.

"I wanted to see how you've been," Victor said. He was trying to keep it light but his voice was strained. "You and Grace still together? Happy?"

"She is wonderful," Lee said, pulling on her dress, "and I am still me. Does that answer your question?"

"You asked me to stay away," he said, "and I have." He didn't look at her. "But nothing is the same. I always feel like something's missing."

"Let's not talk about it. Do you want something to eat?" She got up and walked toward the kitchen. He gently took her fingers in his hand as she went past. She shook her hand to get away from him. He held firm for a moment and then let go. Her fingers brushed his face. She sank to her knees beside him. He pulled her up onto his lap.

"We can't," she whispered.

He kissed her neck and chin. She unbuttoned his shirt. Their breaths grew faster. She bared his chest and kissed it, licked it. He pulled off her tights. Rubbed her gently. So gently. Cupped her breasts, sucked on them as if they held mother's milk. Tears streamed down his face. She unzipped his pants and moved her pelvis down onto his penis. They both sobbed as they held each other, as they moved together, in perfect harmony, faster, slower, "It's only us," he said, "always only us together." They orgasmed together and paused in each other's arms only a moment before they began moving again, faster, clothes torn off, desperate, desperate, calling out for one another. I tried to move away, tried to leave the room, but my ruby slippers were planted again. Lee whispered, "Keelie," and Victor kissed her mouth, "Shhh, it's just us."

Finally, they lay still in one another's arms on the living room floor. Lee cried quietly.

"I love you," Victor said. "Only you. I try with others, but it's never the same."

"It shouldn't be the same, Victor," she said. "It shouldn't be." She buried her face in his chest for a moment and then looked up at him. "This has to end."

"I don't mean to hurt you," Victor said. He seemed so childlike. Lost.

"It's not you," Lee whispered. "It was never your fault. Never."

They fell to sleep. I sat on the porch, finally released from the living room. After a time, Victor left. Lee took a shower. She let the water run for a long time, until it was cold. I shivered as I watched her, wondering why I felt only half here, wondering when I would come back into myself.

When she was finished, she sat at her desk and wrote, "Dear Grace Under Pressure. I hope I come back as a dancer."

She took a bottle of pills from her purse and opened them. She swallowed two handfuls, washing them down with orange juice. I wanted to scream, to rant, to rave. But I could only watch.

She lay on her bed and closed her eyes. Everything was so quiet. Still. She looked like Sleeping Beauty.

"Wake up," was all I could say. I leaned over and kissed her. Then I fell into her. I tripped and fell. Tumbled. I screamed.

And opened my eyes. My body throbbed. I knew I had to be covered with bruises. Cuts. I couldn't move, yet someone was moving inside me. Grunting. Sweating. Swearing. Calling me names. I moved away from the pressure, from the being inside me. I closed my eyes.

"Lee?" I whispered.

"Don't call me that," she hissed in my brain. "That's his name."

"Who?"

"My father, that's who. The man who is fucking us as we speak. I don't ever want to hear you call me that."

The thing inside us roared and tore us. Lee tugged at me and we blacked out.

I was awake again. I opened my eyes. Lee

watched with me. This place where we lay naked and bloody was dark, yet rich with something. What? Money? The sheets beneath my bruised butt were silk. Spotted with my blood. I couldn't move. Lee wouldn't. I couldn't find her. I was trapped in her body and I couldn't get out, couldn't find her. Couldn't find her.

"She's your daughter! How can you do these things to her?" A boy's voice, cracking with puberty.

The man, the thing, laughed. "If you don't do it, I'll do her again."

"I'll tell!" the boy sobbed.

"Then I'll kill us all," the father thing said.

I squirmed. I tried to raise my hand to my chest. I couldn't. I felt disintegrated. Dismembered.

The door opened and the father thing came in, dressed in a maroon smoking jacket. He smiled. The boy next to him cried. He had black hair and sky-colored eyes. Victor as a boy.

The thing pushed Victor.

"I'll beat you both if you don't."

Shaking, Victor took off his clothes. He had done this before. They all had. A sick dance.

Naked and shivering he turned back to the thing one last time. "She's my sister, Dad, don't make me do this."

"She's a slut. Do her."

The father sat. My senses seemed supernatu-

125

rally heightened. Was it the paralysis? I heard the father unzip his pants, heard him sigh. Felt the sweat under my arms, on my buttocks. The wood grain imprinted on my brain. The boy Victor lay next to me.

"It's just us," Victor whispered. "Forget about him. It's just us."

Lee flickered back. Their bodies moved together and then their minds floated away, we all floated out of the room, out of the mansion. Lee and Victor held hands and disappeared. I heard someone behind us, left in Lee's body. I tiptoed back and listened to several someones singing, chanting, "Keelie, Keelie, Keelie."

Orgasms rocked us, and Lee and Victor snapped back into their bodies.

I heard the father zip up his pants. "I told you she was a slut," he said. Then he left the room.

Victor and his sister shivered in each other's arms. I fell away from them. I wished I could cover them up, make it all go away. Instead I put my hand to my chest, and screamed, "I want to go home!"

I fell hard, bumping my head. I opened my eyes to darkness. I sat still, breathing hard and rubbing my bruised head. My body hurt. Hurt. The memories of that man. That thing. The father.

Gradually my eyes adjusted to the dark. Dim light fell through slats in the door. I was in a closet. Clothes hung above me. A girl lay on the floor beside me, asleep, her thumb in her mouth. She was probably ten. Eight? She was surrounded by several ghost children. They were chanting, "Keelie, Keelie."

"I'm here," I said. "I'm here. What do you want?"

The kids stopped and looked at me. They were various sizes, ages, sexes. They seemed almost innumerable but they all fit in that tiny closet.

"Shhh!" one of them said. "She's sleeping. Sleeping Beauty."

"Is that Lee?" I asked.

"Don't call her that."

"Okay, okay. What are you all doing? Why'd you call me?"

One of the children with blackened eyes and long brown hair said, "We are her memories. She gets hurt and we're born. She forgets but we remember. We are her saving grace."

"You said it yourself," another said. "She's dismembered. We are those dismembered parts."

"Why are you in this closet?" I asked.

"She's hiding from the thing," Black Eyes said. "He hurts her."

"Yes, I know. Isn't there anyone to help her? A mother? Schoolteacher. Victor?"

"Momma killed herself. Victor is only a boy.

And we are just children. We help her as best we can." They smile. "Now, shhhh."

They began chanting again, softly, "Keelie, Keelie."

I closed my eyes, exhausted, unable to move, and listened to them. As I faded away, I realized they were not saying my name, they were not calling me into being, they were chanting, "Kill Lee, kill Lee, kill Lee." My name becoming the battle cry for the death of the father.

Ten
•••••

I opened my eyes and felt as though I had been asleep a long while. I sat up and looked around. I was in my room in Victor's mansion. The Chessies slept on either side of me. They sighed as I moved but stayed asleep. I rubbed my eyes and remembered all.

I felt ancient. Older than Eve, older than that raging Goddess Eriskegal Lilith had told me about. I got out of bed and went to my closet and turned on the light. The colors were dazzling. Maybe I should just slip on one of these dresses, find Victor, and tell him I'd changed my mind. I'll be his missus. I fingered a gown and smiled. I couldn't. I knew too much about him and about myself.

I took off the desert dress which was now green and dropped it on the floor. I kicked off the ruby slippers. No matter how many times I clicked my heels together I would never find home. It didn't exist. I was in hell. We were all in hell. No way out. I rummaged through the closet until I came up with a faded blue pair of jeans and a flannel shirt. I even managed to find a white camisole, buried beneath a bevy of wire push-up bras. I put on the clothes and left the room, barefoot, my soles bare. My souls.

Just stay asleep. It works for us.

The mansion was quiet. No Lilith and Griffin wandering the hallways arguing with one another. No piano playing in the distance. Victor sat in his study, the drapes drawn, the fire out.

"Hello, Victor," I said.

He looked up. His eyes were blank; his face dark with early beard.

"Keelie?"

"Yeah, *c'est moi.*"

"I thought you were gone forever," he whispered.

"I am," I said. I sat on the desk and stared at him. "When was the last time you bathed, Vic? You're a mess."

He stared at his hands for long moments and then looked up again. "Hart pulled the plug."

"Pulled the plug on what? Your freezer babes?"

Tears filled his eyes. "They were a part of you. Don't you understand why I kept them?"

I closed my eyes briefly. So the rest of me

was buried, I hoped, becoming fertilizer for MommaEarth?

"You did it to assuage your guilt."

"What guilt? I did nothing wrong."

I leaned toward him. I felt . . . nothing. As if walls had grown up all around me and I would never feel again. Or care. And you know what, I didn't care. What a sense of freedom it gave me. I could say whatever needed to be said.

"I know everything," I said. "About Anna, Belle, and your sister Lee."

He pushed away from the desk and turned to stare out the curtained window.

"They were all so hurt. I wanted to fix them."

"You should have saved them. At least Lee. You could have saved her! You were bigger! You could have kept him from her!"

He turned again and stared at me wide-eyed. "I was a child."

"You fucked her! You fucked me!" Okay, I felt something. Some semblance of rage swelling like a tsunami.

Victor looked as though he had been struck.

"I saved her from my father!"

"You saved her for yourself!"

"It's not true, it's not true. I was a child. I wanted to save her, I wanted to." He was mumbling, his voice a child's. I almost felt sorry for him. Almost.

"You should have saved her."

"Why couldn't she save herself! Why was it my responsibility?"

"Because." She was a child.

"You are her, you know; I even named you after her." He was desperate to please.

"What are you talking about?"

"Your name. Keelie. She used to say it all the time. It made her feel better. I looked it up. It means beautiful." He was smiling, a half-loon smile. This little piece of information was supposed to make it all better.

"Wrongo, brother o' mine. She was singing 'Kill Lee' in your ear. She was thinking about killing Daddy Dear every time you fucked her. It was her mantra. She wanted it to be yours, too. We wanted Daddy Dead."

The final blow. Victor seemed to crumble. I wished I had a broom to sweep him away. How could I be so cruel? He had been a child. It wasn't really his fault—

"Whatever happened to Daddy dearest anyway?" I asked.

"You don't know? You really don't remember?" He summoned up enough energy for those two questions.

"I assume he died of some degenerative disease and is now pushing up daisies."

"He lives in Florida."

He was alive?

This was too much. I screamed.

I hissssed.

I stormed out of the room, hurricane wind forces. The daughter-fucker was still alive! Alive! The mantra hadn't worked. Hadn't worked. He destroyed his son and daughter and he was alive. The rage swept around me, through me, I remembered him inside of me, and I stopped to vomit, and then continued down the corridors, down stairs, down and down, and down. I had to hit bottom. I had to. I kept walking, running, walking. The corridors grew darker. I turned around, but there was nothing behind me. The corridor undulated, pushed me forward, outward.

Finally I came to a door. I tried to open it. It wouldn't budge. I pounded on it.

When my energy was gone, it opened. Rank air wafted out. A woman, dark, huge, black hair everywhere, eyes like Lilith's, stood in the entrance.

"What the fuck do you want?" she asked.

"I got lost. I was trying to find my way out."

"No you weren't, you lying piece of feces. You wanted in. So get your bloody ass in."

She yanked me inside, nearly tearing my arm out of its socket. The door closed behind us and then disappeared. I was surrounded by dripping black walls, mossy and wet, yet the room seemed to go into infinity. A bed stood off to the side of a huge throne, covered in slime. To the left of the throne, embedded in stone, were three pegs and from these pegs, three rotting putrid corpses hung.

"You ain't in Kansas anymore, Dottie, so get used to it."

"I seem to have made a wrong turn," I said, looking for the door.

"Sit down."

"Really, I've got things to do."

"SIT DOWN," she roared. I was surprised she didn't shoot flames; her breath was bad enough. I sat on the cold stone floor. I was naked as a jaybird, whatever that means.

The woman smiled and showed pointed teeth. "My name is Eriskegal. You can call me E. Or Risk. Or better yet, Gal. We are sisters, after all, aren't we? Fellow bleeders. Only you've got every fucking thing you could have ever wanted and I'm left rotting down here!"

"You can have all my things," I said. She kind of scared me. "Gal, really. All yours. We'd probably have to make some alterations on the gowns, but hey, no problem."

"Shut the fuck up. I'm not interested in your wardrobe, you skinny little bitch. You think you can get out of here by bribing me with designer gowns?"

"You haven't seen them. They'll take your breath away."

She roared. Baseball-sized rocks fell from the

ceiling onto my head. She laughed as I covered my head.

"After all you've seen, you think you can bribe your way out of hell. Pu-lease. You came down here of your own accord. After torturing poor Victor."

"Poor Victor? Listen, E, Victor is not poor. He deserved torturing. Is that why I'm in hell? And you're the devil?"

Eriskegal sat on her throne. "Girl, you are as ignorant as the day is shitty. The devil is a patriarchal invention to keep people in line. The underworld ruled by a scrawny red guy with horns?" This time she roared with laughter. "You aren't here to be punished for your so-called sins. It doesn't work that way. I'm not into punishment. Well, at least not in a big way. See those putrid rotting corpses?"

"Yeah."

"Do you know who they are?"

"Larry, Mo, and Curly?"

"What a fucking smart-ass. I like that in a woman. Up to a point. Let me introduce you to your fellow players. There's Anna, and then Belle, and little sister Lee. They're trapped down here in the underworld, killed by my greedy little hand. They'll rot here forever."

"Unless what?"

She cocked an eyebrow at me. "What ever do you mean?"

"You wouldn't be telling me all this shit unless there was an unless." I was getting a headache.

"Listen, you little cunt, don't talk to me like you know what the fuck you're talking about. I'm THE FUCKING GODDESS OF DEATH. SO DON'T FUCK WITH ME."

Get this woman some Valium.

"I heard that," she said. "Now, you whiny little twit, you think you've remembered all there is to remember. You think that's it. You've remembered and now life disintegrates. Life is shit and then you die?"

"I wanted to remember. I thought it would explain the pain."

"You thought it would take away the pain."

"Yeah, okay, I did."

"Like taking an aspirin. I'll remember all this horrible shit, and *voilà*, I am HEALED. Novices, why do I always get novices?"

She shook her head. Were those snakes in her hair?

"Now, you stay here with el sisteros," she said, pointing to the corpses, "or you can get on with your remembering."

Those pegs looked pretty inviting.

"What more is there to remember?"

"Much more." The voice was so kind I wondered if she had really said it.

"Okay. I'll go. I'll remember. But can I have

some control over it? I mean, can I have some linear progression here. Can I have some choices?"

"Linear? What patriarchal bullshit." She waved me away. "Go, go. Get the fuck out of my house."

"House?"

"Yeah, it was in *Architectural Digest* last month. Did you miss it? Get out of here before I change my mind and kill you for the fun of it."

I got up and went in the direction she waved me. A door appeared and then disappeared, showing me stone stairs. A lot of them. Leading up to a pinpoint of light at the top.

"Hope your heart is good," Eriskegal called to me.

I started climbing.

• •

PART 2

THE BURNING TIMES, 1535 C.E.

Eleven

••••••••••

I passed out somewhere between here and there, staring at that fucking light. Climbing. Climbing. I was going to have the best-looking calves outside a slaughterhouse. Until the light went out on my feeble little brain.

"Did she hit her head?" someone asked in French. And I understood it.

I opened my eyes. I was surrounded by what seemed like hundreds of strange eyes; beyond them, the jungle enveloped us, below, above, and all around. I blinked. The eyes revolved and then resolved.

Anna first. She had bright red hair and emerald eyes, but it was Anna. She leaned over and French-kissed me.

Then Victor. He, too, was different. Smaller. Browner. But it was him.

"We were worried about you, Keelie," he said.

Lee stood next to him. She was white-blond, small, and extremely pregnant. She leaned back against him.

I felt slightly nauseated. Where the fuck was I?

A tall almost fair Indian woman shooed them away. "She has been with the Mother. Leave her be." She was not speaking French, but I understood most of what she said, too. And when she winked at me, I knew she was Belle.

"Check please," I said.

Other white people, mostly women, and a few Indians became faces to me. Thankfully I didn't know any of them.

"Where am I?" I tried in English.

Anna stepped forward and took my hand. "No one understands English here except me and your brother, love. Don't you remember?"

I tried to focus, but I was completely confused, more so than when I had awakened on Victor's cutting board cum surgery table. The jungle was an extremely noisy place. I mean, creatures were screaming, roaring, calling out, chattering, singing, chirping, chittering, hissing. And the green. There was so much green. Green above. Green all around.

I squinted. The white women were dressed like the Indians—like the indigenous people.

The aboriginals. The originals. Like their hosts. They looked slightly askew and a bit uncomfortable with their white-bread breasts hanging out, but they were trying. Everyone except Lee. Pregnant Lee. She was completely clothed. I stared at her. She looked much happier than the last time I had seen her. Of course, she was nearly dead the last time I had seen her. And I had a feeling Victor was no longer her brother.

Then there was Anna. My Annie. She was nearly naked except for a tiny skirt covering her crotch. She fit it. She looked like a fucking red-haired Amazon.

"Anna?" Okay, she had a different name—they all did, but I won't confuse you. I saw her as Anna, so that's what I'll call her.

"Anna," I said again. "What happened?"

"You hit your head," Victor said. "You didn't know any of us a moment ago. Do you remember now? I'm your brother."

I closed my eyes. Oh boy.

"Where am I?" I asked.

"You're in the New World," Anna said. "What do you think of it?"

"Don't we all have things to do?" Belle asked. Yeah, let me tell you, it was a bit weird picturing Belle inside the body of this older Indian woman, but I swear it was her. She waved everyone away. Several of the Indian women stayed, conclaved with Belle for a few minutes, and then went away, everyone drifting into the jungle, becoming a part of it. Anna kissed my forehead and then bounced away, her red hair visible for a long while, until she looked like a red bird in the canopy.

I sat up and looked down. Like the others, I was clad in early jungle wear. I was on a kind of hammock, swinging between two thin trees which also provided the beginnings to a thatched roof. Inside was dim with morning light. I felt comfortable here, safe. Even a gorgeous bright green snake hanging from another nearby tree didn't bother me.

Belle brought me something to eat. In the near distance, the jungle dipped to the water; I could hear a stream cascading away from us. Children splashed and laughed.

I drank the cool milky liquid from a container that looked like the shell of a huge nut.

"Not bad," I said. "What's it made from?"

"A little of this, a little of that," Belle said. "You have helped me make it many times."

Slowly, slowly, I began seeing more things in the jungle. Another hut. And another one. In a circle, with a bare spot in the center, for fires and dancing. The canopy filtered sunlight. I breathed deeply: the smells of a thousand crushed herbs.

"How was your visit with the Mother?" Belle said. "Did you learn much?"

"I learned this is all part of a bad dream," I said. I swung my feet around and put them on the ground. The Earth felt cool and solid beneath my hardened souls. Soles.

"A bad dream?" Belle asked. She pushed her hair away from her face. It was a beautiful face. She had been here a long while and seen a great deal.

"Maybe a good dream," I said. "How long have we been here?"

"Who?"

"Us white guys."

"We found your group a time back," Belle said, "but the crazy men have been here for some time. Come. If you're feeling well, you can go out in the river with me."

I stood and followed Belle. She walked with grace, immediately a part of the jungle when she stepped from the village. I glanced behind us a moment later and could not see the huts. We walked down the flora-strewn bank to the water. Trees grew out of and around the stream, vines hanging from them. Brown children swung from the vines and jumped into a still pool amidst the flowing water. When they saw Belle, they called "Mother, Mother" in her language. She smiled and nodded.

"You birthed all these babies?" I asked.

"You went away smart and came back stupid?" she asked.

"I was smart?"

Belle laughed. "They call me mother. I have no children of my own. That is why my husband cast me aside. Crazy men." She stopped and shook a finger in my face and laughed, "But we had the last laugh on them, didn't we?"

We walked—actually, Belle walked, I kind of slid—downstream away from the children until we came to a tiny boat made from what appeared to be a hollowed-out log. Belle pushed it into the water and waited for me. I stared into the tea-colored water and wondered what creatures of the night waited below.

"Keelie?"

"I think I'm afraid of monster-infested waters."

"You're funny," she said. "Now get in."

I shrugged and got in with her. She steered the boat with one oar into the middle of the stream. We bumped against this and that; nothing I could see. Everything seemed ink-colored. Green and ink. I smelled herbs and teas. Above us, birds called out. Orange ones. Red. Green. Were those toucans? Swearing at us as we drifted past. A huge black cat lounged on the bank, in a spot of sunlight, licking her paws. She yawned at us.

After a few minutes, Belle turned us closer to the bank. The stream began moving more quickly. Suddenly, a brown ocean seemed to open before us. I gripped the sides of the boat tightly. We'd never make it: this tiny boat, that huge river tugging at the boat. Belle turned the boat onto the brown water and hugged the banks. In the middle of this vast river, currents pushed the water forward, faster and faster. We were on the ocean of rivers. Unending trees and impenetrable jungle were on both sides of us, before us, and behind us.

"Our Mother," Belle said, using the word "mother" in her own language as though she were speaking of a Goddess.

The Amazon River.

We went only a short ways before Belle ran the boat partway up a bank. Then she leaned over the boat and watched the cloudy water. Suddenly, she reached into the water. In the next moment, a five-foot fish lay in our boat. Belle whispered a prayer and then killed the fish by smacking it against the boat.

"Your turn," she said.

"I've done this before?"

She nodded.

I hunched over the side of the boat and watched the muddy waters. I didn't know what the hell I was watching for when this huge gaping mouth appeared. By reflex, my hand went out, I grabbed the poor creature gasping for breath and threw it on top of its compatriot. It slapped around the bottom of the small boat, nearly knocking Belle out. She quickly grabbed it and killed it.

We did this twice more. Blessing the water before we started and thanking the Mother River when we got the fish. Of course, we thanked the fish for giving up its life. I liked the prayer: we recognized the fishes' right to life and our right to life and somehow we were both all right with it. Of course, the fish couldn't really vote on any of this. I felt invigorated. Alive and lively. This was primal living. I could do it; I was doing it!

The entire fishing expedition didn't take long. When we had four gigantic fish, we pushed the boat back into the water. The vastness of Momma River made me a little scared shitless. This time we both had to steer the boat. Upstream was a bit difficult, but in no time we were back at the village. The children ran up to the boat; two kids to a fish, they carried our catch deftly up the hill to awaiting adults. I pulled the boat up high on the bank and then followed Belle.

"What do you call that kind of fish?" I asked. I wanted to know the names of everything in my new home.

"Stupid fish," she answered.

Before long, the village circle, the village that was a part of the jungle, was filled with people, mostly these tall native women and their chil-

dren. An occasional native man. Victor and
Anna returned carrying what I assumed were
fruit. A fire was started. Fruit was opened,
peeled, cut; fish gutted and put over the fire.
One of the women drew a circle around us
using a brown liquid; they said prayers, and
then we ate. Using our fingers we ate the fish
and some kind of grainlike substance from
bowls. We drank milky liquid and consumed
everything. I was so famished I barely noticed
the people around me. After a bit of sweet cake,
the children found the laps of adults and starting falling asleep. Lee put her head on Victor's
shoulder and went to sleep. They looked sweet
together, almost happy. Too young to know
much. Anna sat across from me, eating with
more gusto than even I did. It seemed to get
dark very quickly. Belle told a story of laughing
monkeys and then people started drifting away.

Women carried children. Couples, men and
women and women and women, went into the
night. The fire slowly died out. I was alone in a
dark that seemed almost total, except for a spot
right above the village. Stars shimmered there.
Pinpricks of light. I heard things slither and
splash and whisper and cough and cackle and I
wanted to stand up and scream, "All right,
lights please! Let me wake up." Just then, someone touched my arm.

I jumped.

"It's Anna. How are you doing?"

"I'm about to go stark raving mad, how do you think I'm doing? Why are we here? How did we get here? I can't imagine there's an airport nearby. Whose idea was it?"

"Darling," she said in her beautiful Irish drawl. "I don't know what an airport is but we came by ship. We stole it, remember?"

I could just barely see her next to me. But I could smell her. What was it? She leaned toward me and French-kissed me again. I felt the shivers clear to my toes. Then she moved down and kissed my bare breast.

"You taste like salt," she whispered. "Sweat. I like it."

I remembered the first time we had made love, she and I and Victor. I glanced around. This time it was just the two of us. Her fingers tickled the insides of my thighs. I was hers, all hers. We sat on each other's laps, our crotches kissing, legs around each other, and we kissed and petted and nibbled and drank until the jungle seemed to undulate with our orgasms, which, of course, it didn't, busy with its own orgiastic pleasures. We fell to sleep wrapped around each other, like snakes twined around one another, our own snake dance. I thanked Eriskegal. These. These were the good old days.

Twelve

•••••••••

W hen I awakened the next morning, Anna was gone. Victor sat next to me in the gray of dawn. Or was it gray? More misty, indistinct, as if the jungle had to be recreated this morning after disappearing in the night.

Victor looked as though he had not slept.

I sat up and rubbed my eyes and hair. This was only the second night's sleep I had gotten in a long while. I stretched and sighed. Felt nice.

Victor stared at me, waiting for me to ask him what was wrong. So I did.

"What's wrong, brother dear? Have a close encounter with a jungle creature last night? You don't look well."

"You know what's wrong. I'm tired of this. I did what you asked. I stayed with Lee, pretended to be her husband. She's better now.

How long are you going to torture me this way?"

This Victor was equally as intense as the one from the twentieth century.

"I can honestly say, bro, that I haven't a clue as to what you're talking about."

He grabbed my upper arm and held on to it too tightly. "You and Anna."

I jerked my arm from his grasp. "Listen, I don't know what our previous relationship was, but I don't give a fig if you are my brother, don't you ever, ever touch me unless I want you to."

"And I guess this means you don't want me to? You prefer Anna? You prefer the woman's touch?"

"I prefer not to have this conversation," I said. "We are brother and sister aren't we?"

Victor stared at me. "Of course we are. What's the matter with you?"

"I—I told you, yesterday, the accident, or whatever happened, it's left me without all my marbles."

"Your what?"

"Victor, I don't know where we are or why we're here."

"We escaped on Lee's father's ship," he said. "You don't remember that?"

"Where was this ship?"

"Spain!"

"All right! I got that. And you're saying we rowed this ship across the ocean until we got to the New World, i.e., the Americas?"

He nodded.

"And where is Lee's father? The owner of this little Spanish galleon?"

"We threw him overboard. Keelie, this isn't funny. Don't you know anything?"

"I know a lot of things, just none of them would be very useful now. Who are these women we're living with, the natives?"

"The Coniupuyara, the grand mistresses of the jungle, they're called. They've left their villages and created their own."

"Like us?"

"Keelie! Stop teasing me. You're just trying to change the subject."

As I gazed out at the jungle, it began moving. People emerged from the mist, like ghosts suddenly becoming incarnate. One of the few Indian men brought Victor and me some kind of cake. I devoured mine. Belle nodded to me and then sat in a circle with her Coniupuyara friends, deep in conversation. Lee lay in a hammock not far from Victor and me, her eyes closed, fat and uncomfortable. I didn't see Anna.

"She went out fishing early," Victor said.

"Who?"

"Anna! Anna! That's who you're looking for, isn't it?" His voice was raised in anger and several of the villagers stopped to watch us. He turned red and quickly ate his cake.

Obviously something was going on with Victor and me that I wasn't picking up on.

"We haven't been alone in such a long time," Victor whispered. "Won't you come with me today?"

I hesitated, wondering what else I had to do, or how long I was going to be staying in this place and time. What the heck.

I shrugged. "Fine with me."

When we were finished eating, we got up and went to Belle. Victor told her where we were going.

"Be careful," she said. "The crazy people are coming down the Mother. They are stopping along the way to rob and kill."

I didn't know what she meant but no one seemed unduly alarmed, so I followed Victor away from the village. We walked a short time in the dense undergrowth before Victor climbed a vine-wrapped tree. I went after him, my feet doing what came naturally. Like making love with Anna, I was certain I had climbed these trees before. Once we were in the canopy, we paused to look around. Multicolored birds gazed at us momentarily and then looked away. Insects crawled around and away from us. The sunlight was bright; I closed my eyes and tilted my head to let it warm my face.

When I opened my eyes, Victor was watching me. He started to say something but changed his mind, apparently. He grabbed a vine, tugged on it, then stood, put it between his legs and swung. "Oooooh weee!" he called, disappearing into the canopy.

"Victor! Are you all right?"

"Come and find me!"

I got another vine, pulled on it, and then jumped into space, holding on to the vine with all my strength. The ride only lasted a few moments but it was exhilarating. Free. The air rushing across my face. My hair flowing behind me. The vine against my chest. It was glorious!

I laughed as Victor grabbed me and pulled me next to him.

"Watch what you're doing!" he said. "You could get killed that way!"

"Sorry," I said, "I was just having fun." We were about six inches away from one another. I felt that old sexual attraction. His arms and chest were muscled, nice. I wanted to touch him, but I didn't. I moved away. We jumped to the next tree. And then the next. And the next. By the time we had gotten to wherever we were going, Victor seemed to have relaxed, too, and was laughing. We climbed onto a banana tree next, or something like a banana tree. Victor cut a bunch of long wine-colored fruit from it. We climbed down onto the jungle floor again. Monkeys screamed at us.

I turned and waved. They waved back.

Victor grabbed a reed growing near one of the trees and broke it open. He tipped it up and let the clear liquid run into his mouth. I did the same. It was the sweetest water. Then we sat against one of the huge vine-covered trees and ate a couple of bananas. Or whatever they were. Being Tarzan and Jane was hard work.

Our shoulders touched. Victor leaned over and kissed the top of my arm.

"I've done everything you've asked," he said. "But it's too hard. You're the only one."

I shifted away from him. This reminded me too much of the last conversation he had had with Lee. And she had ended up dead.

"Victor, you're always wanting to put your dick where it doesn't belong."

He turned to face me. Now we were inches from each other. I could smell him. I knew his scent. It was so familiar. I knew the feel of him.

I kissed him. I thought this would end it. I mean, I'd have to feel revulsion. If he was my brother. But I didn't. He kissed me back, pressing himself against me.

"Victor," I whispered.

He pulled away from me. "Now you want me? God *damn* you. You were sent from hell to torture me!"

He stood and left. Disappeared into the jungle.

"Yes, I was sent from hell all right," I said, but I was alone, completely alone. Except for the millions of insects, reptiles, and mammals all around me. I put my hands between my legs and squeezed. This place certainly aroused me. Or the people in this place. I felt in a constant state of heightened . . . awareness.

A bright green frog hopped from behind a tree and stared at me. We watched one another, motionless, for a long while. I felt as though I were becoming a part of the jungle as I looked into the frog's black eyes. Roots growing from my butt, my feet, heels. I smiled at the frog.

"They're coming," the frog said. Then she broke the stare and hopped away. "They're coming, they're coming."

Who was coming? What did it matter to me, anyway? I had grown roots, I was a permanent part of the jungle. Nothing mattered except being here.

Then a toucan flew down and stood next to me. "Haven't you got ears?" the toucan said. "That was the Paul Revere of this particular jungle. Get your white ass moving."

I closed my eyes. No. I liked it here. Alone, yet a part of everything.

"Yeah, yeah," the toucan said. "That's very Zen and everything but you're skipping a lot of steps. You've got places to see, people to be. People to warn."

I opened my eyes again. It was almost dark. Had I fallen to sleep?

Belle appeared before me. "Come, Lee is having her baby. She's calling for you."

She pulled me up. I think she pulled roots off my butt.

"Is this a dream?" I inquired.

Belle laughed, "What do you think, honey?"

I came fully awake about the time we reached the village, in time to hear Lee screaming. She was pissed and in pain.

I stopped in Belle's tracks. "Hey, I don't know nothing about birthin' no babies."

"She doesn't know our ways," Belle said. "We don't know what to do for her. It is up to her to bring the child across, but she is fighting it."

I went under the thatched roof. Inside Lee lay on a mat, writhing. Two of the Coniupuyara squatted behind her. Another was at her feet.

Lee screamed again and flung her arms out, trying to hit everyone close to her.

The woman at Lee's feet stood. "She is dreaming," the woman said. "She needs to be with her child. She must help her across or they may both die. She isn't very strong."

"She's a fucking child," I said. When I saw Victor again, I'd kill him, knocking up a poor girl like her. "What can I do?"

"Bring her back," the woman answered. She knelt down again.

Bring her back from where? There she was, plain as anything was around here. One of the Coniupuyara behind Lee stood and motioned for me to take her place. She was bigger than I was and certainly better equipped to withstand Lee's blows. But I squatted next to the remaining Amazon.

"Lee," I said to her, "it's Keelie. I'm here."

Her face was streaked with tears, her eyes nearly swollen shut. She groaned.

I glanced outside. Anna and Victor stood close to one another, watching. If I clicked my heels together three times would I go back? Forward? Find the place I needed to be.

"Keelie?" Lee whimpered.

"I'm here," I said. Lee reached up. I took her hand; she squeezed mine. And we melted. Fuck. I hadn't melted with Anna or Victor this time. Why now? I tried to pull away. Lee screamed.

Someone was inside us again, battering us, ramming us, grunting and sweating, whispering obscenities. Fuck, fuck, fuck. Not again. This fucking hurts! Stop it, you bastard. STOP IT!

"Lee, listen," I said. "It's not happening now. Not now. You're having a baby. You're not being raped."

She whimpered in my mind. Teetered toward insanity. "I cannot do this," she said. "It will be just like him. Don't you see? Just like him. Killing and raping. Pillaging. If I kill it now, if we both die now, it stops."

He was ripping her. Doing it again. What was this thing that drove men like him? The testosterone craze?

"I have to stop it now," she said.

"It can stop, sweetie. Come on. Come back. It's not someone's dick in your vagina. You're trying to give birth."

The man inside us was gone. Snapped away. Lurking in the background.

"Momma!"

I remembered Belle in modern times talking about reaching across to the other side, pulling Pearl into this world. I reached out, Lee screamed and pulled my hand away.

"It will be a demon child!"

"I don't believe in demons!" I reached out again.

"Momma!" It was a girl's voice.

The man was getting closer.

"No," I said, "Lee, listen to your child's voice. Bring her home."

Lee reached across the chasm and together we pulled the child toward us.

Lee released my hand, and we were no longer one. I fell back against one of the Coniupuyara. The midwife laid the bloody baby on her mother's breast. Lee was almost unconscious. She didn't touch the baby.

"She needs to break the cord," the midwife said to me.

"She can't."

"You, then."

I moved to Lee's side. The baby whimpered on Lee's breast, trying to suckle. Her face was wrinkled; her hair white. Pearl.

"Pearl," I whispered. I took the cord where the midwife showed me and I bit through it, as if I had done it a thousand times before, and maybe I had. I tasted blood, salt, my flesh and blood. I tied the cord and then picked the baby off Lee's breast and held her against my shoulder, warm, present, and listened to her breathing. She was strong. Healthy. I kissed her bloody face and then gave her to the midwife who gently wiped her off and then handed her to another woman, who offered the baby her breast.

Lee birthed the placenta and then turned on her side and fell unconscious. She looked too much like the Lee back in the twentieth century after Victor had left her, after she had taken the pills, curled up on her bed, ready to die.

"You can help her," the midwife said.

"No. I got the baby here. I'm tired of trying to save everyone."

"It is yourself you save," she said.

I don't give a fuck. I don't give a fuck. Why

does it always involve so much fucking pain? I liked being rooted in the jungle.

"You are still rooted here," Belle said. "Always here."

I looked at Pearl pulling on the other mother's breast. Demanding, pulling already. And then at Lee. I sighed.

I lay down on the mat next to her and then spooned myself up against her back, felt myself falling into her, melting. We were being battered, torn, thrown aside.

"It was awful," I said. "It was so awful. Let's just kill the bastard."

"But he's my father. I love him, too. I hate him. Hate him. Hate him."

"Remember," I said, and we were in the gym together watching Lee dance across the shiny floor, moving to her own rhythms, until we two were moving with her, across the gymnasium, across the plains, dancing with the long grasses, the buffalo, down to the desert, dipping and baying with the coyotes, down to the jungle, deep down, dancing to the beat of Momma-Earth. We laughed. Three old crones, dancing as one. One and the same. "I want to come back as a dancer," she whispered. "Why not be one now?" I asked.

When I awakened, Lee was sleeping next to me, Pearl at her breast. Everyone else was asleep, it seemed. The jungle was bright with full moon. I got up, stiff and achy, and went down to the riverbank. The moon spotlighted Victor sitting alone.

I went and sat next to him. Across the stream, green eyes blinked at us.

"How come you're awake?" I asked.

He shrugged and stared off in front of him. "I tried to sleep, but I kept seeing you and the way you looked at me when Lee was in labor. I've never seen such hatred."

"I'm sorry," I said. "I thought you had caused Lee's pain."

"Me?"

"It's all right," I said. "Don't worry about it." I rested my head on his shoulder.

He stroked my hair. "It was never like that with us, the way it was with Lee and her father. He forced her. You saw."

I saw?

"You and I were different. It was just—it was just us. No one else."

"No one forced us?"

Victor laughed uncomfortably. "No one had to force us. We just did what came naturally."

"Sorry, but that's not what comes naturally for most brothers and sisters."

"Come, Keelie," he said. "You're exhausted. You need to sleep. Lie down."

I laid my head on his thigh and closed my eyes.

"What about you?" I asked.

"I'm on watch," he said, petting my hair. He began humming and then softly singing some song from our childhood. For a moment I could remember being brother and sister, alone against our parents, who were either beating one another or one of us.

"On watch for whom?"

"Haven't you heard?" he whispered. "They're coming, the crazy men are coming."

Thirteen

•••••••••••

When I came awake again, the jungle had changed, shifted, held its breath. It seemed still yet anxious. I imagined monkeys above chewing on their fingernails, snakes drinking too much of the tea-colored water, jaguars gnawing on cocoa nut.

I went to the village center where the Coniupuyara were gathered, spears in hand. It was no wonder the river was named Amazon; when the explorers—the crazy men—saw these women they must have thought they found the mythic Amazon nation. Perhaps it had not been so mythic.

"We can't go," Anna said.

"Gee, that's too bad," I said. "I was looking forward to killing today."

"If they see any whites," Belle said, "they would come and try to rescue you."

"Mother Belle will stay, too," the midwife said. "She will lead you and the children to safety in case we don't return."

"Why are you going after them? If we leave them alone won't they pass on by?" I asked.

"We have heard from the Frog People that this man is particularly vicious."

"Frog People?" I asked. "Are these frogs that talk or people you call frogs?"

The midwife ignored me.

"The men on this ship are nearly starving, nearly dead, yet they kill with ferocity. And he knows our languages. He has many people as his slaves."

Anna and Victor glanced at each other. I frowned.

"May the Mother bless and protect you all," Belle said.

The Coniupuyara left quickly, quietly, slipping into the jungle.

I went to find Pearl.

She was in her mother's arms nursing. Lee had circles under her eyes, her skin was ashen. She smiled. I wondered what business the midwife had going off to war when she had a patient to tend to.

"Are you eating?" I asked. "You don't look well."

Victor and Anna followed me into the hut.

"Keelie, you're always so diplomatic," Anna

said. She sat next to Lee and took her hand. "You are a little pale. How do you feel?"

"Extraordinarily tired," Lee said. "But look at my baby. Isn't she wonderful?" She grinned at Pearl and then up at Victor. He sat on the other side of her. "I'm glad you're all here with me. I've decided on a name for her. I'd like to call her Keelie, after you, Keelie."

I sat next to Anna and stroked Lee's damp forehead. "Honey, that's a sweet idea, but how about Pearl? Don't you think she looks like a precious pearl, born from her mother-of-pearl?"

Lee gazed at her child. At our child. It felt as though I had birthed her, too. Hadn't I felt her tiny hand across the great divide? My child.

"Yes, I like that. She is our precious pearl, here, in this place, our New World."

Lee put her hand over mine and squeezed. I smiled at her and then looked outside. What was happening to our great protectors now. These ladies of the jungle?

I left the four in the hut and went outside and down to the river. The children played quietly on the banks, throwing something back and forth between themselves. Belle was squatting on the sand nearby.

I got on my haunches next to her. This was becoming my place. A real beach hound.

The jungle sounded the same again. Unmoved by our particular catastrophe.

"We have never wanted to fight," Belle said, listening as she talked. I listened, too, but heard only the water and the jungle, the children whispering. She listened beyond us, she listened to the Mother. "But from the beginning we had to. Just a little, but enough to frighten them." She laughed, "And our men frightened easily. They always did. They knew their power was false, that they could fall any moment. We won many battles, even some with the crazy white people. They look the most surprised. They who are the most crazy. They come all that distance without women and children. I think they leave their minds behind, too.

"We took over a place north, the ruins of another people. Circles everywhere. Place to birth our babies." She made circles in the air. "A place where we could be wilder." She laughed. "They have come to fear us over the years, make up stories about us—that we kill our male children! What mother would do that? We raise them to be good men." She looked around. "I wasn't certain why some of us decided to come closer to the Mother for a time. I thought maybe it was to rescue you. Maybe it was to fight with the crazy white men. Maybe it was to die." She closed her eyes and sighed. "Sometimes I want to just wish them all away, all back to where they came from."

"Us, too?"

She opened her eyes and smiled. "Especially you!" She put her arms around me and held me tight, for only a moment. "No matter what happens, we will meet again."

"You can bet on that," I said.

This day, time nearly stopped. I tried imagining the women on the edge of the jungle, coming out to frighten and slay the Spanish sailors. I tried to imagine them victorious. The ship carried away on the fast currents of the Mother.

Belle tended to Lee. She seemed to get weaker. Anna and I fed the children. And the adults. We waited. The children cried. Pearl drank and drank while her mother was barely conscious.

Everything felt unreal.

Near dusk, the Coniupuyara came out of the jungle, tall, bloodied ghosts, holding on to one another, some staggering, some not, all awash in sorrow. We tended to them in hushes. The jungle shivered beyond us, but we moved in slow motion, wiping the blood, pressing juices or salves on places where Belle showed us. Sadness filled the village, made us all ache. I knew many had died on both sides. I hadn't known their names, yet I felt their presences missing. As if pieces of a body had been cut off. We would never be whole again. Could never be. Why didn't people see that?

"They have no souls," the midwife said. "We fought dead people. They will return. We must leave in the morning."

This was all that was said. At least all I could understand. The women stayed to themselves, embracing, weeping, eating, only letting us wipe their tears and blood away.

"Mother, where do these beings come from?" Belle whispered as the sun disappeared, dropping night onto the jungle.

We were safe from them, the soulless men, for now. They would never venture off their ship in this dark. Their terror, our safety.

I checked on Pearl and Lee. The midwife was feeding her herbs and roots. Anna slept next to Lee, tears staining her dusty hands.

I walked deep into the jungle, away from the sounds of crying, toward the cats in the distance, roaring and yawning, swatting phantoms in the night, past a line of fluorescent insects marching up a tree. When I grew tired and was certain I was lost, I followed the sound of water, found a clearing near the edge of the stream, and sat down. The moon was not quite overhead yet.

I pulled my knees up to my chest and put my head on my knees. This was only the beginning of the death and destruction. Only the beginning. What was it like for the rest of them, to know the past instead of the future? To have hope that safety was possible, resurrection the norm?

"Keelie?" A whisper in the dark. Was I dreaming again?

"What?"

A shadow sat next to me. I recognized his scent.

Victor. "How'd you find me?"

"I was just going to ask you the same thing." He laughed. "We were always doing that kind of thing when we were kids. Remember? The parents thought we were the devil's spawn!"

"Gee, that doesn't say a lot for them, now does it?"

He laughed. "I never thought of that. You always have looked at the world a little differently than most people."

I leaned against him. He put his arm across my shoulders. It was so dark, I wondered how we had ever found this place at all.

"We've seen so much death," Victor whispered. "Been to so many places where people destroyed one another. I thought we had left that all behind."

I snuggled close to him. I suddenly didn't care if he was my brother, I wanted to wash away all the blood, all the hurt.

I kissed his stubbly cheek. How did he keep himself beardless out here in the nether regions? He turned his face to me and we kissed.

I felt no revulsion, no sense of past or present, as Victor moved into me, as we rocked together on the darkened beach, the jungle beasts our bored spectators. For a time, I just wanted to connect with him, find why we kept ending up in each other's places. And though this had been a long time coming, we moved slowly, whispering to one another, forgetting everything except these moments when there was just us. Only us. Skin pressed against skin, in loving embrace, I felt unspeakably contented.

We slept near to one another, embracing. Just before I fell into my dreams, Victor whispered, "I will always love you. I will never leave you," and the Frog People sang, "They're coming. They're coming."

We walked back to the village together, when the jungle was still made only of mist and we were a part of the mist, characters in a dream.

Anna looked up at us from the fire, puzzled, watching as we released the other's hand and went to opposite sides of the fire.

"How is Lee?" Victor asked Anna.

"She seems better," Anna answered.

Belle crouched near us. "We will leave as soon as everyone has eaten."

I heard a toucan snort; I looked up. The mist dissolved and men of steel were walking toward us, spears and swords raised. They looked ridiculous in their conquistador costumes and I almost laughed. Several of them held torches, burning black in the morning.

What I had trouble with, have always had trouble with, was how the natural world seemed to stay the same when horror abounded. The apocalypse was upon us, yet the sun continued to shine. The birds sang. Insects chirped.

Or maybe it all stopped and I didn't notice.

The remaining Coniupuyara appeared out of nowhere, it seemed, screaming their Amazon cry, still bloody and battered from the day before. The men advanced. Belle ran after the children. Anna grabbed a spear. Pearl began crying.

I ran into the hut. "Can you move?" I asked Lee.

She nodded. I took Pearl from her and pressed her against me. What safety would I provide against a weapon? We started out of the hut. Victor and Anna stood in front of us.

Suddenly. He was there. Out of the mist. Out of bounds. Out of place. The father. Father Lee. His wretched spirit in the wretched body of the leader of these crazy men. This was the father. The father of Lee and Victor. The father who raped his child in this century, fathered a child called Pearl. The daughter-fucker who was alive and well in Florida in the twentieth century. Bent on destruction. Or just bent.

The men were afraid of the women. And they

hated them. They desperately tried to kill them. I heard people dying, screaming, but I could not take my eyes off the father. He looked at Lee.

Seeing him, she screamed. And screamed.

"Lee!" I cried, shaking her, trying to stop her, but she was now frozen in horror: the madman had returned from the dead. "Let's go!" I said. "Run!"

"You don't belong here," Victor called in Spanish. "Leave us in peace."

The father laughed while the men around him died and killed. "You left me to drown. And now you expect me to leave in peace? Besides, you have my daughter." He glanced at the baby at my breast. "Or should I say you have my daughters."

Time slowed again. I wanted to stop it forever. The father raised his sword and took careful aim. Holding it as though the sword were merely a dart. I tried to reach up through time, I tried, I screamed, I tried to stop it, to stop it, to stop it, but the aim was true.

The sword sliced through Victor's heart.

He spun toward me, surprised, reaching for me.

Our fingers brushed, touched.

He died as he fell to the ground.

"Victor!" I screamed. Lee took the baby, which nearly fell from my arms. I dropped to the ground. Pulled at Victor. Shook him. Screamed at him. Kissed the blood from his lips.

Anna and Lee pulled on me.

"Victor!" I screamed. "This is too fucking cruel!"

They jerked me away.

We slipped into the jungle, sobbing, wailing, we joined the cries of the other jungle creatures, and followed the Coniupuyara away from the crazy men. North.

I closed my eyes as I ran and sang, "There's no place like home, there's no place like home."

I tripped and the sounds of the jungle faded away and all I knew was the taste of Victor's blood on my lips.

Fourteen
• • • • • • • • • • • •

A pause. Then I opened my eyes. The jungle was gone. I was in another memory, held firmly in place by chains and shackles that dug into my wrists and ankles.

My body hurt. Everywhere.

I was naked. Blood and other bodily fluids stuck to my legs. I reached up noisily and felt my head. I had no hair.

The dark damp room smelled of fear. I hadn't really understood that expression until now. But I smelled it. Someone moved in the corner. A window let a square of light onto the dirt floor.

Outside, people were shouting in French, "Kill the witch! Kill the witch!" A woman screamed. I tried to look out the window, but it was too high.

"You don't want to see, sister," the huddled mass in the corner said. "It'll be us next."

The door I hadn't seen until now rattled and then opened. A man dressed in blue and purple robes, a square hat on his head, strode into the room, his fingers on the beads tied to his belt. Hart. The little bastard had once been a part of the Inquisition. What a surprise.

"Well, witch. We have given you the first and second degrees," he said, moving close to me. His breath smelled like rotten fish. "You have yet to confess. Once we give the third degree, the devil's tongue is loosened and you will tell all."

"My guess is anyone would confess to anything just to stop the pain, is that how it works?" I said.

He put a finger on my chin. "She talks." He dragged his filthy finger down my chest. So this was the way it was.

"Is this the only way you can get girls? To put them in shackles? How romantic."

He slapped my face.

I slumped to the floor. I was weaker than I thought. Hart put his hands in his pants, started to pull out his dick, when the door banged open. The room filled with four or five people, all dressed in heavy clothes, their heads and hands covered, too.

One of them hit Hart over the head. This time it was he who slumped to the floor. Another one unshackled me and gave me a shirt and slacks to put on; another helped the woman in the corner.

The one who had hit Hart took off his head covering. Victor. My brother!

Alive!

I ran to him and we embraced. I kissed his cheeks, his forehead, his mouth. He laughed.

"Come, we must leave!" Anna's voice, muffled by her disguise.

"You're alive," I said to Victor.

"Cover yourself," he said. "We must get you out before they finish with the other killing." He pulled a blanket around my shoulders. "Of course I'm alive. I'm sorry we couldn't get here sooner."

I held his face between my hands. His skin was white, his eyes bright. This was before the Amazon journey. How could I have forgotten? I remember backwards, backwards.

Maybe I could change history. Maybe I could keep him from going to South America. Keep him from dying.

He spun me around and pushed me forward. "Move!"

The sunlight hurt my eyes. It didn't matter; a moment after stepping out of my prison, I was gently thrown into a wagon full of straw. The wagon lurched forward as they covered me in straw. Someone began singing. I felt Victor sit on the side of the wagon; he reached his hand down into my golden world and took my hand.

I knew, for the moment, that I was safe.

We stopped hours later by a stream in the woods. Anna helped me out. I could barely walk. I wouldn't let go of Victor's hand.

"It's all right," he said. "I'll be right here."

Anna put her arms around me, along with another woman, Beth, and took me down to the river. They washed me off, cooing when I moaned, wiping my tears. My body remembered what they had done to me; I was glad my mind didn't. At least not yet.

I started shivering from the cold water. Beth gently pulled on my clothes again.

Anna took my arm. We staggered back toward the wagon. Victor was still there, talking with the other two rescuers, one man and one woman. Victor. My eyes filled with tears. He was alive. And my body hurt.

I started to cry.

Victor came to me, picked me up, and put me in the bed of straw. I couldn't stop crying. I wrapped myself around him, wouldn't let him leave, felt him relax in my arms, hold me tight. He was alive. Alive. I could stop that sword. Could and would.

Only hold me forever.

I sobbed myself to sleep, my wails mingling with the lamentations of Eriskegal, Lee, Anna,

Belle, Pearl, Victor, my own, down through time. I was tired. And everything hurt.

I awakened in a dimly lit room, warm blankets beneath and on me, a lumpy pillow under my head. A crucifix hung on the wall opposite the bed. Across from the high window a kind of dresser or wardrobe stood with a pitcher and bowl on top.

I was all alone. I touched the top of my head. A bit of fuzz was growing out. I curled myself into a fetal position. I was never going to leave this room. It was warm, had a bit of light. I wasn't thirsty or hungry.

"I've never seen her like this." Victor's voice, outside the door. "She's always been so strong."

"She'll be all right." A woman's voice. "She just needs time."

I don't need time. I need a new life. Lots of new lives. Ones where women weren't constantly being raped or beaten or otherwise abused. I sighed. I was never getting up.

Someone tapped lightly on my door and then it opened. A dark woman dressed in the purple robes came in. She had the prettiest bronze-colored skin and black eyes and when she smiled at me, Lilith was there. Lilith!

"How are you feeling, Keelie?" she asked, sitting on the edge of the bed. She was so beautiful. And powerful. Nobody was going to mess with her.

Victor followed her in. He stood apart from us, his hands folded in front of him.

"I am glad to meet you," Lilith said. "We hoped you would be able to stay with us a long while, but we fear we have a traitor among us, and the abbey is in jeopardy."

I sat up a little bit. "I never saw you as the Catholic type."

Lilith laughed, "I never have been." She patted my hand. "We're going to have to start making arrangements for you to leave. Maybe sooner than we like."

"I just got here," I said. "I want to be still for a while. I want to be safe."

Lilith glanced at Victor. "I know it's been difficult."

I pulled my hand away from her. "How can you know? How can anyone know!"

"Sister, I watched my entire family be strangled and then burned as witches. None of us is a stranger to agony."

"And that's supposed to make me feel better?"

Lilith sighed and stood. "No. It shouldn't make any of us feel better. I'll have someone bring you food. You've been asleep for nearly three days. Welcome back."

She strode from the room, the robes swishing

behind her. When she had left, Victor quietly closed the door and then came and sat on the bed.

He cleared his throat and looked uncomfortable.

I took his hand. At least he was alive.

"I'm sorry I didn't get to you before—before they hurt you."

"Victor, I'm not your responsibility."

He looked surprised.

"Of course you are. You are my baby sister."

"I don't think of you as a brother," I said.

He got up and began pacing.

"I heard you were in jail, and someone put me in touch with the abbess. We tried to get to you sooner but we couldn't. I hope he didn't hurt you too badly."

"I don't remember what he did."

He stopped pacing and looked at me.

"I'm so sorry," he whispered. "It reminded me of when we were kids. How I could never stop them from hurting you."

Just then the door opened and another woman dressed in robes brought a tray of food. She set it on the bed.

"I brought enough for your brother, too," she said and then left us alone.

The food smelled so good that I sat up and began eating. Soup. Bread. Fruit. Cheese. More bread. I pulled Victor onto the bed with me, and he ate, too.

"That was the best meal of my life," I said when we had finished. Victor put the tray on the dresser.

"I should be going," he said. "You need your rest."

"Why are you treating me like a stranger?" I asked. "I'm your sister. I'm—I'm your best friend. What's going on?"

Victor stood by the door.

"It's hard being so close to you," he said.

I tucked the covers in around me. "Why? Because I'm bald? Because you can't control your erotic impulses? Why?" I just wanted him to get into bed and hold me. I just wanted to feel him next to me so that I could sleep. Sleep without dreams or memories.

"None of those things," he said. He walked over to the bed and sat next to me. "Even in this place, this place that does not judge, this place where they love the land, the Mother, the way we do, we must hide how we feel about one another. And you, you made me promise to stay away."

"I changed my mind," I said. "Go lock the door if you're worried about the others, and then please get into bed with me. Tell me a story. Rock me to sleep. Just be with me. Everything else is too strange."

He leaned over and kissed my forehead. Then he kicked off his shoes and got under the covers with me. He put his arms around me and I lay on his chest. I could hear his heartbeat through his clothes.

"What story would you like to hear?" he asked.

"How about Sleeping Beauty?" I said, closing my eyes.

"I don't know that one," he said.

"She slept for a million years," I whispered.

When I woke up, I was certain, the world would be cured. Healed and whole again.

I rested for another day, and then I began taking walks around the nunnery. Although the place was replete with crucifixes and the women all wore nun's habits, this was unlike any convent I remembered. I would often catch women French-kissing each other in the hallways, holding hands at dinner, or making love under the stars. I even found Lilith and Anna necking in Lilith's office one afternoon.

They had an extremely fruitful garden and on more than one occasion I went out and helped, not really remembering what to do, just letting my fingers do what they wanted to do. Gradually I even allowed Victor out of my sight for more than a few minutes.

I felt rested and numb. I knew we were just passing time. Here it was more difficult to find the heartbeat of MommaEarth, buried beneath the cultivated hills and the stone foundation of the churches and abbey. I felt it only when I was with the women.

I knew it wouldn't last. Only a pause in the drama.

I felt as though I had no say. No choice. I had to go forward.

One evening after dinner, Lilith said, "We were right. They are looking for you, Keelie. And Victor. We think they're coming here. We are to have the company of Father Michael in a couple of days. He has always wanted to find a way to close us down. It'll be a pity to have to tell him I own the land. I will stay here no matter what happens, but you must leave, Keelie. I have heard rumors from the New World, of a land where women rule."

My heart started racing.

"You aren't suggesting we cross the ocean, are you? There must be safety here, somewhere?" I said.

"The New World?" Victor said.

"We might have a ship available," Lilith said. "Not with a willing captain but a willing crew. Some of them are women."

"On a sailing ship in the sixteenth century?" I said. "Please, you're stretching the bounds of my imagination." I think I was screeching.

I pushed away from the table. They all watched me. "I'm tired of fighting. I'm tired of the battles. I just want to go on with my life."

"That's what we're all trying to do," Anna said. "Go on with our lives. If we stay here, we'll probably be tried as witches. You already have been! You are as good as dead."

"And what the fuck does that mean!" I cried.

"I mean, you have been sentenced to death. If they find you, they need no one's permission to kill you."

"Since when is permission ever needed!"

This was ridiculous. I wasn't even safe in a nunnery.

I must have said that last bit out loud because Lilith said, "Remember who started the Inquisition, my dear, the Catholic Church. It was his highness the pope who allowed the *Malleus Maleficarum* to go forth and multiply, the torturer's bible, telling all who will listen that women are inherently evil so anything that is done to us is justified in the name of their god! Have you forgotten, love?"

"I haven't forgotten anything," I said. "I remember more than any of you could possibly remember."

Victor stood and put his hand on my arm.

"Don't tell me to calm down or I'll kill you."

I turned and ran out of the dining room, down the dim hallways to my room.

I slammed the door and leaned against it. What was wrong with me? Kill him? I didn't want him dead. I wanted him alive. Alive. I didn't want him on that ship. I wanted him in my arms.

My brother.

He knocked on the door. I knew it was him.

I pushed away from the door and swung it open. I pulled him inside, shut the door, and put my arms around him.

"Everything will work out," he murmured in my hair.

"No, it won't," I said. "Not if we get on that ship."

Full moonlight bleached the meadow. I looked down upon it from my darkened room. Victor lay in my bed asleep. The moonlight touched his face, smoothing out time, until he looked like a boy, lost in a fairy tale. Only I could kiss him awake again. My own Sleeping Beauty.

I looked out the window again. Women filled the meadow: Lilith, Anna, Beth, and all the women I didn't know. Naked. Their brown and white and black and beige skins all sharp and clear under the moon, yet hazy, as if I were watching a dream.

I slipped a robe over my head, kissed Victor's forehead, and tiptoed out of the room, out of the abbey, and into the night.

The women were dancing, singing, laughing, moving in a circle, fluid, together, and separate, their faces shiny in the night.

"Join us," Lilith sang.

I dropped my robe and stepped into the circle, naked, became a part of the women instantly, knew the words to the song, felt their heat, blood, energy, pulling me closer to the earth, deeper into myself. Lee's legs, my legs, kicked up their heels.

We stopped, spread our feet apart, centered our hips, and raised a hand up to the moon until she sat on each of our palms. I pulled her light down my arm, down into my heart. Pulled her into my body and soul. Planted myself in the earth, in the moment.

"We call upon the Goddess to bless this circle," Lilith sang. "To keep us wise. To let us harm none."

"To let us know when to be still," another said.

"And when to run."

"To keep us healthy."

"To let us leave this life readily when it is time."

"To bless those we love and keep them safe."

Yes. Yes. Yes.

We danced again. Under MommaMoon. Laughing. Kissing. Embracing. Calling to ourselves and the world.

These were the real witches.

We were the witches.

I could save Victor. Myself. Anna. Belle. Lee. The world.

When the circle was dissolved, the women moved away in pairs. Anna came to me, took my hand in hers. I kissed her hand. "Not yet," I whispered, knowing it would happen one day, knowing what her mouth felt like against mine, her legs wrapped around mine.

I watched the women disappear into the night, and then I started back up to the abbey.

An owl hooted at me from an old oak. "They're coming, they're coming."

"Who?" I asked.

"Shouldn't that be my line?" the owl asked. "But you know who's coming. They. This time shouldn't you tell someone? They're coming, coming, coming."

Fuck.

"Lilith!" I screamed.

They who wanted to capture and kill me. And Victor. Anna. All of us. We must escape. We would escape. But I would keep us from that ship.

Victor looked down from the bedroom window. He had heard my scream. The women came running.

I would keep us from that ship.

I felt myself fading.

"No!" I must stay here. Here.

Fading.

189

"They're coming, coming, coming."
"Victor!" I screamed.
I must keep us off the ship.
The world whipped past me in a spiral of vertigo. I couldn't keep hold. I closed my eyes.

Fifteen

❖❖❖❖❖❖❖❖❖

I gasped for breath and opened my eyes. The wood floor beneath me moved, rolled. I smelled salt air, heard the wind in the sails. I was on the ship. The ship! Had I jumped forward in time?

Someone was beneath my skirts, kissing my knees, licking my thighs. And laughing.

Victor's laugh.

Shit. Shit. Shit. I hadn't been able to keep him off this ship.

He came up from beneath my ridiculous frilly skirts laughing, his black hair tousled, his clothes slightly rumpled. I had to smile.

"I don't like these dresses," he whispered. "I liked it much better when you wore pants."

We were in what appeared to be a tiny cabin. Sunshine streaked through the closed window. Outside I heard voices singing. The sun was sinking.

"Victor," I whispered, putting my arms around his neck, holding on tightly to him. "What are you doing here?"

"Trying to get into your pantaloons," he said. "If the captain catches his first mate trying to bed his daughter's companion, we're both in big trouble."

My body wanted him. I pulled off an inordinate amount of underclothes. Both of us giggled quietly as I guided him into me. Leaning against the wall, I wrapped my legs and arms around him. We were together. Together. He would never leave me.

We moved faster and faster, and still laughing, we orgasmed, pushing deeper into each other, reaching up until I had his heart in my hand. "I will not let you die," I said.

"Where is my first officer!" a voice boomed in Spanish. The father. I stiffened. Victor gently slid out of me. He kissed me hard on the lips.

"I've got to go," he whispered. "I love you."

He straightened his clothes, opened the door, looked both ways, and then I heard him go up the steps.

I rubbed my crotch. He felt too right, we felt too right together. How could it end on the floor of the jungle?

I shook my head. No. I wouldn't think about that.

"Mademoiselle?"

I turned around. Lee stood in the doorway. Her blond hair curled prettily. Her dress neat and tight. She wasn't pregnant yet. She looked so young.

"*Mon chère!*" I said. "I was just coming to look for you."

"*Mademoiselle*, you are speaking partly in Spanish. Remember Papa wants me to learn French."

"How *stupide of moi!*" I said. Lucky for me I was multilingual in this lifetime.

"And I will continue to teach you the languages of the savages," she said.

"That's *les* savages to you," I said.

We went up on deck. As I looked out across the ocean, I was struck with a bit of vertigo.

"*Mademoiselle?*" Lee held my hand to steady me.

"I'm all right," I said. "Please, call me Keelie."

The ship was smaller than what I would have expected. I mean this tiny thing was traversing the globe? At least part of the globe. The wind was in the sails and we moved rapidly over the roiling water. Blue skies. Sinking sun. No land in sight. Deckhands sat at one end of the ship. Was that fore, aft, a poop deck, the prow, the bridge? I hadn't a clue. But they sat eating. One had red hair sticking from his cap. He looked up at me and I realized it was a she, Anna, disguised as a sailor.

On the other end, near the steering wheel, or whatever the fuck it was, Victor stood next to the man, the father. The bastard. He smiled as he spoke with Victor. I wanted to kill him. Kill him now and it would all be over. Victor would be safe. Lee would be safe. Pearl would never be born, but she'd be born again in the twentieth century. I'd been there. I knew.

The father glanced up and met my gaze. I turned quickly away.

"Shall we play chess before supper?" Lee asked.

"Certainly." Anything to get away from him. I followed her down below. Her cabin was much bigger than mine but it still wasn't very large. Two beds. A place for her clothes and her father's. A place to eat. Was that called the captain's mess?

"You and your father sleep here together?" I asked. I nearly tripped over my dress as I went into the cabin.

She laughed and sat at the chess table. "You've been in here many times before; why do you ask that now?"

"Just curious."

"Yes, my father and I share this cabin. Do you want to be black or white?"

"Your choice. Don't you find this game boring?" I asked.

"Actually, yes, but my father wishes me to be

good at it. He says every husband wants a wife who is stimulating, and chess is such a stimulating game!"

"Where is your mother?" I asked. I moved a pawn forward. Lee did the same. I did something with my knight. Or rook.

"My mother is back home," Lee said. "You met her. Don't you remember?"

"The sea has sucked out my brains," I said. *"Lo siento."*

"You are very funny," Lee said.

"I'm a riot," I said. She moved a chess piece and then I moved.

"That's a new strategy," she said. "I've never seen it used."

"It's called the not-knowing-what-you're-doing strategy," I said. "My mind is on other things."

Lee leaned back and wrapped a curl around a finger. "Mine, too."

"Oh?"

"Have you noticed the first mate?"

Victor.

"Yes," I said, "I've noticed him."

"He's very nice," she said. "He's quite polite and he seems interested in me. He never tries to take advantage."

I thought of our recent get-together in my cabin. "No, he never takes advantage. Do others aboard try and take advantage of you?"

She looked down. "Oh, no. I only meant. You know how men are." She smiled and moved one of her pieces. "Checkmate," she said. *"Lo siento."*

"Not at all. I should be going."

"My father is expecting you for supper," she said.

"Please send my apologies," I said. I was not going to break bread with that man, no matter what. "I have a bit of a headache."

"I'll have some supper sent to you," Lee said. She sounded so much older than she was, playing her father's little hostess. I couldn't wait to kill him.

I picked up my skirts and left the cabin and went into my own. I had to figure out what to do next. I had to keep the father from killing Victor. The only way I could think of doing that was by killing the father first. How?

Anna leaned into the room. "Quick!" she whispered. "We'll have landfall in a few days. Wait for the word." Then she was gone.

I looked around my cabin for some sort of weapon. Nothing. I could go down to the galley. Had to be a knife there. Easiest thing. Wait until everyone was asleep.

The cook brought me dinner. But no sharp objects. I ate the food. Afterward I sat in the dark, waiting for everyone to go to sleep. Instead, I fell to sleep.

I dreamed. I was locked in a room, naked, my head shaved. They were torturing me. Doing things to my feet, knees, fingernails. Hart was there, directing it all. The inquisitor. In between torturing my extremities, he raped me. Until finally he pushed me to the floor. "I told you I would have you on your knees," he laughed and forced my mouth open.

I screamed and screamed. I had had just about enough.

I screamed again. I would scream my way out of this fucking nightmare.

"Keelie, Keelie." Victor's voice. "I'm here. It's all right. What's wrong?"

I was shaking, couldn't stop trembling.

"What's wrong?" he asked.

"What's wrong? What's wrong is that I'm the butt of some cruel cosmic joke." I was so cold. "Victor, please, I'm so cold."

He sat on the bed and put his arms around me. I pressed my face into his chest. The memory of the dream still stung.

"I dreamed I was accused of being a witch, they were torturing me, raping me."

His arms tightened around me. "Sweetheart, that happened to you."

"I know! I know! That doesn't make it any easier." I couldn't stop shaking. "The world is a cruel place," I said.

*   *   *

The next morning dawned exquisitely. I hadn't slept at all. Victor sneaked out of my room before his watch. The sun changed the colors of the sky over and over again before settling on blue. Porpoises rode alongside the ship, jumping out and diving in, jumping out and diving in. What glorious freedom!

Victor waved at me from his post at the helm.

I went down below to get a shawl. I passed the captain's cabin. Heard grunts. Knew what was happening. I'd kill him. Kill him. I opened the door.

He was on top of Lee, fully clothed. She had her face turned to me, her eyes staring vacantly ahead. Her spirit gone.

I picked up the heaviest object I could find. I don't know what it was. A paperweight? I struck the back of his head.

He groaned and fell on Lee. She screamed. I struck him again and then pulled him off her, sent him sprawling to the floor. Lee quickly pulled her dress down. The room stank of him.

I thought of Lee and Victor being forced to make love in the twentieth century, forced to couple so the father wouldn't rape any longer. I hit him again. Blood flowed. I thought of Lee, pregnant in the jungle, almost dead from birthing his baby. I struck again. I thought of all the times I had been raped and I struck him again and again.

He had to die. And die. And die.

"Keelie!" Victor grabbed my arms, pulled me away.

Lee sank into a corner, whimpering.

"You'll kill him," Victor said.

"That's the point!" I screamed. "He must die!"

"Keelie!" Victor wrapped his arms around me, pulling me farther away from the prone man. Anna was suddenly in the doorway. "It's now or never," Victor told her. "Mutiny!"

No one died when we took over the ship. The men were too surprised and the women too quick.

The father lived. Bastard. Victor wouldn't kill him. They put him and the ones who didn't want to join us into a boat with provisions. Hadn't they ever read *Mutiny on the Bounty*? The motherfuckers would survive. The father would kill Victor. I had changed nothing. Accomplished nothing.

Anna and I cleaned Lee up. It hadn't been the first time. But it would be the last. Something to be said for that. She fixated on Victor. As the ship sailed toward the land we could now see, she wandered around behind Victor. Sometimes she sat in a corner mumbling, drifting between here and there. Only Victor seemed to be able to bring her back. She seemed so sad and lost.

Sometimes she danced on the deck, all by herself, her eyes closed, hands high, moving to unheard music.

I watched the land come nearer and knew the boat would break up. We would stumble ashore. I remembered it all now. Many of us would die of strange fevers and starvation. Until the Amazon Amazons came through the jungle, our heras, our Valkyries, saving us with herbs and potions, taking us into their house and home. I would ask Victor to stay with Lee, at least until she had the baby. She had never had anyone to protect her. Ever.

I asked Victor to make love to me at night as our mutineered ship sailed toward the Amazon. I cried as we moved together, wishing I could remember the first time, the real first time, wondering if this would be the last. "You promised never to leave me," I whispered. "I promised," he said, kissing my ear.

It was a promise I knew he would break.

I held myself as close to him as I could.

"I want to stay here, in this moment, forever," I prayed.

I closed my eyes and bit my lip. "Please." This time I tasted my own blood.

And then I spiraled back in time once again.

Sixteen

❖❖❖❖❖❖❖❖❖❖

My brother Victor was walking away from me, down the road and up the hill. He stopped and waved. He looked younger than the last time I had seen him, infinitely sad, a bag over his shoulder. I called to him. He didn't stop. Didn't hear me. I had sent him away.

I turned around. A stone cottage stood behind me. Meadows and forest surrounding it. In a valley beyond I could make out bits of a village.

This must be the home where we grew up together.

I walked around to the back. Two fresh graves and crosses. Dearest Mother and Dearest Father. They had died within months of one another. I felt no sadness as I stared at their graves.

I went inside the house. It was dark. Dreary. Stank of cruelty.

I put my hands on my hips. "I think I'll stay a spell."

I cleaned out the cottage, throwing almost everything away, watching it burn up and turn into smoke. I opened windows and doors. Made bright curtains. Cleaned it top to bottom. Planted wildflowers around the house.

I talked to no one.

I let the cow go. Sometimes she came into the yard and I milked her.

The chickens left me eggs. Brought me chicks to pet.

I went into the forest and dug roots. I knew what each of them did. How to cure this or that.

Occasionally someone would wander by and trade me something for my herbs.

Sometimes I went and eased the pain of a woman in childbirth. I even helped one or two bring their children across the divide.

I was content.

Then Hart came to my cottage.

"I would like to marry you," he said. He had left his inquisitor robes back in the village.

"I am happy alone."

He shook his head. And left.

I gathered more herbs. Sometimes the trees whispered to me, but I couldn't quite understand them.

Hart returned.

"Your brother is away at sea."

"Yes, I sent him away."

"It isn't good for a woman to be alone," he said. "Will you honor me by marrying me?"

"No."

He left and brought by another man. "Mr. James would like to buy your property. A woman alone cannot work a place like this properly."

"No."

When Hart returned again, he wore his robes. "Will you marry me?"

"No."

"You gather in the forest with other witches."

"I gather herbs in the forest," I said.

"You and the devil meet in the forest to couple," he said.

"I couple with no one. Couple means two, right? There is only one."

"You will be on your knees to me."

I closed my eyes momentarily, knowing what he said was true.

"Never," I answered, despite the reality.

I closed my cheery little cottage and went into the forest. I lived there until one morning when one of the villagers found me.

He pointed at me. *"J'accuse!"* he cried.

I closed my eyes and spun away down the spiral.

Seventeen

٠٠٠٠٠٠٠٠٠٠٠٠٠

Victor and I run through the meadow together. Children. We hold hands and fall to the ground, the wheat becomes our golden bed.

"Put your ear to the ground," he says.

I do.

"You'll hear the Earth," he whispers. "Just like listening to a seashell. You can hear the ocean then. Now I give you the Earth."

We hold our breath and listen. I do hear the beat, feel it. Is it my own? Victor's?

Someone calls for us.

We kiss each other.

"Maybe one of us is a foundling," I say.

We breathe the other's breath.

"Wouldn't they tell us?" he asks. "They must see how we love each other."

Have always loved each other.

How young are we? How old?

Someone screams for us again.

Victor pulls me up. We race through the gold, toward the darkness ahead. Laughing, pulling at one another.

We step across the line between light and green darkness. Green-gold darkness. Slanting into the forest. Shafts of light that fairies dance down. See them? He sees what I see and I see what he sees. We have never been apart. Maybe even together in our mother's womb? No. The womb of the Earth?

The trees are taller today. Whispering to us. Flowers wave. Birds sing to us.

Life is absolute magic. How could I have forgotten that?

We lie on a cushion of moss. Tiny white flowers tickle our bare butts. We kiss. Touch. His touch is so gentle. When I close my eyes I am certain I am being kissed by a thousand butterflies.

When I open them again, we are surrounded by butterflies, flying in a spiral around us.

Protecting us.

He kisses my bare barely breasts. I kiss his. I tickle his belly with my hair, watch his penis grow a bit. To never be touched by him. Ever. I can not imagine that in a million nightmares. A trillion.

He is small and not too hard and I open to him. We transform. Moving with the butterflies.

Tasting each other. Spiraling to the stars and back into the earth, deep, until we hear the heartbeat of the earth, become the heart of the earth.

There has never been a moment of sadness. Ever.

The butterflies kiss us a thousand times and when we finally draw apart from each other, we know—

"I will never leave you," he whispers and I, "I will never leave you."

We will be with each other forever.

Eighteen

••••••••••

I am too young to know more than this: they have taken my mother away. I know she is gone from me forever. They call her witch and she shoves me into the forest. "Run," she whispers, "run."

I am running. My fat little legs carry me deeper into the forest, where I have lived since before I was born.

The trees protect me at night. In the morning, the birds try to get me to eat.

I try to pick a wild rose. It pricks my finger. I cry.

A man appears. He bends down to me. I see a bit of kindness. A bit.

"What's your name?" he asks.

"Keelie," I say.

He asks me other questions, but I am too young. I only know my mother is gone and I am hungry.

He picks me up and puts me over his shoulder. I bounce around with him all day while he does something. Hunts for mushrooms? Quail? I probably never knew and the memory doesn't stay long.

When it is night and my momma has been gone too long, the man brings me to his cottage. He sets me on the floor and shows me to his wife. She laughs and claps her hands. She, too, has a bit of kindness, though I think I remember it doesn't last.

Then you come into the room. Sucking your thumb? Just a little older than I was, I think. Creatures the same. Don't you remember either?

"Victor," your mother says, "this is your new sister."

"Keelie," your father says, "her name is Keelie."

You come to me and smile. Then you kiss my finger where the thorn had pricked it.

As you taste my blood, we become instant kin. Forgetting that we have ever been apart.

PART 3

•••••••••••••••••••••••••••••••••••

RE-MEMBERING

Nineteen

• • • • • • • • • • •

A n eon passed.

I opened my eyes to purple, undulating purple, with streaks of orange here and there.

I sat up.

I recognized this dungeon. Eriskegal screamed her throaty laugh. I looked behind me. She sat on her throne. She was dressed in purple and orange, too. The black sheets beneath me moved as if alive.

I quickly stood.

"Welcome to my humble abode," she said, waving her hand to encompass all. "What the fuck brought you back, you lifeless little tit—I mean twit." She smiled and revealed the moss on her teeth.

"I can't be back here," I said. "I climbed out. I got out! Why am I here?"

"To see what you have learned along the way," she said.

I glanced at the pegs. The corpses continued to rot. Had no time passed?

"A fucking eternity has passed!" Eriskegal roared. Then she smiled, "But enough about me, how did you find yourself? What great lessons did you learn?"

"I saw a lot of horror. And love. I am connected to many people through time."

"Including the father?"

I shook my head. "I am not connected to him. He is slime. He is nothing."

The purple-and-orange decor was really making me sick.

"You don't like it? *Better Homes and Gardens.* I did it *moi*-self."

I slumped to the charred floor. I wasn't up to this banter. I just wanted oblivion. Or a meadow. Sunshine on my face. Something. Else.

"Can you envision it?" Eriskegal asked. She stood and the room shed the black. Now it was gray. Spinning. We were all spinning. Not the fucking vertigo again. I shut my eyes.

"Can you envision it?" she asked again.

"What? Envision what?" I opened my eyes.

We were standing in the mountains, in the ruins of a kind of amphitheater. Gray pillars here and there. Steps. All looking out away from the mountains, down at the foothills, the olive trees. Was that a bus in the distance, tires squealing as it rounded the twisted roads?

"Well?"

I looked next to me. Eriskegal had changed. Literally. She wore white. Her black hair was piled on her head. Her skin shiny black. She smiled.

"Who are you?"

"Eriskegal. Athena. Artemis. Yemaya. Maat. Medusa. Hecate." As she spoke each name her visage changed, her skin color, eyes, hair. "I am She of a Thousand Names."

"Where are we?"

"You don't recognize it? This is Delphi, in Greece. This was a place where I was honored, worshiped, until I wasn't. Delphi means womb in Latin. Did you know that?"

I breathed deeply. The air quivered with ... memories? Songs? Whispers?

She nodded. "You remember it, too? Women were honored; life was honored. The people were connected with all around them."

"What happened?"

"Don't you remember?"

I shook my head. The world spun again. I put my hands out to steady myself, covered my eyes. When all was still, I looked around me again. We stood on golden land now, treeless. Bits of ruins lay beneath our feet.

"Anatolia," she said. She was dressed in lavender, her breasts exposed to the sun. "This is where the story of the Amazon women began.

Like your women in South America, only many millennia before."

I shook my head. "It is difficult to imagine a world of Amazons."

"It is said the world gets the gods humans imagine. And the gods shape the world. In your present, the twentieth century, most people believe in desert gods, so the world is fast becoming a desert."

"A kind of gods-are-us?"

"The world has not always been ruled by those who worship the desert gods."

"What has this to do with me?"

The world shook, cracked, parted. A fissure opened between us. Eriskegal stood on the other side, body black, eyes flashing fire. The open ground between us belched sulfur fumes. "Do you wish to continue?"

"I want some control!" I cried.

"You've learned nothing!"

"Can't I at least go forward? Remembering backwards is too hard."

"Don't be so linear. That's not the way the world goes round!"

"That's my offer!" The ground was really shifting now. I could hardly keep my balance.

She screamed, tossing her head back, back, back, until she curved into a bird, a vulture, huge wings spreading. Her red wrinkled feet bounced her up. She grinned as she caught the air, spiraled up, and then down, down, diving for me.

I opened my arms wide. I could play this game. I had always been able to. I was a survivor. There wasn't anything she could throw at me that I couldn't stand. Nothing.

Her beak missed my eye by a millimeter. She laughed and flowed back into Eriskegal. Then Medusa. Hera. Artemis. Oya. White Buffalo Calf Woman. Spider Woman. Eriskegal. She was making me dizzy. She quivered and then I was staring at myself. Dressed in green, I didn't seem quite as tired as I felt, quite as haggard-looking as I knew myself to be. I looked rested, powerful, standing steady on the Earth.

She who was me smiled.

"Now do you get the point?"

Suddenly the lights went out.

I was utterly alone. In darkness.

"Eriskegal? Hey, anyone there?"

Nothing.

I hurt. My stomach hurt. My eyes. Throat. Belly. Crotch. What the fuck? I doubled over.

"Eriskegal!" I screamed. "Hey, She of a Thousand Names! Help!"

A window of light appeared. Fingers extended.

"Sweetheart?" Lilith's voice. Lilith! Yet different. Not the mess of flesh from the mansion or the abbess from France. A new Lilith. "Keelie!"

Have fun! The Chessies meowed at me from the great beyond.

The fingers reached for me. I grabbed hold of them. I tumbled forward. Forgetting most of what I had remembered. Cells shrinking. My mother pulled me into the world.

Twenty

• • • • • • • • •

I remember
    They pulled me slowly from the water
where I had dropped from my mother's womb.
Surrounded by laughter. Caressed. Kissed.

"Welcome, Keelie," they all said.

My first taste was the sweet milk of my mother's breast.

I remember
    The world as it was.
    Pieces of sunlight, shafts of moonlight. Purple hills. Flowers the color of the rainbow. Turquoise. More laughter. Songs. Dances. Kisses.

    Sitting on Grandma Belle's lap, sucking on the beads around her neck, listening to words I did not yet understand, singsong.

    Voices of women and men, joined together in

song, the moon reflecting my mother's smile back to me.

Sister Lee smelled of mother's milk and cream. Peaches. Olives. Butterfly kisses.

I remember

Mother Lilith and I stood in the fields. Four times the Earth had circled the sun since my momma pulled me from the other side.

To the north, hills shaped like women's thighs and bellies lay, crotch side up. I tried to reach across the distance and stroke their velvet green sides. To the south, valleys criss-crossed one another, streams like giant snakes, coiling and uncoiling as they slithered up and down the hills. To the east and west, in between trees and stone, the fields opened before us. My toes dug into the cool furrowed Earth. MommaSun stroked fairy mist from the ground, teasing them upward to her embrace.

My tiny hand held on to Mother Lilith's fingers. She was a tall woman, her skin dark, her hair cut off at the nape, the way of those who cultivated the land. Multicolored beads circled her neck and fell between her breasts. Today she wore a purple skirt, woven especially for her by Grand Keelie, the woman I was called after.

"All that you see, Daughter Keelie," my mother said, "is a part of you. The hills, valleys, trees, stone, all manners of creatures, crawling, flying, walking, they are you. Treat all as you would wish to be treated."

She squatted down, and her long fingers dug into the Earth. I knelt beside her.

"This is the Mother," my mother said. "She provides all for us and she is all of us. Everything. You and me. We create her daily and she creates us."

I slipped my fingers into the Earth. Warm and cool at the same time.

"Can you feel her breath?" my mother asked.

I closed my eyes.

I felt her breath on my cheeks.

I nodded.

"Can you feel her heat?"

I tilted my head to the sun. Her light and heat warmed me through to my toes.

"Can you smell her body?"

The air was fragrant with many aromas. Mostly the flowers just beyond the fields, purple on the outside, yellow inside, with bees dancing in and out of them.

I looked at my mother and smiled.

"Can you feel her in yourself?"

I settled on my haunches. The wind and sun and fragrances washed me in pleasure, and I felt my heart pounding in my toes that had sunk into the Earth.

"A little bit," I said.

My mother laughed. "Well, my dearest child,

your body is a gift from the Goddess and the Goddess is a gift to you. Your body is yours. Take pleasure in it!"

She touched the ground once more, whispered a blessing, and then we stood. My hand in hers, we walked away from the hills, toward the sound of water. As we walked, my mother pointed out flowers I would have missed had she not been with me, insects I had not seen before. I wanted to run ahead to the water, yet I wanted to stay at my mother's side. I sensed the water would always be there, but I would not be this age always, able to keep still at my mother's side. So I remained with her, my hand sweating with hers.

The river appeared between the hills and trees, a slash of green silver, splashing away from us. The river breathed cooler air, and gurgled something at us. My mother stayed still for a time, listening, and I wondered when I was her size if I would be able to understand the water.

We walked toward the whirlpools on the east side of the river. I had seen them before, spirals of water, endlessly spinning around and around, making smaller circles and then larger and larger ones. They were almost separate from the river, attached to her by a small rivulet. Stone circled the whirlpools. Beyond the pools, inside the hill, were the caves where the women went during the dark moon. Today I could not see the mouths of the caves through the spring-time foliage.

We stood on the stone and looked down at the swirling water. The pools looked huge, and the water below bottomless.

We sat on our haunches again.

"Look into the water," my mother instructed. "This is the blood of the mother. It feeds and nourishes us all. All the world. Look into the whirlpools."

I stared and stared. I wobbled with dizziness. My mother put her hand on my arm to steady me. "Can you see beyond the spirals? Below are rocks. It's not very deep, even though it appears bottomless."

"I only see the water," I told her.

She nodded. "The spirals are like the dance of life. We spiral into and out of this world, into and out of good times and bad, into and out of one another's lives. This is life."

She dipped her hands into the water. I got onto my knees and did the same.

"For time beyond time, our women have come to these pools or ones like these. It is here each month we give the Goddess some of our wise blood. It is here we squat and the spiral of life flows around us, making us a part of us. Each month we are reminded that we are part of all that is."

"You go into the pools?" I asked.

My mother smiled. "There are rocks beneath the surface, my daughter. You will be safe, and you will be linked with all of us and all those who went before us and will come after."

"Can we go in today?" I asked. I wanted to stand on the invisible rocks.

"Not yet," she said. "The time will come soon enough. Know that you are blessed to be in this world, and the world is blessed to have you in the world." She leaned over and kissed my cheek. "And I am especially blessed."

I smiled.

"Now, child, you have been patient. You may run to your heart's content."

And so I did, splashing in the river, running up and down the hills, until, happily exhausted, I fell into my mother's arms. She lifted me onto her shoulders and carried me home.

I remember

White walls, curving around us. On some of the walls, my mother's brother Griffin painted women and children, animals, trees, grains, all connected, growing into and around one another. On the altar, along with flowers and stones, was a statue of the Goddess. She changed as the seasons changed, my mother always choosing one of Grace's creations. Though none of the art was signed my mother could always tell.

Many people lived with my sister Lee, my mother, and myself. Sometimes they stayed a few moons, sometimes longer, shorter. Griffin lived the longest time with us. He painted and cared for us. Slightly built and quiet, he was perfect. He never tired of wandering around with us. While we played for hours in the river, he would watch us with part of his eyes and wander away with the other part. Yet if some danger appeared, he snapped to attention and took us firmly in hand and away. I once saw him come out of a dead sleep when a poisonous snake coiled near me.

"We bless you, Mother of Snakes, and we'll be on our way," he said, gently pushing Lee and myself up the hill.

When we were out of danger, he said, "There was a time when we could talk to the animals. Some people still can. But I cannot, so I could not tell her that we meant her no harm."

"Talk to them?" I remembered how my mother listened to the river, the wind, the animals. Perhaps she really did understand what they said.

That night, Griffin painted the snake onto the wall, blessing our house with her powerful presence.

*   *   *

Grandmother Belle was a storyteller. When the city became a market once a month on the full moon, my grandmother told her tales. They said her words were magic, able to keep the children within the bounds of her voice, always, safe and cared-for. Her singsong voice often put me to sleep. I would sit on the ground with the rest of the children, surrounded by merchants trading cloth, tapestries, pottery, and food; by grandmother's second story I was asleep on a spot of grass nearby. Grandmother always came into my dreams with me, weaving stories even as I slept. When she was finished, I would awaken, along with most of the other children, in time for the ceremonies.

We would gather into circles, or spirals, depending upon the mood of the community, and give thanks, dance, bless ourselves, and draw the moon down into our hearts. I would stare up into the face of the moon and drink her down until I was full of her light. Then we would eat. More singing. Drumming. Dancing. Couples would go off by themselves, and then Griffin and my mother would carry Lee and me home.

As we got older, Lee, myself, and Grace's daughter Camie would devise ways to run off without Griffin. Every once in a while, we'd run up to the menstrual caves to see if we could hear anything the women said. Several times we found boys up there trying to do the same thing. Outraged, we chased them away. After they were gone, we would hear the women laugh at us. Embarrassed, we'd run back home.

In the city, we played, too, running from place to place to watch the potters or weavers or bread makers. Sometimes we ran to Grand Keelie's house. She lived alone and had no children. She often wove in her garden. Surrounded by flowers and trees, she pulled colors through the loom, creating tapestries more realistic than any painting. Unlike most of the adults, she didn't seem to care for children. It wasn't as though she hated us; she didn't pay us any attention. Of course, this made her fascinating.

Lee, Camie, and I would hide in her bushes and watch her create, waiting for her to cast a spell or disappear or mumble her tapestries into existence. Yet all we saw her do was sing softly to herself and move the loom back and forth, back and forth.

One day, after we had spied on her several times, she said, "Camie, Lee, go home. Keelie, come from behind there. I wish to speak with you."

Camie and Lee fled without a thought for me. I stood up and thought about running, too. But I didn't. I stepped around the bushes and into the cool green of her garden.

Grand Keelie continued to pull threads into and out of cloth.

"What is it you want from me?" she asked.

I stood before her, my hands folded in front of me. I could feel the blood in my face.

"Nothing," I said.

"I heard you were a bright child," Grand Keelie said. "Is that the only answer you can give me?"

The wind rustled the olive leaves. A tiny bird hovered near me and then flew away. Beyond, I could hear nothing. We were on an island, myself and Grand Keelie.

"I—I wanted to watch you weave," I finally said.

She glanced at me and then back down at her cloth. "So you wish to become a weaver? I don't take apprentices."

"Oh." I didn't want to become a weaver, but I wondered why she didn't take apprentices. How else was one to learn if the elders did not teach?

"I have tried to teach my weaving," Grand Keelie said, "but I'm not good at it. I have no patience. The gift of my tapestries will have to be enough."

I looked at the piece she was working on. She was weaving a spider at the center of the web.

"You may look closer," she said. I stepped

nearer. The lines of the web were so delicate. How had she done that?

"I have been working on this for a long while," she said. I noticed a few gray hairs growing amongst her black hair. She was becoming a crone. Someday I, too, would be a crone. I would be wise enough then that people from all over would seek my counsel.

"She is a beautiful spider," I said.

"I have known your family for many years," Grand Keelie said, her hands moving up and down. For a moment, it seemed as though the threads were coming from the tips of her fingers, like the spider herself. "Though I have not visited for many years."

"I am named after you," I said.

"Yes, I am your Goddessmother," she said.

"Why don't you see us? Why are you always alone?"

She looked up at me again. "You are bold, aren't you? Your mother has taught you well. Some people like being alone. There is nothing wrong with that."

No, but I had difficulty imagining it.

"When you are older, when you come into your wise blood, you will discover you like being alone, too."

I knelt on the ground next to her. I reached into her basket and began arranging her spools so they would not tangle.

"Your mother and I were in love once," Grand Keelie said, "but it did not last."

"You and Mother? You would go off together after the celebrations?"

Grand Keelie frowned and then smiled. "Oh, yes, I see what you mean. Yes, we went off together. We were lovers."

I nodded. "And now you don't like each other."

Grand Keelie laughed. "Of course we do. We just aren't lovers anymore. I liked being alone too much. That's difficult when someone loves you and wants to be with you."

I liked sitting on the ground talking about love with this strange woman. Although I had not had my first blood or initiation, I found great pleasure in my own body and looked forward to being with someone else soon.

"Were you ever in love so much you didn't want to be alone?" I asked.

Grand Keelie stopped her weaving for a moment. "Yes, I was. Many years ago."

"What happened?"

"You ask many questions."

"Please!"

She laughed again. Why had I thought she was a cross woman?

"When I was just a few years older than you are, I met a warrior from the north."

"A warrior?" I asked.

"They are a different people than ours," she said. "They do not recognize their connectedness to all things. They do not live with sacredness."

I could not imagine letting someone like that touch me.

"We had gone to the City, to trade, and he was there. We fell in love. I thought we would be together forever."

"What happened?"

"I went to live with his people," she said, looking down at her weaving again, her fingers moving in and out. "They were obscene. He would not come here, so I returned alone."

"Did you ever see him again?"

She shook her head.

I sighed. It was a sad story, but I felt relieved. I would never fall in love with anyone like him.

"Do you miss him?" I asked.

"I wish I had never met him or seen what his people were like. I sometimes still dream of it. The Earth is charred, the air choked with their smoke, bodies decaying where they have killed them."

I shuddered. For the first time in my life I felt a twinge of fear.

"Are they near? Will they come here?"

"They are far away," Grand Keelie said, "but not far enough away."

We were silent for several minutes. I felt chilled.

"Why was I named after you?" I asked.

"Your Grandmother Belle is a seeress, I'm sure you know," Grand Keelie said.

"I know she can see things I cannot," I answered.

"Before you were born, she saw that you, too, would fall in love with a warrior."

I stared at the spider on Grand Keelie's cloth. I hoped Grandmother Belle was wrong.

Twenty-one

•••••••••••••••

I remember
Feeling seamless. As if all flowed together continuously. Learning pottery from Grace, feeling her smooth brown skin, gritty with clay, guide my hands over a pot. Watching Ben fish, listening and watching for what he heard and saw, laughing at his jokes, learning. Painting with Griffin, seeing a dot of red create a skirt, a spot of green a bird, peering at the hair on his face and wondering why his wasn't smooth like mine. Or listening to Grandmother Belle's stories, laughing so hard I would cry. Grand Keelie taught me weaving and was not as impatient as she believed herself to be. Others taught me arithmetic and music and conversation, cooking, and diplomacy. My mother knew about the Earth, the winds, herbs, and roots. Always if I fell down and hurt myself, someone was there

to pick the dirt off my knees and reassure me. As I got older, someone was always there to explain the changes in my body.

Lee, who was a year older than I, had her first blood after her twelfth birthday. She waited two years after her menarche celebration before being initiated. After that, she became an initiator in the art of love. Camie, who was a year younger than I, started when she was thirteen. Every month they would go with the women to the menstrual cave. I was left alone—with all the other people who weren't bleeding!

I was fourteen and still hadn't seen my first blood. The ground lay fallow, the crops stored, the leaves turning crimson and orange and gold before drying up and falling to the Earth. The city prepared for the harvest's end celebration.

I sat on the edge of the field, my feet digging into the ground. My mother touched the top of my head.

"It was a good year," she said. "We will have supplies well into next spring. It'll be a great celebration!"

I sighed. Mother sat next to me. "Child, you needn't rush things. All things happen when they need to."

"How old were you when you started?" I asked. I had asked this question many times, hoping the answer would be different.

"I was just twelve, I think."

"Mother! You know exactly when."

She laughed. "I have been in this world many lifetimes, I get them mixed up."

"Don't make fun of me," I said.

She leaned against me. "I'm not. I just hate to see you so serious. It's a beautiful day, season, world!"

"Mother!" Lee came running up the hill toward us. We both stood and waited for her. She stopped breathless in front of us, holding her sides.

"Mother, it's finally happened!"

Mother and I glanced at each other. Another lover? Lee was in love with a different person nearly every day—depending upon with whom she had been that day as they practiced the arts of love.

"What has happened, daughter?" Mother asked. She was suddenly formal, a slight smile on her face, as if she knew what the answer would be.

"I am going to have a child, just as I wished!"

My mother and sister embraced. Lee let my mother go and hugged me.

"You won't be the youngest for very long!" Lee said. She squeezed me and then she and my mother walked away, arms around one another.

"Are you coming, Keelie?" my mother called.

"Soon." I sank into the ground again. I wanted to be alone. I just wanted to be by myself, sink into the Earth, have my own thoughts, figure out why I was the only thing not fertile!

I curled up on the ground, my ear to the ground, and fell to sleep.

I dreamed about Lee. She looked different but it was her, dancing in a large room, sunlight her only audience. Then she changed again; surrounded by dense foliage, she gave birth to a giant pearl.

When I awakened, it was nearly night. The moon was beginning to rise above the hills. I felt something on my thighs. I lifted my skirt to the moon. A bit of blood was smeared on my thigh.

No. It couldn't be?

I reached my hand up and touched myself, felt the moisture, not much but a little. I looked at my fingers: blood.

My blood. Bleeding every month and never dying. I reached up again and got both hands as bloody as I could and then wiped them on the fallow ground, dug my hands into the Earth. This field would be blessed for years now, blessed with the magic of first blood. I had started my blood in the field! This would have great meaning to the whole city!

I raced through the dusk until I reached my mother's home. The house was empty. I touched the Goddess statue with my bloody finger and kissed her and then ran outside again, toward the meadow where I knew most everyone would be gathered. The city was deserted, quiet, fallow like the fields. The setting sun and rising moon streaked the outside of the buildings a milky red. Bloody. My blood. My celebration!

I ran down the street until I saw the grove of oak trees, heard them whisper welcome, smelled the food and wine, called out to my mother.

"Lilith!" I cried.

The circle had not yet been joined. Something in my voice caused them all to stop and look at me. Even babies stopped crying. Seph and my mother Lilith stepped toward me, they who were leading the circle this night.

"What is it, Keelie?" Seph asked, his hand on my shoulder.

Lee, Grandmother Belle, and Grand Keelie circled me. They knew. Everyone must know.

"I fell asleep in the field," I said, suddenly self-conscious as everyone listened to me. "When I awakened, I was bleeding. Bleeding my first blood. Onto the field."

The cry that went up from my people was one of pure joy. Leaping into the night. The circle spontaneously joined. All knew next year's crop was assured. I was next to my mother as she led the spiral dance. The moon gazed upon us as finally I was raised onto the hands of the tallest people and shown to the moon, shown to the world. I had given the community a great gift.

I would never forget it. And none of them would ever forget me.

When the couples began moving off together, Grandmother Belle came and put her arm across my shoulder.

"What did you dream as you blessed our fields with your blood?" she asked.

"I dreamed of Lee, only she was different, and she was dancing and then she was pregnant. She gave birth to a pearl."

My grandmother nodded. "We have all been here many times, granddaughter. Perhaps you saw her in another life."

"You think I have the gift?" I asked. The night smelled of the Earth.

"We all have the gift of sight," she said, "only some of us have forgotten how to use it. You will discover how you wish to share yourself with the world soon enough."

"Grandma, do you think I will fall in love with a warrior?"

Grandmother Belle laughed. "Perhaps my sight was cloudy that day, what do you think?"

I remember

Being dressed in white, following the women dressed in red following the crones dressed in black. We walked barefoot to the river and the whirlpools where my mother had once taken me so long ago. My heart raced. Soon I would be in the caves where all women before me had gone each month during their bleeding time. Those of us dressed in white took off our garments and stepped into the whirlpools. We squatted in the cold water, giggling, as it whirled around our legs and the soft hair between our legs. Tickled.

"Feel the blood of the mother," said one of the crones, one of the women who held her wise blood within her. "Feel the life of your sisters, mothers, grandmothers, and Goddessmothers. Feel the life of the world pulsing through your body, the body of the Goddess."

"You belong to yourselves," Grand Keelie said, "and you are Goddesses all. Use your wisdom well. You are creators—creators of children, of art, of the world. Of yourselves."

Then we stood and the mothers, the women in red, helped us on with our clothes. Shivering slightly, we followed the wise women and mothers up the path away from the whirlpools and toward the black holes of the caves. The crones first made an arch for us, and then the mothers, and we went under their arms, through their arms into darkness. For a moment, I could not see. None of us could. We bumped into one another, struggling to see forward, and feeling only each other, smelling only ourselves, and then we looked behind us at the light in the opening of the cave and to our mothers and grandmothers and sisters and Goddessmothers and they came to us and showed us the fire, lit the lamps, and we followed them through the golden blackness, back away from the opening to the cave, away from the outside world, away from all we had known before. Holding hands, we walked. The crones and mothers began singing and we joined in, "We all come from the Goddess and to her we shall return." Our words undulated all around us. I smelled the sweet scent of women bleeding. The corridor opened into a large cave. A room. Along the walls were openings, large enough for a woman to lie down or sit, meditation chambers. Other corridors snaked away from the room. Large oval containers with flat bottoms were arranged throughout the room.

We sat in circles, circles within circles. We began singing softly at first, and then more rhythmically, rocking slightly from side to side, my buttocks fitting into the stone floor.

"Some of you will have visions," one woman said as the rest of us sang. "Some of you will sleep. Some of you will talk. What happens to you is what happens to you; it is your unique experience, no one else's."

We closed our eyes and hummed. "Feel the heartbeat of the Earth," someone whispered, the voice coming almost from beneath me. I rocked and felt a twinge of energy at the base of my spine, felt it creeping upward, upward, I breathed deeply and tried to move the energy up, but it stayed in my buttocks and stomach.

When the humming stopped, we blessed the circle and moved away, into smaller groups. My mother, grandmother, Grand Keelie, Lee, and Camie stayed with me. We ate cheeses, breads, fruit. And talked.

"I remember my first time in these caves," my mother said. "I slept nearly the entire time!"

"I remember that," Grandmother Belle said. "You had wonderful dreams."

"And I danced most of my first time," Grand Keelie said. "I had so much energy."

I smiled, imagining Grand Keelie twirling around this room, weaving a tapestry of movement with her hands and feet. Now the room was subdued, only the light of the lamps gilding the walls of the cave. People talked in hushed voices.

"I have felt many things here throughout the years," Mother Lilith said. "Sometimes sad, happy, angry. And always I feel more like myself than I ever do."

Lee got behind me and began combing my hair. The baby inside of her was beginning to stretch her belly.

"Did you attend your initiation right after your menarche?" I asked.

Grandmother Belle, Mother Lilith, and Grand Keelie laughed.

"They just begin bleeding and already they're ready to jump into the initiation!" Grandmother said. "Young people are in such a hurry!"

"I am attending this year," I said firmly. "I'm ready."

"Before we leave here, we will show you ways not to get pregnant and ways to get pregnant," Grandmother said. "It is always your choice."

My mother laughed. "The herbs do not always work the way we want them to. I got pregnant with you, my dearest Keelie, during my bleeding time and when I was taking Grandmother Glee's herbs. I felt the moment, some hours later, when you began making yourself. Even then I could have started you at a different time, but I thought it was magical, being conceived during the bleeding time."

"You weren't here? With the rest of the women?" I asked.

Grand Keelie smiled at my mother.

"I didn't always come here," Mother Lilith said. "Just as you may choose not to always come here. When I was younger, I felt very sexual during my bleeding time."

"And, of course, the men liked it," Grandmother said. "They can more easily connect with the Goddess during lovemaking on our bleeding times. They felt honored to be chosen by Lilith."

"Do you still feel like that?" I asked.

"Sometimes. And if you wish to make love to yourself or another woman, there are places within the cave for your comfort," Mother explained.

I smiled. I couldn't imagine being more comfortable than I was right now.

Later. Much later. One of the women was chosen to be the Goddess. We sat around her and she danced for us, for herself, naked, pulling the energy of the Goddess up into her body, transforming herself before us. I watched in awe, knowing someday I would be able to do this. I felt the Goddess always with me, a part of me, yet this seemed different, watching the woman change, dancing faster and faster, seeing the blood, black in the light, trickle down her legs, fall on us as she whirled, becoming a part of the stone, the cave, the Earth. She was mother, Goddess, creating herself in her own image.

I slept in the meditation chambers. I breathed the air of all the other women. I breathed the air of all the women and Goddesses who had gone before me and would come after me.

I dreamed. I was blond and light-skinned. Scars ringed my neck and thighs. I was crying as I cut my hair, cutting it until it was black. A raven flew behind me. "There's no place like home," the raven said. I nodded and looked into a moon-shaped mirror. I was myself again. I smiled. "There is no place like home," I said. "And I have found my place."

I helped my mother and most of the community turn over the Earth and gently awaken her. We planted seeds, and plants emerged from the soil. The land seemed more fertile than it had ever been. So everyone said. With the crops safely in and growing, we prepared for the initiation. People came from communities all around us. Those of us who were to be initiated, and the initiators, were housed in the city Center: the round labyrinth building where I had never been. The rest of the city celebrated outside; the days were filled with lovemaking.

Inside the city Center, the female initiates stayed in one part of the building, the males in the other. The initiators prepared themselves at the Center.

I readied myself in a room filled with women. Lee, her child belly almost bigger than she, wove flowers into my hair. Mother Lilith fed me grapes. Grandmother Belle washed my feet. Beyond us, Camie waved. This year she was going to be initiated, too.

Lee squeezed me from behind. "You'll love it! There's nothing better."

Grandmother shrugged. "It will be a wonderful experience, but personally, now, I enjoy food more."

"I will never forget my initiator," Grand Keelie said. "She was the most beautiful person I had ever seen. Her soul shined through her beautiful blue eyes." Grand Keelie sighed.

"Mine was from the south," Lee said. "He had a nice accent. And great moves."

Mother Lilith laughed. "It's almost time. Do you want to ask anything?"

"What about you, Mother Lilith, do you remember your first time?" I asked.

Mother glanced at Grand Keelie and then at me. "Yes, I remember my first. We knew each other before and after. She was the best." My mother's eyes filled with tears.

"Momma?"

"Joy, child. I am feeling joy. This will be a wonderful experience for you. Any more questions before you go?"

"Who should I choose? How will I know?"

"Choose someone handsome!"

"Someone with breasts."

"Someone who smells good."

The older women shouted all around me. Had every initiate asked the same question? They started gently pushing us out of the room and down the mazelike corridor.

"Choose someone dark."

"Someone blond."

"Someone small! This is your first time!"

"Someone big! This is your first time!"

The women laughed as they pushed us. Lee dropped behind. Camie grabbed my hand. I squeezed it and then let go. Grand Keelie waved.

"You'll know," my mother whispered.

And then she and Grandmother dropped behind. They all seemed to stop and we went forward, girl-women I had known all my life and others I had never seen before.

Suddenly the corridor opened and we were in a huge room. Sunlight poured in from overhead, highlighting the tiles painted with scenes of lovemaking. The room vibrated, pulsed. Young men and women moved around one another, watching, not watching. Choosing, not choosing.

The initiators were dressed in red so that we would know who they were. I think I would have known anyway. They seemed to glow, like Lee had when she was an initiator. I looked, and looked away. So many people. Dark and light, male and female, blue-eyed, brown-eyed, green-eyed. Small, tall. All in between. Couples began moving away into the labyrinth. Hands linked. Some kissing. Some petting. Mother Lilith said I would know. How?

I walked and turned, and a young man, blond, a little smaller than I, his skin almost white, smiled at me. He wasn't from our city. I could tell he liked me. My mother said I was beginning to look like the Amazon women of old. Tall and dark. Strong.

I liked his smile.

I went to him and held out my hand. "I am Keelie."

"I am Atwan." He took my hand in his.

"I choose you," I said.

"And I you," he answered.

Together we left the others. Within moments we were walking down cream-colored hallways. Everything seemed so light. Light and pulsating. Quiet. The noise from the central room was gone. Atwan stopped and opened a curtain.

"This is our place," Atwan said. "Only ours."

I went under his arm into the room. Pale blue. The light subdued but not dark. Almost like early-morning sunlight. On the floor were blankets and cushions, oils and candles, water and fruit.

My heart was pounding in my ears.

Atwan came into the room and took my hand again. "I bless this room and ask the Goddess to join us on our journey," Atwan said.

"Blessed be," I answered.

We went to the cushions and sat down. Atwan took both my hands in his and looked into my eyes. He had beautiful blue eyes and smooth skin. I wanted to stroke his face.

"Keelie, this time is for you, to help further the transition from childhood to womanhood.

You come here of your own choosing and I am here of my own choosing."

I nodded.

"It is normal to be nervous," he said. "But that will pass."

He leaned forward slightly. What did he smell of? It was exquisite. And his arms. Small and muscular. He untied the cord around my dress and helped the cloth fall away from my body.

"I will bathe you," he said. "Will you lie down?"

I lay naked on the cushions. He took off his top. I sighed involuntarily. He was so pretty.

He gently washed me with warm water. Stroking me up and down. Taking my fingers in his and washing each finger. My ears. Neck. Back. Buttocks. Legs. He washed each toe and then kissed each one. He took my toes between his teeth and I thought I would orgasm right there, but I didn't. I closed my eyes and groaned. He leaned over and kissed my ear and gently turned me over. He washed my breasts and belly, my cunt and thighs.

Then he began massaging me with warm oil. I felt stimulated and relaxed all at the same time. I sank deeper into the cushions and into the moment, into the feeling of his hands on my body. Stroking me. Touching me. Massaging me. He kissed my breasts, flicked his tongue over my nipples, kissed my belly button. His fingers gently ran through my pubic hair, pulling it softly, teasing me. I opened my legs. I wanted him inside of me.

He ran his little finger between the lips of my cunt. I gasped as his finger went inside me, into that deep wonderful moistness. And then he was out again and his fingers rubbed me gently. Excited me. I wanted him. I wanted him.

I reached for him and we kissed. He pressed against me and I could feel his erection. His tongue explored my entire body. He knew where to touch me, where it felt best.

I was nearly exhausted with pleasure when Atwan took off the rest of his clothes.

"You are wonderful," Atwan whispered, nearly breathless.

I pulled him toward me. I wanted him on top of me. Covering me with his wonderful body, becoming a part of me. I opened my legs and his penis slid easily into me. We moved together. I felt no momentary twinge of pain which Mother Lilith said occasionally accompanied lovemaking the first time. I felt only exquisite pleasure. We moved together. I felt as though we were reaching toward something. Moving toward some thing. We kissed and he moved over me, in me, we moved together, me surrounding him. The room seemed to fill with light. Or was that only me, only us? The pleasure mounted. I had never made love like this to myself. Never this long. Never this—the energy vibrated in my cunt, wrapped itself around Atwan's penis, exploded throughout my body and his. I felt the Goddess surge through me, become me, I was the Goddess. I felt her heartbeat roaring through us, her blood cascading through us, keeping me moving and moving. Atwan cried out in pleasure. I felt her press herself into my soul. The orgasms seemed endless, glorious, imprinting the Goddess on my being again and again.

And then the lights faded and Atwan and I fell against one another, exhausted.

After several minutes, Atwan whispered, "It is always wonderful, the first time. But this, here with you, has been extraordinary. Thank you for choosing me."

I embraced him and we lay in each other's arms. I sighed deeply. I had touched the face of the Goddess.

We made love several times afterward. It was not quite as earth-moving, but nearly so. We slept for a long while. When I awakened, Atwan was watching me. He smiled. I smiled, too, and pulled him down next to me.

"This has been the best time of my life," I whispered. "Thank you so much."

He kissed me. "I sense greatness in you."

"We all have greatness," I said.

"And you especially so. You will be a healer of some kind."

I laughed. "My grandmother believes I will fall in love with a warrior."

"She has seen it?" Atwan asked.

"She has," I answered. "And she is rarely wrong."

"Can't one fall in love with a warrior and still be a healer? Since when does love end healing?"

"When that love involves a warrior, how can there ever be healing?"

Atwan laughed. "I am a seer, too. I do not question or doubt your grandmother's vision. I will add my own. As we found the Goddess together, I had a vision of you, older, and I sensed you were a healer. What kind of healer I couldn't really tell."

I grinned. "I like your vision better. Do you think I have a choice?"

"You always have a choice."

I frowned. "Where have I heard that before!"

We slowly got dressed and then stood in the middle of the room, hand in hand.

"The circle is open but unbroken," I said.

"Blessed be," he answered.

We kissed for a long time. And then I left.

Alone I walked through the labyrinth of the Mother until I found the entrance and ran out into the sunshine and the arms of my family.

Twenty-two

♦♦♦♦♦♦♦♦♦♦♦♦♦♦♦

The child within Lee grew. I walked around in a daze for many weeks. My family laughed at me. They had experienced the same daze; they, too, had touched the Goddess, and they understood. I walked alongside the river, sat in the whirlpools. Danced alongside the fields, sometimes ran between the rows of golden green stalks. The hills surrounding our city turned lavender and then green and then began transforming to gold. The white hat of the mountain slowly got smaller.

We decided to go to the City. Lee had been born there and wanted to give birth to her child in the Sacred Well. Mother wanted to be with her and talk to the Elders of the City about the upcoming crops. Because of my first blood, everyone was convinced we would have extra grain to trade this year. Grand Keelie decided to come along to trade some of her tapestries, she said. I was certain she wanted to come because of my mother. I had noted they were "accidentally" spending more time together. Grand Keelie had even started coming to community meetings. At the bleeding time, my mother and Grand Keelie would sometimes meditate together.

"Grand Keelie said they loved each other very much at one time," I told Griffin. We sat on the floor of my room trying to figure out what to take for the trip to the City. "Do you remember when they loved each other?"

Griffin unfolded the garments I had just folded and carefully folded them again and put them in my bag. "Yes, I remember it. They did love each other very much."

"And then they didn't?"

"And then they couldn't live with each other. That's just the way people are."

I brushed a strand of hair off Griffin's forehead. Blond and gray. He was getting older.

"What's it like?" I asked.

"What?"

"Becoming wise?"

Griffin laughed. "What is the matter with you? You are acting like a child again. Is it because it's your first time going to the City?"

I grabbed the bag from him. So what if I was a little more talkative than usual.

"You have no sense of order," he said, taking the bag back.

"Thank the Goddess!" I said.

Griffin smiled. "You grew up so fast." He shook his head. "I remember when you came out of your mother's womb."

"You've been saying that my entire life, Uncle," I said. "And you always look so sad. Are you sorry you are getting older?"

He laughed. "No! I am only sorry we won't be doing the things we did when you were younger."

I had never thought of these things before. Everything had seemed to be such a natural progression from one event, one day, to the next. "Maybe I will be a painter and become your apprentice."

Griffin shrugged. "You can be whatever you wish to be."

I leaned closer to him. "But a bit more artistic talent from the Goddess would've helped, eh, Uncle?"

He laughed. "Keelie, it is enough just to be yourself. That in itself is artwork."

I kissed him. "I love you, Uncle Griffin. You are one of my favorite creations of the Goddess."

"I feel the same way. Now let's finish this."

The night before we left, I dreamed the sun exploded. The world I knew was white and then gone. Disappeared. I woke up in a sweat, shaking. Alone. For the first time in my life, I didn't know who to call, what to do.

I called no one.

I eventually stopped shaking and slid under my blanket again and went back to sleep.

We left before dawn, a group of twenty or so. Griffin stayed behind, to finish the painting, he said, but I knew he did not like to wander far from home. I turned to wave. He stood against the white walls of our home, his face obscured by the graying light of dawn. He smiled and waved. I wanted to run to him and make him come with us, but I knew that was childish. I would see him soon.

We were a sleepy bunch. I felt depressed and stayed near the back of the group. As the sun rose, frosting the land with gold, my mother led us in song. I stared at the sun and wondered if it would ever really explode. I shuddered and walked faster. No. The dream meant something else. Later, I would ask Grandmother Belle.

Midday, we reached the port. Ben and some of the other fishers awaited us. We climbed into two of the bigger fishing boats. I helped Ben put up the sails, watched the wind catch them, and then helped sail toward the City. We stayed within sight of land. People talked excitedly all around me. I wanted to join in. I wanted to notice things. This was a new adventure. New places.

The dream kept exploding in my brain.

Grandmother Belle put her arm across my shoulders. Together we watched the land move past us. White cliffs. Green-and-gold hillsides. Some black beaches. The prow of the boat slipped through the water quietly. The breath of the Goddess stroked our faces.

"The Dark Goddess has a hold of you, eh, my Grand Child," she said, kissing my cheek.

"I dreamed the sun exploded," I said, "and life changed for us all. It disappeared."

She squeezed my shoulders. "Perhaps it was you exploding."

That hardly sounded reassuring.

"Perhaps you are about to explode upon the world."

"I was so frightened," I said. I wanted reassurance from her, but I did not believe the dream was only about myself. "Grandma, did you always know who you are? I mean, did you always know how you would help the community, how you would truly be yourself in this world?"

Grandmother laughed. "Did I always tell stories? Or have I always been able to see?"

"Both."

A huge white bird flew above us. Goddess of the Waters. I waved and Grandmother sang a blessing. The bird dipped toward the boat and then flew onward.

"I could always see what was to come. It was only later that I learned to tell stories. We all have gifts, but it is up to us to find what about the gift makes us become ourselves more fully."

"And what is my gift?" I asked. "Mother is a farmer. Grand Keelie has her tapestries, Grace her pottery. Ben is a fisher. Lee will have children and teach. Griffin paints. I don't know what my gift will be. My initiator said I would be a great healer to my people. But how? You say I will fall in love with a warrior."

"It doesn't matter what any of us says," Grandmother Belle said. "It only matters what your heart tells you. What your body tells you. You don't have to do anything! It is enough to be yourself—and be a part of the community in any way you wish."

"That's what Griffin says."

"Naturally he has great wisdom; he is my son." She smiled.

"I feel so sad, Grandma. I don't know why."

She kissed me again. "If the Dark Goddess has you, you might as well sit with it. You can't shake her until she's ready to leave!"

She let me go and walked to the front of the boat, where Mother Lilith and Grand Keelie sat talking. Lee leaned against my mother; Kide rubbed her feet. Her belly was a giant ball, almost separate from her, it seemed from my viewpoint.

I sat, my legs crossed, and closed my eyes.

I dreamed I was alone on the boat. Except for a man wearing gold. His hair was black and I could not see his face. He held a shiny gold sword. He reached up and grabbed the moon. He dropped it into his mouth like a silver candy and swallowed it. I screamed, "Momma!"

I opened my eyes. I was curled on the floor of the boat. It was nearly night. Ben leaned over me.

"Are you all right, Keelie? You were talking in your sleep."

I sat up. I didn't feel well. "Are we in heavy seas?"

"Smooth as one of Gracie's plates. Why?"

The boat was moving too much. Or I was. Dizzy.

Dizzy. Sweaty.

I stood. Wobbled. And fell.

I remember little of the trip after that. Shadows of people rushing toward me. Getting me to drink this herb or that potion. We tied up to dock. Blurry. Everything slowed down or sped up. Cottony. I know that it was sunny and probably warm but I couldn't stop shivering. They carried me, I believe, and yet I remember the feel of the Earth. Tiny gold stones pressed against my feet. Which shouldn't have been bare, but were.

I remember colors. Everyone wore such vivid colors. Hair styled differently. Or else they wore snakes in their hair. Buildings whiter than clouds. Tall. With columns to support them. Vines and flowers creeping down them. Waving to me. Asking me how the day was.

Whirling away. Sunshine. Sheets softer and cooler than anything I had ever felt. The Goddess pressed my flesh.

Mother: "What is the matter with her? How can we help her?"

Grandmother: "She is sick with destiny."

The sun winked off. That's right. It had to be night. Didn't it? Somewhere.

I slept.

Dreamed the land was charred. Burning. The sun had eaten everything. I tried to wake from the dream.

Tried.

Sat up.

Grand Keelie wiped the sweat from my face.

"These are not my dreams," I whispered. I could not see the room, only Grand Keelie's eyes.

"What is it you fear, child?"

I stared at her. Who was she?

"I fear this."

257

I could not keep a hold of this world. I tumbled away.

I wanted to be with my sister. I wanted to see the place where she had been born and where her child would be born, surrounded by women and water, bathed in love and the blood of life. I walked down the spiral stone, around and around, slowly, heard the women cooing, singing, calling the child into the world.

"Keelie's spirit is with us," Grandmother Belle said. Lee squatted in the water, supported by woman after woman. The world was filled with women. Each sucked on a silver candy moon until they swallowed it and it filled their beings. Glowed until the birthing place was the moon. The child emerging from Lee's womb was the moon. A shiny pearl moon.

"Pearl," I whispered.

I gasped myself awake.

The room was dark, wrapping me in shades of blue.

Stroking me. I could not tell if there were bodies attached to the hands. I was bathed in sweat.

"I am sick with destiny," I whispered. The room wavered. In a dream? I walked away from it all. From the room and the blue hands. The City that sang and danced. The bull leapers prepared in the Center as I walked by. Two of them, their hair pulled away from their faces, their breasts covered. They sang songs to the bull. Preparing. Preparing. And then they disappeared.

"Mother Goddess," I whispered. Walking. The fever blurred my vision. Visions.

I think. I remember. Did I fly? Too hot. Too hot.

I just wanted green. I wanted water.

I must have walked.

Golden sand. Green. Green. Green.

I fell into the green.

The Goddess Eriskegal screamed at me. She tore out her hair. Gnashed her teeth. "Do you remember nothing? NOT A THING!"

I opened my eyes. I was blind. Until I saw the stars above. And the silvery moon.

"Momma," I whispered.

The grass was cool against my skin. I was weaker than any baby ever born. I turned my head.

And saw gold. Exploding everywhere. I tried to get up, to scream. To let the universe know all was wrong. I could do nothing.

My vision cleared and I saw the gold was only a fire, close to me. A shadow sat behind it.

I felt a blanket over me.

"The ground is cold." A male's voice. "But you wouldn't let me move you. So I built the fire. You are safe."

I closed my eyes. I could do nothing more. Nothing less. The sickness was fading. Destiny sat across from me. The warrior. The man of my grandmother's visions. Except destiny always involved choices. Didn't it? And hadn't I decided not to meet this warrior. Not to know him?

I kissed the Earth. "Blessings," I whispered, and slept.

Twenty-three
••••••••••••••••••

I awakened at the edge of a meadow, sheltered by trees. I heard a stream nearby. Sand edged the green. The man was gutting a fish. I sat up. The man looked up.

I felt as though the wind had been knocked out of me. A thousand things flashed through my brain. Pieces of memory I did not understand. He stared at me. He did not know me. But I knew him. Had known him forever. Or would.

Sick with destiny.

His eyes were hard. Barely a man. A boy really, about my age, maybe a little older. His eyes were so closed. It hurt to look at him.

"Who are you?" I asked.

"Victor," he said. "I found you feverish, trying to crawl into the river. What were you trying to do?"

Get to you. Get away from you?

"I must have been thirsty. Thank you for taking care of me."

He nodded and looked back down at his fish. He pretended he was not interested in me, that the fish was more important. But I knew. Why did he pretend?

"Where are your people?" I asked.

"They are trading in the City."

Warriors came to the City?

"And you stayed out here?"

"My father thinks I am not ready for the City," he said. "Too many women."

"Too many women?" I tried to stretch but I was too weak. I needed food and water.

"Do you have anything to eat or drink? My strength has left me."

He dropped the fish. "I apologize. Certainly."

He pulled a jug and fruit from his bag and came closer. He smelled like jasmine. He held the jug up to my lips. I tried to take it from him but he wouldn't let me.

Juice. I immediately felt strength returning. He pulled the jug away. It was a pale blue with flecks of gold in it.

"Beautiful work," I said.

He glanced at it and then away, shrugging off the compliment. Were his people not honored by their artisans?

"Did your people create it?"

"Yes," he said, "it is necessary work. We all do what we have to do." He moved away from me again.

"Did you have to care for me?" I asked.

He looked at me and shook his head.

"A woman alone? My father would wish me to take you."

"Take me? Take me where?"

"Take you home with us."

I laughed. "I would not wish to go with you."

He frowned. "That would not matter."

I laughed again. "It would most definitely matter. Would you wish to be carried away from your home by me?"

He stared at me again and then looked back down at his fish. "Eat your fruit. We'll have fish soon. It will help get your strength back."

It? The fish was an it?

I slowly looked around. I had no idea where I was. Perhaps the man had already started the journey back to his home. My heart started racing. I tried to stand. My arms and legs would not help me.

"Where—where are we?" The fear spread throughout my body. Filling every cell. I had never felt this way. Ever. At least not yet. Not yet. The world shifted. I was not prepared for this.

Not prepared for this man. This boy.

"The City is just beyond the rise," Victor said.

"I found you down by the river." He looked up at me. His face seemed to relax. "You have nothing to fear from me."

I stared at him. He relaxed as soon as he saw my fear. Something was not right. I wanted to go back and be with my family.

But I couldn't walk.

He couldn't carry me.

I saw no other means of returning.

Unless I could fly again.

I bit into an apple and chewed. Watched him put a stick through the fish, build up the fire, hang the fish over the fire. He didn't bless the fish. I hoped he had blessed her before taking her from the river. Or after.

A few minutes later he wrapped leaves around pieces of the fish and handed me one.

I whispered a blessing.

"What did you say?" Victor asked. He sat cross-legged several feet away from me. Perhaps he was fearful of me.

"I blessed our meal. I don't mean to be rude but I didn't hear you bless the fish."

"The fish is there for me to kill. Why should I bless it? It should thank me for killing it." He bit into leaves.

"Do you really believe that?" I asked. I said another prayer. I closed my eyes and breathed deeply and drew a circle around myself and the fish. Maintained our sacredness. Then I bit into the fish. I tasted her death and gagged.

I spit the food into my hand. I reached out to the sand and easily dug a hole. I carefully placed the fish into it. I said a prayer and covered the hole.

"Blessed be," I said out loud.

"That was good food you wasted," Victor said.

I stared at him. My grandmother's vision had been all wrong. I could not imagine ever falling in love with this creature.

"You were wrong in your manner of killing," I said.

"Do you think a bear prays before it kills a fish? Or a man?"

I nodded. "Of course. And a bear doesn't kill people."

"A bear killed my uncle."

"If he was anything like you, he probably killed her cub!"

He blinked. "How did you know that?"

"Anyone would know that!"

"You need to eat. You don't see how pale and weak you are."

"You only think I'm weak because you're losing the argument!"

He picked up his bag and carried it to me. "Please, eat whatever you can. My mother would never forgive me if harm came to you."

At last. A reasonable statement.

I reached into the bag and pulled out bread, dried fish, fruit.

"Did your mother prepare these foods?" I asked.

"She did."

I nodded. "Then I will eat them."

I had to pause often, and he made me drink his mother's juice, but I managed to eat quite a bit. Then I lay down, he put a cover over me, and I fell to sleep.

It was hot when I awakened. The tree fanned me. Victor sat under the tree, staring across the sand.

I sat up. I was stronger, but still so weak.

"I have never been this sick," I said.

"I have," Victor said. "You will be well soon."

"Thank you for that reassurance. But I am concerned about my family. They will be worried about me." Except Grandmother Belle would probably tell them where I was. She would know. She had predicted it when I was born. "Do you like being without your family?"

"My mother is back in the village. My sisters and brothers, too. It is only my father and the other men."

"I do not recognize your accent. Where are you from?"

"The north," he said. "I learned your language as a child. My father thought we should.

We need to know the language of the conquered."

"Conquered?" The fear began again. "What are you talking about? We are not conquered. We are not warriors."

"Then it will be easier to conquer you."

"But why?"

"Because."

"That's an intelligent answer! A three-year-old would have more to say than that." Fury had tickled my feet and was now rising to my throat, throwing off the weakness. Victor just watched me.

"My mother's people fought," he said. "She's told me stories when my father isn't around. They were prepared, her people. They fought. Like Amazons. But in the end"—he looked away from me—"in the end they lost."

"I wish you to go away from me. I do not need your food or water, dear conqueror. The Goddess will provide. Go away!"

"As you wish." He got up and walked away, disappearing over the rise in the sand within seconds.

I was alone. My heartbeat slowly went back to normal. The fear stayed. I had never heard such hideous things. I wanted my mother, my grandmother. I wanted to be back in my home.

I ate more of the food the man had left, and then I went to sleep.

I awakened to the smell of fish cooking.

I sat up. Victor squatted across the fire from me, watching the fish.

"I gave a blessing, the way my mother taught me," he said quietly. "Does that satisfy you?"

"Perhaps you are more your mother's son than your father's?"

Now his eyes came alive. With anger.

"If you weren't a woman!"

"What does that mean? Why are you so angry? I was complimenting you!" Strange, strange creature.

He poked at the fish and a piece fell into the fire. He reached for it and then yelped when the fire bit him.

"Leave it! The fire will eat it," I said. He sucked on his hand. "There's probably some plantain growing nearby. Break the leaves and press the juice and leaf onto the burn."

I said a blessing, certain he wouldn't, and watched as he pulled at the plantain and put it on his hand. After a moment, the pain left his face. I scooted toward the fire and took the rest of the fish off the sticks and put them on the leaves Victor had waiting. I wrapped the fish up and handed Victor one.

"Thanks," he said. I eagerly bit into the fish. She tasted much better.

"Do you taste the difference?" I asked.

"It does taste different," he said, "but I don't know why."

"Your people must be exceedingly ignorant. You can't just go around killing things just because you're hungry or you want that something dead!"

"Do you always talk so much?" he asked.

I would be well soon. Very soon. And then I would get up and walk back to my people. Away from this person.

We ate in silence for a few minutes. A wind picked up, the Goddess breathing on us, blessing us. The copse of trees shook. The fire went out. Out toward the ocean, darkness gathered. Lightning flashed. I suddenly noticed I had hardly seen or heard any birds in the last little while.

"Is there a cave nearby?" I asked.

"Why?"

I pointed out to sea.

"How long before it hits?"

"I think it'll come ashore before dark." Which was soon.

Victor stood up. Now he looked frightened. "I will look for shelter."

I tried to push myself up but was just barely able to get on my knees. I shook my head. This was infuriating. The Goddess was sorely testing my good humor.

"I can't come with you."

"I'll be back," Victor said. He hurried away. "I promise."

I finished eating and then carefully put the remaining food and drink in Victor's bag. I covered the embers of the fire with sand. Then, exhausted, I pulled the blanket around me and waited. The humidity went up, and the wind grew in intensity.

I watched all around me for Victor to return. There wasn't time to dig a hole, to crawl anywhere. The clouds came ashore. Darkness mixed with storm. I could not see much beyond the copse of trees and green. I protected my face from the pelting sand.

The temperature dropped. The wind lessened.

Then, Victor was there. I got onto his back—my arms around his neck, my legs around his waist. He held on to me and ran away from the trees and over the sand. The wind started again. Howled. Sand and twigs whistled past us. Victor stumbled, regained his balance, and ran again. Away from the river? Toward the river. I could not see anything. Hear anything except the wind. And this terrible roar. This deafening scream of the storm. I buried my head in Victor's back, wondering how he could see. Tripping forward.

Suddenly the howling lessened, and we were inside darkness. Victor walked a ways in the darkness and then carefully let me down. I put my hand up against cool stone. He had found a cave! We were safe.

In total darkness. I could hear Victor trying to catch his breath close by. His teeth were chattering.

"I hope we're the only ones in here!" he said.

I smelled no other animals.

"We're alone," I said. Victor was breathing hard. The storm crashed all around us. Thunder cracking. Shaking the ground. Us.

"Victor," I said, "come closer." I put the bag of food down. I had managed to keep the blanket. I felt Victor next to me, trembling.

"Are you cold?" I asked.

I put the blanket across his shoulders. He pulled it away and put it around me. "Don't be stubborn," I said. "I'm not the one shivering!"

"I—I'm not cold." The wind whistled through the cave. Thunder shook us again. Victor moved closer. He was afraid of the storm! He was terrified. Yet he had come back for me. I put my arm across his shoulders.

"It's all right," I said. "Here. Move closer so we can keep each other warm." I pulled him closer. I liked the feel of his body next to mine. "We used to tell stories during storms. Did you do that? My sister Lee and Uncle Griffin and Mother Lilith and Grandmother Belle. Grandmother Belle is the best storyteller."

"W-where was your father?"

"My father? All the men of the city are my fathers."

"All the men? Your mother was a whore then?"

"A whore? What is that? I've never heard that term."

"Your m-mother had sex with a lot of different men."

"Of course she did. And women, too. Is that a word from your native language? I guess all the people of my village would be whores."

He shifted next to me. His shivering seemed to be lessening.

"No. I'm sorry. It is not a polite term. I didn't understand what you were saying. Please go on."

"Grandmother Belle would tell stories. Sometimes the thunder scared Lee, so Grandmother would tell silly story after silly story."

"Do you remember any?" he asked.

"Sure. Would you like me to tell you some? I like the ones about the tricksters. Every village or city has one, don't you think? Ours is Wils. She's our town clown!"

"What does she do?"

"She makes fun of people who are getting too full of themselves. Or during ceremonies she'll pull some stunt to make us all laugh, or to remember to laugh, in case we're too serious."

"My father would kill anyone who laughed at him."

"I don't think I like your father. Promise me you'll never introduce us."

"So tell me a story about Wils."

The storm screamed outside our cave while I told Victor children's stories of the trickster. After a time, he stopped shivering. I moved my arm away but he stayed close. He laughed at all the funny places in the story. We ate and drank.

The storm blew away.

Silver light came into the cave. Victor helped me up. I leaned on him and we walked to the entrance of the cave. The moon silvered the landscape. A cool breeze blew across my face.

"It's beautiful," I said.

"Yes, it is. I've never gone out after a storm."

"Never?" I looked at him. His face was much more relaxed. His eyes had warmth and humor.

"I'd usually fall asleep. I'd be afraid for such a long time and then I would go to sleep."

"Didn't anyone comfort you?" He stiffened next to me. I knew he wanted to move away, but I would have fallen had he done so. "My father usually drinks too much when it storms," he said, "and then he beats my mother. Or one of us."

"Your community allows this?"

"This isn't the way of your people?" he asked.

We slowly walked away from the cool entrance of the cave, but not as far in as we had been.

"Of course it isn't the way of my people or any people I know of!"

"My mother tried to leave but she is in a strange country and knows no one. He always brings her back."

"If your mother cannot protect herself, perhaps you can."

"He isn't home enough anymore to hurt her," he said.

We sat down again. Close. I did not like talking about his father. He reminded me of the exploding sun.

"Why do you go with your father?"

"Because it is my duty as a son."

I shook my head. "I don't like that he is in the City."

"The City is well protected. My father and his armies will not attack it. At least not now."

But my city. My people. This felt like a dream. None of it could be true, could it?

"I don't think you're like your father," I said. "I think he made you stay out here because he knows you have listened to your mother all these years, that you know her way is right. I will pray the Goddess changes him or takes him into her bosom soon, before he can hurt anyone."

"It is too late for that," Victor said. "He has hurt many. Killed many. So have I."

I moved away from him. "You are sick. Perhaps our healers can help you."

Victor laughed. Snorted. "Maybe he won't come back for me."

"You'd like that?"

"I don't really fit in. Not yet. My father is trying to make a warrior out of me. He has shown me how to kill. How to die."

"And has anyone shown you how to live?"

He didn't answer.

We ate again. I felt stronger by the minute.

"Let's sleep under the stars," I said. "It's probably warming up now."

"It doesn't make you nervous to sleep under a full moon? She steals men's hearts, you know."

I let him help me up. "What nonsense. But I'm not a man, so I guess I have nothing to fear."

The air was warm. Victor brushed away the sand until he found a dry spot. Then he laid the blanket on top of it. I dropped onto it and he started to walk away.

"Where are you going?" I asked. "Come sleep with me."

He stopped and looked back at me. "I don't think that would be right. I—I might take advantage of you."

"What are you talking about? There's enough

blanket for both of us. You are the strangest person I ever met." I patted the spot next to me. "We'll keep each other warm."

He hesitated and then returned to my side and sat next to me. "I'll stay up as lookout."

I lay down. "There are no harmful beasts in this area. Sleep. We will dream together."

"You aren't afraid?"

"I wasn't afraid of anything until I learned of your existence. I'm tired. Blessings."

I pulled the blanket around me. Victor sat up for a few moments and then lay down next to me. I closed my eyes. I felt infinitely comfortable with him, even though I thought his ideas and people were totally strange. I pressed my back against his back. I smiled. The sickness was completely gone. Tomorrow I would return to my family.

I dreamed of Atwan. His tongue in my ear. His stomach against mine. Together. Reaching for the Goddess.

I opened my eyes. It was still night. Victor slept next to me. I pressed closer to him, trying to warm myself. I put my hands between my legs; I was moist with my dream and my blood.

Victor shifted in his sleep to face me. His eyes opened. He sat up quickly.

"What happened? Is everything all right?"

"All is well. Victor, do your people practice the arts of love?"

"The women still do. The ones we call 'whores.'"

"I would like to call the Goddess to us, with you."

He blinked. "You want to have sex with me?"

"Is that what you say? It is a sacred magical act for us."

"What do you mean?"

"First," I said, sitting up, "I bless this spot. I call upon the Goddess to bless us and make this union sacred. You, too." I pulled him into a sitting position. "Go on."

"Blessings?" he said. I nodded. "Please bless this circle."

I shrugged. Better than nothing. I reached for his hand. It was warm in mine. "I choose you."

"I choose you," he said.

At first, we just looked at each other. Then, I leaned over and kissed him. Our lips met and I felt myself sinking into him. He pulled away.

"I don't think we should do this," he said. "I like you too much."

"What? Of course I like you, too. It surprises me but I do. Why else would we do this?"

He lay down and turned away from me. "Good night."

I lay down, too. My cunt ached for him. I wanted him to feel the Goddess. How could he ever want to kill again or follow his father if the Goddess touched his heart? And I wanted him.

I didn't even know why. The dream? Or because he had laughed at my stories? Or had run across the sand in a storm to rescue me? I put my hand between my legs.

Victor turned to face me. "You are the strangest person I've ever met."

"I choose you."

"And I you."

I remember

It didn't happen slowly, as it had with Atwan and me. It seemed almost instantly we were naked. His mouth was on my breasts, mine on his. His penis slipped into my cunt, and something happened, the world shifted, doors opened, closed, people whispered. I had felt this man against me a thousand times, this man with me. I had held his hand, wept with him, screamed at him, loved and hated him through time. We rocked each other, moved, undulated. Snakes across the sand. Eagles tumbling through the sky, locked in intercourse. Orgasming and then breaking apart before impact. Only I reached ahead of the orgasm, reached into the ether, into the Earth, called to the Goddess, turned Victor over and was on top of him, moving my hips slowly, his hands on me, and then faster, faster, the Goddess descended, I kissed her face, and Victor felt her, She rocked him, bloodied him with my blood, shocked him with pleasure, until we both screamed out in the supreme glorious joy of it, and exploded into the silvery night with orgasm after orgasm.

We couldn't stop. Couldn't break into two people. We stayed together, our souls and cells meshing, until light.

The light of dawn colored our skins, turning us into rose petals. Victor kissed my bare butt and then ran to the nearby stream. He stood in the water, naked, his feet spread apart. He looked up the hill at me and cried, "Grant us the blessings of the water of life, Mother of us All!" He looked like a god himself, brown and powerful, straddling the stream. He watched the water, his body still, and then he dipped into the water, quickly, quietly, and then cried out and showed me the rainbow-colored fish flapping in his clenched fist. "We are blessed!" he cried. He thanked the fish for her life and then killed her. He ran up the hill to me.

I pulled him down next to me.

"Is that the way of your people?" he asked, showing me our morning meal.

I kissed him. "Close enough."

He laughed.

I took his face between my hands. "You look so different today. You are in your eyes."

"I will make us something to eat."

"Is that all you know how to cook? Fish?"

"I wouldn't complain. You are well, aren't you? It was my cooking that did it."

We ate and drank and made love as the sun rose in the sky.

"I have known you before," he whispered as we lay pressed against one another. "This is not the first time we have met."

"In this lifetime, it is the first we have met. I would have remembered otherwise."

"I want to stay with you."

"Then stay," I said. I wrapped my arms around his neck. "Stay."

"My father would be furious."

I did not understand his ties to his father.

"He would hurt my mother. Or my sisters."

"He hurts his own daughters?"

"He beats them," Victor said. He held me tightly. For an instant I could not breathe. "He has sex with them when they don't want to."

"Your world is too frightening. How could such sickness be allowed to continue?"

He kissed my cheek. "He would hurt them and he would hunt me down. If he found me in your village, he could kill everyone."

I closed my eyes. "I could not live in your world."

"I wouldn't ask. I have seen what it's done to my mother."

"I miss my family. I want to return to the City soon."

"I will go with you to the edge. It's just south of here."

We got dressed slowly, splashed each other in the stream, gathered water and fruit for the short journey.

Then the world changed. I felt the sun exploding in my brain again. Voices. I fell to my knees, trying to blink away the sun. Victor's face changed. Joy fell to fear.

"Hide!" Victor said. "You must hide."

The cave was too far. Nothing else would hide me except the trees. The voices were coming nearer. Any moment they would crest a hill and see us. Victor grabbed my hand and we ran toward the copse of trees. When we reached them, I put my foot in his hands, and he pushed me up into the leaves, where I was, we hoped, hidden from view.

"Victor! You can reach. Come up."

Victor looked up at me and smiled. "I can't let him hurt you. I must go with him."

He moved quickly away from the trees. I parted leaves until I could peek out. The men came over the hill. Nearer and nearer. Victor walked to greet them. One man walked ahead of them all, toward his son. He smiled and grasped Victor's hand in his. He wore metal everywhere. He took off his helmet and I saw his face. The tree seemed to tip, the world swirl. I had known him before I knew him. He was the father. I remembered. I remembered something. I remembered him. Lee. We had called him Lee. Like my sister. Only he wasn't like her. He was the father.

I held tightly to the tree. I never wanted to see him again. But Victor. I had to see Victor.

Victor who walked away without a backward glance. Protecting me. Keeping me from the father. For now. I would have to find a way to protect myself in the future. I was certain we would meet again.

Twenty-four

❖❖❖❖❖❖❖❖❖❖❖❖❖

I remember
  Finding my way back to the City and my family. The newest member was Baby Girl Pearl. No one could stop the constant tears that flowed down my cheeks, not even me. When Grandmother asked what was wrong, I said, "I'm still sick with destiny."

We got home and life settled into a routine again.

Except I had nightmares and woke up crying nearly every night for weeks. I decided I wasn't a good influence on the baby and went to live with Grand Keelie for a while.

I sat at her feet as I had done as a child and unraveled her thread.

"So you met your warrior," Grand Keelie said as she spun her tapestry of gold, blue, and green.

"Yes, I met him. He was a boy, really. Not much older than I am."

"You didn't go with him."

"How could I? Leave you all behind? I could not live as he does. It is too horrible to think about."

"Perhaps they do not think it is awful," she said.

"How could they not? Now I just feel lost. I didn't get to see Pearl come into the world. I don't know what I want to do. Atwan said I would be a great healer, yet I only have a rudimentary interest in herbs and flowers. I don't know how I will help my community."

"Maybe you already have. You made love with the warrior. Maybe that will save us all. We never know what gesture the world turns upon."

"I want life to be as it was. Before I knew such horror existed."

Grand Keelie nodded and spun her web.

I dreamed of charred ruins. I called to the Goddess. Sometimes she walked with me over the desolate landscape. "Soon no one will hear me." "No!" I cried. "Never!"

Then my bleeding stopped.

A child grew within me.

Mother Lilith came to Grand Keelie's house. Not to see me. She and Grand Keelie laughed together. Sometimes kissed. I blessed their happiness and returned to my mother's house. All welcomed me and my becoming child.

The nightmares continued.

I prayed.

Griffin brought me a painting. He left it covered while he spoke to me.

"The Goddess asked me to paint this," he said. "I do not understand it and I'm afraid it might frighten you."

I put my hand on my belly. "You can show me." I took his hand in mine. He looked so frail. Had he always been so thin? Pale? He had always seemed awkward to me, even when I was very young, but so tall. Had he shrunk? Or had I gotten bigger?

He let the covering drop from the painting. The backdrop was night purple. The Dark Goddess screamed at the center of it. Her teeth green. Her hair made from worms. Three corpses hung from three hooks. The Goddess pointed at me and screamed.

"What is she saying?" I asked.

"Remember."

"What?"

"That's what she wants you to do. Remember."

I kissed him and took the painting from him. "Thank you, Uncle."

I remember

I put the painting near my bed.

Several days later, Griffin fell to sleep and never awakened. My uncle who had always been there was gone.

We mourned our loss and celebrated his life. We walked from house to house looking at the art he had painted throughout his life. His last was the painting of Eriskegal, screaming at me to remember. Remember what? As far as I could tell, I hadn't forgotten anything.

We put Griffin back into the womb of MommaEarth.

Somehow, through all the grief, the cycles of life and death, life took hold. I began the apricot dreams of pregnancy. The nightmares grew further and further apart. I passed much of my time with Grandmother Belle, and she told me tales from long ago, before any warriors existed. Life had gone on as we lived it today for thousands of years. I found great peace listening to these stories. Peace in knowing.

We gathered the harvest, celebrated it, dug in for the winter, celebrated menarche. This year I wore red. I felt old and new.

When my baby's water broke, I crouched down close to the Earth and the other women. The baby fought life. He screamed and clawed and refused to come. Exhausted, I followed him to the other side.

"Child Hart, come with me," I said.

He shook his head. "I know what I will become."

"Many lifetimes from now," I said.

"So you remember?" he asked.

I shook my head. "I only know it is time for you to come into the world."

"Or you to leave it."

"Or me to leave it. There is much love waiting for you. You will live in a peaceful and loving world."

"Always?"

I started to answer yes. I felt my heartbeat slowing. I heard Eriskegal singing my name in her raspy voice.

"Hart, my dearest boy, come with your mother. All is not lost yet."

He tentatively reached out for me, and I grabbed his hand and pulled him over, wrenching him and myself back from the other side.

Leaving parts of ourselves behind, I was afraid.

Hart came screaming into the world. I drifted back and forth between here and there before deciding to stay with my son.

My breasts wouldn't give milk at first, so Lee suckled my son.

Grand Keelie sat next to me as I lay recovering and took my hand. "I'm sorry you ever heard the story of my warrior or met your own.

You will never be the same. I'm so sorry." Her tears fell upon the hand she held.

I watched Lee feed her daughter and my son and wondered when I would begin feeling again. Grand Keelie went back to her house, to stay, alone. My mother watched the four of us with arms crossed. The warrior had affected so many of us.

Finally, my breasts began giving milk and my son took nourishment from my body. I watched him suck and felt a deep love for him. I gently petted his head and wished I had never heard about the warrior people, either.

I remember

I started to forget. Or go on. My son grew quickly. I studied with several herbalists, to see if that was my calling. Though I could talk to the plants and quickly learned their healing properties, I did not seem to be a traditional healer.

Hart followed me as I left the healers and worked with Grace. I shaped pots, taught Hart how to do it, and then quickly lost interest. I worked with Grand Keelie for a time but Hart seemed to trouble her. So we farmed with my mother. Hart loved digging in the Earth.

"I'll be a farmer like Grandmother Lilith," he told us.

We all knew from the beginning that Pearl

would be a dancer. She danced into all our hearts and continued throughout her childhood. Even Hart, who was never still, became quiet when Pearl danced. Lee watched her, and every time, she wept.

My child Hart and Lee's child Pearl knew how they would live and grow in the community and they were children! I floated from one interest to another.

Pearl had her first menarche. Mother, Aunt, Grandmother, and Great-grandmother Belle all celebrated with her.

Not long after, Hart celebrated his coming of age with the men. Seph, Kide, Ben, and the rest taught him the ways of men.

Soon they both had their initiations and we saw little of them. Lovemaking took up much of their time.

After Hart's initiation, I stood at the edge of the sea, staring out. Maybe I was destined to be a fisher.

Ben came up behind me. "You want to go out? You haven't been since you were a girl." He put his hands on my shoulders.

"Do you think I was meant to be a fisher?" I asked him.

"I think you were meant to be whatever you want," he said. "You want to come fishing with your old friend?"

I nodded.

I loved the smell of saltwater, the wind in the sails, the pull on my muscles. I enjoyed Ben's company, and each time we blessed and thanked the fish, I remembered Victor and the fish he had caught during my sickness. I remembered Victor's eyes, his fear and joy. Him against my body. I watched Ben all day long and realized it had been many years since I had celebrated with anyone. Initiation after initiation had passed without me finding a partner.

So then and there, I took the sails down and asked Ben if he wanted to make love with his old friend.

He did. We did.

We stayed in each other's company for a long time.

I had another child. She needed no coaxing to come into this world. She ran laughing into my arms. I called her Anna.

When I looked at her, I saw myself.

Years of blissful peace, celebration, and love followed. Grandmother Belle took leave of us one winter evening, right after a story. After she kissed me good night and said, "Atwan was right, you will be a great healer."

I laughed and told her to go to bed. I had long ago given up the search. It was enough to raise my children, be with friends and family, and help the community in all ways.

*   *   *

Then we began hearing the stories of the warriors and their sun gods. They lived like no others had lived before. They did not hear the call of the Goddess. The rivers and trees did not talk to them. Or they were deaf to their language. They killed without mercy or reverence. Women and children were property. They believed nature was there for their pleasure, theirs to conquer and subdue.

Most thought the stories were untrue.

I knew they weren't.

I waited for the warriors to come.

Twenty-five

＊＊＊＊＊＊＊＊＊＊＊＊＊＊＊

"We need to learn how to defend our- selves," Seph told the community. We gathered on the steps of the city Center. My mother sat next to him.

"The City has been prepared for this eventuality for decades," Kide said. "They can teach us."

"We don't have weapons," someone else said. "We don't know how to manufacture them. This is ridiculous. What could they want from us? The land is good but not that good. Maybe if we remain as we are, they will go away."

"That is what many have said, only to be overrun. Their crimes are horrible. If we stay together and defend ourselves, we will be able to overcome them."

"We could leave and find another place to live," another woman said. "Where they can't find us."

"That is how we came to be in this place," Grand Keelie said. "Long ago our great-great-grandparents came here. We cannot keep running forever. Before long, they will conquer the whole world."

Hart sat on one side of me, his sister on the other. I glanced at him. How like Victor he had become. Except his face knew no killing. Knew only love.

"Maybe when they came, we could hide," my five-year-old Anna said, "and they wouldn't know we were here. Wouldn't they go away then?"

Everyone laughed, a little nervously. I kissed the top of her head. Behind me, Ben rubbed my shoulders. "Maybe she's right," he whispered.

"Lilith," Grace said. "What do you think?"

"I am as confused as all of you," my mother said, "but I think we should be prepared to defend ourselves. Perhaps we should send a group to the City. When they return, they can teach the rest of us."

"Is there enough time?" Sister Lee asked. "I wish we knew when they were coming."

We sat in momentary silence. Since Grandmother Belle had died, no one else had come forward as seer. It was a great loss to our community.

"All agreed to sending a voluntary group to the City?"

"Agreed!" the group cried. "Blessed be!"

"The circle is open but unbroken," Lilith said, standing. "May we cause harm to none."

"Well, maybe to some," Hart murmured.

I put my arm across his shoulders. "You really wish to go to the City and learn these things?"

He hugged my waist. "What choice do we have, Mother? My father and others like him will try to kill us, will kill us, if we don't fight back."

"You don't know that your father has anything to do with it."

Hart nodded. "Yes, I do know."

I dropped my arms. Lilith and Lee came to stand with us. I leaned back against Ben. Anna pulled on her brother's hand.

"How do you know?" I asked.

"I dreamed it," he said. "I dreamed he was at the head of the army." Hart pointed north. "They were camped not far from here. They left behind rubble. Nothing more."

We were silent.

"Perhaps it means nothing," Ben said.

"Or perhaps he has Grandmother's gift," Lee said.

I saw the same fear in their eyes I had seen so long ago in Victor's.

*　　*　　*

After the crops were planted, a group left, my son amongst them, for the City.

Everything remained the same, yet all was different.

Anna cried in her sleep. During the day, she danced with Pearl. Watching Pearl's colorful skirts swirl around her legs, I believed that all was well with the world.

Then a man stumbled into our city. He was badly beaten, bruised and bleeding. He crumpled into a pile and whispered, "They killed us all. Killed us all."

We tended his physical wounds, but his mind was broken. We couldn't discover where he had come from.

I dreamed of the exploding sun again. And then Victor ate the moon.

I bolted upright in the darkness. Anna slept quietly next to me. My clothes were damp with perspiration. I wished Ben had stayed the night.

I got up and went outside. Dark moon. Deep deep darkness, broken only by the tiny stars. I walked along the path I knew so well, away from the buildings, down toward the river. I heard the water long before I saw it. And then I saw it only as swirling blackness. I stepped into the water, cool between my legs. Bleeding time again.

"I am ready, Mother," I said, sinking into the water, "to know what the dream means."

I breathed deeply and felt the water flow around me and into me. Felt the Goddess stroke me. After a few minutes, I got up and went into the menstrual cave. No one used light this night. Complete darkness. I sat on the stone, felt its coolness, listened to the other women bleed with me, pray with me. They all sought answers.

I closed my eyes and dipped deep into the darkness.

In my own darkness, I walked a long time. Until I was more exhausted than when I had met Victor. Finally, the darkness ended. A sickly gray light appeared. I went through the opening.

Into a black-sheeted room. A black throne. Deep dark glorious wonderful blackness.

"Hey, so, the bitch is back, eh?" Eriskegal. She stood with her hands on her hips. Enormous hips. Long legs. Her head touched the ceiling.

"Have you figured it all out yet?"

"Horror ahead."

"Very good, my dear. But we KNEW THAT!" She screamed.

"Have we met before?" I asked.

"Still have that little problem with memory?" She spat and then delicately sat in her throne. "Yes, we've met, you brainless thoughtless memoryless shit."

"Go to hell," I said and turned from her.

"I'm sorry, but you don't even know what

hell is in your particular time period so that curse is quite meaningless. Now I've met Hel. She's a gem. Truly. Love her wardrobe. Black on black. Can you beat it? She's got this little cocktail dress I would just kill for."

"I came to you for help," I said. "I've been praying to you forever. They are going to destroy all that is. Forever."

She nodded. "Not forever. Not necessarily. There are things still that you can do. Can you envision it yet? Do you know who you are?"

I had a flash, a piece of something. Hadn't someone asked me that on a mountaintop a lifetime ago?

"Envision a world without fear," she said.

"Yes! I lived it for years."

"And for thousands of years before that. Can you remember that, yet? Maybe others need to remember that, too."

"We are arming for the battle."

"It is inevitable. Know you are more than the sum of your parts, but no less. Gods-are-us."

I turned again and walked into the darkness.

I spun up into myself and the bleeding room.

"We remember," the women whispered all around me. "We remember it all."

Suddenly, the ground beneath me shook. All the energies of all the women vibrated around me. Filled me. Their whispers tickled me, pushed me, prodded me. The room spun and spun until I vomited and vomited and suddenly the flashes and pieces and explosions and wandering from there to here and here and there, the herbs, fishing, pottery, everything pulsated through me. Exploded. A mirror shattered before me.

I screamed.

I felt Griffin sewing the pieces of Anna, Belle, Lee into me. Me. Me. Lilith reaching for me, keeping me from falling, dressing me in white. Laughing. Other pieces of me frozen in time. Hating Victor. Screaming at Victor. Running away with Hart. Picking up the pieces.

Dying. Again. And again. Plunging the knife into Hart's back. Not killing him. Wishing I had. Running into the woods. The Raven taking me back. Back. There's no place like home. No place like home. No place home. As they battered my body and soul again and again. Victor trying to reach me. Protect me. Save himself.

Time and time again. The burning times. The jungle. Ship. Prison. Abbey. Field. Cottage.

Trying to remember a time when all was not lost. Trying to find a place like no other. A place like home.

Finding it. Finding it.

Here. Until Victor.

But before. Before.

We walked timeless across the forests and deserts and jungles and plains. We walked the Earth. Blessed the Earth. Were blessed by her.

I held out my hand and all the people climbed onto me. Ate from me. Blessed me. Blessed themselves. Made love. Food. Babies. All was sacred. I lay down on the Earth and was the Earth. I was alive with all that was sacred. Which was all.

I remembered the peace of being still. Of being here.

I remembered it all. All my lives. All life.

That was my gift: memory.

Memory.

All of those people, all their lives, were in me. Were me. I was more than the sum of my parts, but no less: Gods-are-us. God us. Goddess.

Me.

When I opened my eyes the other women slept. I carefully stepped around them and went into the daylight.

Hart was right. His father was near. And his father had to see.

I would find him. It was time for his trip to the underworld.

Twenty-six

••••••••••••••

My mother wanted to come with me, but I persuaded her to stay with Anna. I got together some food and water and then started out on my own. I walked along the river, listening to her whisper to me for a long while, before she veered east and I continued north. The trees sheltered me and birds whistled at me until midday. I sat under an old olive tree and ate lunch. Then I left the woods and traveled across the silvery green hills.

I would find Victor and remind him of who he was. Who I was.

Of what had been and would be. Could be.

I passed no human beings. I longed for the company of family, yet I enjoyed the solitude as I continued to remember many lifetimes.

Near the end of the day, I felt the army before I saw it. My heart started pounding in my ears.

I broke out into a sweat. I slunk nearly to the top of the next hill and then got on my belly and crawled through the grass and purple wildflowers until I could see to the other side. The setting sun draped gold across the hills and valley. Spread out below me was what appeared to be endless rows of tents. Tentlike structures. Completely vulnerable to attack from the south, I noted, but they were not afraid of the south. Just a bunch of societies with a lot of peaceful women and wimpy men. A layer of smoke from their campfires hung over the encampment. Add pollution to their crimes.

I pushed myself to a standing position.

"Though that's nothing to what they're going to do. The future awaits."

A bit away from the rest of the tents were two larger tents. Undoubtedly the leader of the pack. Or Victor's father. Father Lee. I hoped not. I didn't want to see him. Not again. We'd had too many face-offs. And he had always won. Always. He had killed Victor and myself life after life, body and soul. He had to be stopped. Someday.

But today. Today it was time for Victor's trip down memory lane.

I waited until darkness. Then I stayed within the trees and walked down the hill toward the big tents. I encountered no sentries. I heard the boisterous laughter of men who had killed. Finally I reached the tents. From the first one, I heard nothing. I moved to the next one. I heard murmurs. Laughter. Brief. Forced.

Victor.

I sat on my haunches and waited until the tent had cleared. Victor coughed. He moved around a bit, and then I heard him get into bed. Sleep. Breathing deeply.

I took the knife from my bag and silently cut a slit in the tent, just big enough for me to slip through.

He always was a heavy sleeper. No matter what lifetime.

I waited for my eyes to adjust to the tent's particular darkness. Victor was alone. Good thing or I'd probably be dead by now. He slept on a kind of cot. Good Goddess, they just couldn't stand being close to the earth.

I moved closer.

I could just make out his face. His beautiful wonderful face that I had not seen in twenty years! I wanted to smother him with kisses.

This man who was destined to kill my people? To change the whole world?

No. It couldn't be.

I knelt by him.

His breath warmed my hands.

He smelled glorious. Like the great outdoors.

"Victor," I leaned and whispered in his ear.

He didn't move.

"Victor," I whispered, "it's Keelie."

He smiled in his sleep.

I couldn't resist. I kissed his cheek.

A moment later I was flat on the ground and Victor, wide awake, I might add, was over me, pinning me to the ground.

"Victor, it's me, Keelie. Your one and only true love."

He stared at me, his eyes wide, for too long a time. I was tempted to knee him but was afraid his screams might draw a little attention.

He slowly released me.

I sat up. "Brute force is not very attractive in a man. I come by to say hi and you try to break my wrists."

"I—I'm sorry," he whispered, moving away from me. "You shouldn't be here. My father would kill you."

"Same sorry old tune, eh? All grown up and still doing Daddy's bidding?"

He just stared at me. "You look the same."

I ruffled his hair. "You don't. You've got gray hair. And wrinkles. We can't stay here. Someone will hear us. Like Daddy dear. Will you come with me?"

I stood and took his hand and he let me lead him through the slit and into the new moon darkness. Owls and crickets and frogs covered the sounds of our leave-taking as we crunched and tripped into the nearby woods. I walked until we were a safe distance from the camp and then I stopped.

"Well, Victor, old friend, aren't you glad to see me?"

He shut my lips with a hard, warm, wonderful gushy kiss. I returned it and pressed my body against his. It had been a long, long twenty years. A long time for two people who kept getting thrown together through history again and again.

I lifted my clothes, he tore off his, and we sank into each other. The pleasure of it, the enormous perfection of his skin against mine, him inside me, made the universe spin just a little faster. Why did it always feel so good to be in his arms? For us to be together.

"What are you doing here?" Victor asked when our breathing had returned to normal.

"I wanted to get laid, why do you think?"

"Pardon me?"

"Never mind."

An owl screamed in the distance.

Was someone going to die tonight?

Yeah. The owl's dinner.

"You know where your army is going, don't you?"

I could just see the outline of his face, the whites of his eyes. I wanted to see him clearly. Imprint his being onto my memory. My memory that remembered every time we had ever been together. For better or for worse.

"South."

"South! Yes! That's where my people are! That's where the City is. Don't you remember any of the time we spent together? Anything your mother taught you?"

"My mother is dead," he said. "I remember our time. It was nice."

"Nice?" The son of a bitch. No. The bastard. No. I couldn't even call him a name without casting aspersions on his mother's character. "Listen, that was the best time you've ever had in your entire life."

He sighed. "Yes. A wonderful childish memory. Is that supposed to change how I live my entire life?"

"You're fucking right it better change your life! For one thing, we created a child. You have a son. Not that he belongs to you or anything. Or to me. But he is part of your flesh and blood. A tiny part. A tiny fucking sperm. Yet, he looks like your twin."

"I don't understand you!"

Twentieth-century slang didn't translate well.

"Sorry. I'm just trying to say, you have a son. A grown-up boy. His name is Hart."

"I have many children."

I wished I could see his face. I wanted to slap it.

"And you speak so warmly of them." I sighed. "This isn't working, is it? You feel nothing, do you?"

"Of course I feel something." He pulled me toward him. I put my head against his chest. Yes. Yes, this was the place. The spot. *Never let me go.* "I have always loved you," he whispered.

"I know," I said, "but it won't keep you from destroying my people, or yourself, will it?"

No answer. Only night-in-the-forest sounds.

"I want to show you something then," I said.

"I can't leave here."

"You won't have to. I promise. Your body will stay right here." I reached into my bag and pulled out a couple of berries. "Here, take these." I pressed them onto his palm. Mild relaxants.

"What are they?"

"Trust me. Just take them."

I could feel him staring at me, weighing the possibilities.

"Victor, I have loved and hated you for thousands of years, but I have never tried to kill you. Please, trust me."

A shadow of his hand moved in the shadow of the night and he swallowed the berries.

"They will connect you to MommaEarth and to me."

"Keelie—"

"Just sit. Relax." I stood. I planted my feet

firmly on the ground and raised my arms upward. "I call upon the Goddesses of the east and the air, help me to dare! I call upon the Goddesses of the south and fire, help me with my desires! I call upon the Goddesses of the west and water, help me to be a healed and healing daughter! I call upon the Goddesses of the north and the Earth, help me with my rebirth!" I crossed my arms over my chest. "I call upon the Goddess that is me, help me to be, help me to see." The earth shook, the air quivered, electricity moved up through the ground and grabbed my feet, rooted me to the earth. I cried out as the energy moved up through me, as the Goddess of a Thousand Names enveloped me. Waves of pleasure undulated through me. Light moved out of my fingers toward the stars. I felt older than existence. Younger than my daughter. All of my daughters. Powered with remembering.

I drew a circle in the air, above Victor and me, encircling us. As I moved, a line of pale blue came out of my finger, until we were surrounded by a cool blue light.

I could see Victor's beautiful face. He looked up at me, dazed.

"The circle is closed," I said.

I leaned down and put my hand on Victor's chest. "There's no place like home. There's no place like home."

As I moved my hand away, a tiny z of lightning went from me to him. I took his hand and pulled him up. He tried to reach for his clothes.

"You came into this world naked, and that's how you'll leave it," I said.

"Who are you?" he asked.

"I am your Keelie," I said, "and we're going on a journey. Think of yourself as Scrooge, and I'm the ghost of things past, present, and future. All wrapped up in this beautiful package."

The world filled me and I pulled Victor toward me. "Come," I whispered.

We stood on a sun-drenched hillside, surrounded by time. It moved quickly around us, circling us, looping back into itself. Babies were born, grew, died, folded themselves back into the womb of the Earth. Seasons spiraled in and out. Communities built homes that were a part of the landscape, not separate. The people made love, art, held ceremonies, honored life and death, felt passion and peace. We were surrounded, held by all. Loved.

I gasped at the pleasure of it, at the seemingly endless time of love and peace. I re-membered it all. Victor watched. After a time, an eon? he let go of my hand and sat on the earth. He looked at me, "May we stay here?" Tears flowed down his face.

"Come," I said, holding out my hand to him.

"I don't want to leave."

"There's more," I said. "There is the present."

I took his hand and the sun exploded. Blinded us. When the light faded, it was night. But we could see and hear all.

We stood in the sand, near a copse of trees, emerald grass, a stream. Two young lovers laughed together, moved, made love. Created love. Kept love between them. Created the Goddess each time they chose love.

"I wanted to stay with you," Victor whispered.

I looked at the face of my earlier self and wondered if I had ever been that young.

"I loved you instantly," he said. "I had never loved anyone, except for my mother, until I saw you. I was terrified you would die before I got to see you open your eyes because I knew—"

"Knew what?"

"That you would be my salvation."

I laughed. A Goddess laugh. The world shook. "You must save yourself, Victor. And we must save the world. Isn't that what this is all about?"

"Can't we stay here?" he asked.

"But you know how it turns out."

We moved through time and the night again. We stood overlooking his encampment.

"Feel their dreams."

Dreams of killing.

We floated down to his father's tent. Lee, the father. We went inside. Lee was pushing himself

309

into some young girl. Her face was buried in a pillow as Lee grunted over her.

"My sister," Victor said. He tried to reach for his father but he was only spirit without form.

"All women are your sisters, Victor."

We drifted away, over the countryside, flying together. Ethereal night birds. To my village.

"Feel their dreams," I said as we walked alongside our homes.

Dreams of love. Ben on his boat. Grace spooned up to her lover. Grand Keelie alone. Lilith. Lee. Pearl.

I kissed my daughter Anna. She smiled in her sleep, knowing she had been kissed by the Goddess.

"We still live as they did in times past. The world you wished to stay in still exists. Today."

We flew to the City. A barrier had been erected around it. We walked through the darkness until we were beside Hart. He lay sleeping. His face smooth. He looked like a boy. I kissed him. He smiled in his sleep, just as his sister had.

"This is your son," I said.

"My son. He looks like you. Beautiful."

"He is beautiful, but he is your twin. He is you. And it is you you are destroying."

"We could take him away from here. All of us could go someplace, where my father would never find us."

We floated away again and looked down over the City.

"Perspective, Victor. Perspective."

We tripped through time. It battered us.

Fire raged. Death. After death. After death. The land was scorched.

Victor put his arm across his eyes to hide from it all.

"The father won, Victor. He was victorious. And behold, this is his world."

Body upon body piled up, skeleton after skeleton, until they reached to infinity.

"Nine million women, give or take, killed during the Burning Times."

Flames licked Victor's feet, kissed him.

Time slowed. Snapped still.

We watched.

As children we ran through a meadow and listened to the heartbeat of the Earth. Grew. Made love.

The inquisitors beat and then raped me.

Victor screamed.

"Stop them!" Time.

He rescued me. We made love in the abbey. Ran through the French countryside. Got on a ship for the New World.

"We were looking for a better place then," I said, "running away from it all."

"Did it work?" he pleaded.

Time snapped us into the jungle. The sword

sliced through the air and into Victor's chest. Cut away his life.

The jungle burned and the survivors ran. I ran.

"I can't watch," Victor said.

"There's so much more."

Time spun again. Killing after killing. Genocide after genocide. Air and rivers choked. Dying. Dying. Dying.

Time snapped still.

We were brother and sister again.

While Daddy watched, we did it.

I split into too many parts.

Danced into suicide.

Drowned in suicide.

Bled onto the carpet.

While Victor tried to stop it all. Run from it all. Hide from it all.

I fell into pieces.

And he tried to put me back together again.

He sat alone in the ruins of his mansion, the light in his eyes nearly extinct.

"And the father. Where is he?"

"Living it up in Florida."

We floated away from it, above it. The air we hung in was dirty. Tasted of metals.

"Is nothing sacred?" Victor asked.

"Nothing," I replied.

We spun back through time again. Watched

it all unravel. Until we were on the forest floor again, his camp walking distance.

He was shivering.

I turned off the blue light and let him put on his clothes.

"The circle is open but unbroken," I whispered.

An owl hooted above us.

We shook off time lag.

I sank down onto the Earth and let the energy flow back into her.

I was Keelie again.

Victor reached for me. I knelt next to him and put my arms around him.

"I will try to stop my father," Victor said. "I promise."

We fell asleep in each other's arms.

Twenty-seven

••••••••••••••••

I opened my eyes to morning light and the sight of Lee the father and screamed.

He grabbed my arm, and I jerked away. Victor and I jumped to our feet. He pushed me behind him and I stepped out next to him.

"Whoring again, Victor?" Father Lee said.

Four or five of his troops surrounded us, all dressed up for war.

"You are not setting a good example for your men," Father Lee said.

"I apologize," Victor said. He looked at me. "You may be on your way now, madam."

Father Lee laughed. "You are foolish, Victor. Don't you recognize her clothing? She is the enemy. She's probably a spy. We shall have to kill her at sundown. Or thereabouts. Maybe after breakfast."

Victor stepped in front of me again. I wished he would stop doing that.

"I lied, Father. She is my wife."

Oh, really?

Father Lee's face flushed dark red.

"You fool! She will be nothing but trouble!"

"But she is mine, and you have no right to touch her."

"I have the conqueror's right!" Father Lee screamed.

"She is my wife," Lee said quietly, "and I lay claim to her life and death."

All of this went against everything I believed, of course, but I sensed he was saving my ass, so I said nothing.

"I told you, as leaders, we should be without women!" Father Lee screamed.

"Then why is my sister in your tent?" Victor asked.

Father Lee looked as though he was going to hit his son. But he did not.

"This woman, this wife of yours, cannot travel with us," Father Lee said. "I want her confined and guarded."

"The other women can watch her," one of the other men said.

"I am responsible for her!" Victor said.

Father Lee turned away. "I have said all I wish to say on this matter. We are leaving soon." He walked away. The other men remained until Victor and I followed Father Lee.

Victor put his hand on my arm. "I will try to stop this, I promise you."

I watched the back of Father Lee. He would not be dissuaded; his troops would not follow Victor.

I took Victor's hand and squeezed it.

They threw me into a tent crowded with women. It stank of urine and perspiration.

"She is the enemy," the guard said. "But she must remain alive."

The mass of women watched me. I backed against the tent. I could see their bodies, could see they were breathing, but the women were gone. No soul. Battered and hunted and degraded. I closed my eyes and tried to breathe in the Goddess, tried to feel the energy of the Earth. Just a twinge.

I opened my eyes and looked at the women again.

Then I wept. I sat on the ground and cried. Soon the whole world would be filled with women like these. With men like those outside. I sobbed and sobbed. Wailed.

Alone. None grieved with me. None of the women knew what had been lost.

I heard the army leave. Most of the women went outside to say good-bye. They wept and then started cooking. I tried to leave the tent, but a woman bigger than I pointed a knife at me and pushed me back inside. When I tried crawling under the tent, another woman punched me in the face.

So I sat on my haunches and waited.

And hoped against all I knew to be true that Victor could succeed in changing his father's mind.

Hopeless. Hopeless.

I tried to feel the Goddess, bring her into my heart.

All was dead around me.

Near dark, while they ate supper, the women actually laughed and told a story or two. They wandered in and out of the tent and seemed to ignore me. I slowly moved to the darkest corner. When they were making a good deal of noise, I took out my knife and made a slice through the tent. No one heard. In the next moment, I stepped outside into the almost fresh air and ran up the dusk-covered hill toward home.

I hadn't had food or water all day, so it wasn't long before my run dropped to a slow walk. I had to conserve my energy or I'd never make it, yet I had to reach my city before the army. I had to protect them. Somehow. All my instincts and intuition seemed deadened. I tried to smell food and water, listen for a stream. But I heard nothing! Smelled nothing!

Terror washed over me. I kept walking. It would all come back to me. Just as soon as I got away from the dead women.

Then I realized I was walking over dead ground.

The army had come this way. No wonder I felt nothing.

I continued through the dark.

After a time, I heard a stream.

"Blessed be!" I cried and ran toward it. I tripped over bushes and roots two or three times before I reached the water. I fell to my knees and cupped water into my mouth again and again. I had no container, so I couldn't take any with me. I drank my fill and then left the riverside for the open meadows once again.

I walked and walked. I developed a stitch in my side and could barely walk for about an hour. Finally, I had to stop and rest.

I closed my eyes. "Mother Lilith! Mother Lilith! Please, hear me. Get everyone out! They're coming! They're coming!"

I listened. Tried to sense her. Or any thing. Any body. Nothing.

I had never felt so alone in my life.

I have heard that when a mother's child is in danger, she gets superhuman strength: she embodies the Goddess and saves her child. My entire world was being threatened and my strength ebbed away. When daylight came, I found some fruit trees. I chewed on the food of the trees and my body ached and throbbed with pain. Agony.

I screamed.

They were dying.

I

knew

they

were

All

dying.

I called upon the Goddess. The Earth. Eriskegal. Raven. Everyone and everything I knew.
If I was God-us why was I powerless?

I had to be there. Help them. Help them.

I hurried. Ran. Fell into a cramp. Walked
again.

Then I smelled it.

Fire.

Smoke rose above the hills in the distance.

I wept and ran. Fell and wept. Walked. This
was land I knew. I could see where the army
had walked. Stalked. Tramped.

The air was heavy with smoke.

I ran.

The fields. The fields.

I stopped on the scorched Earth. The fire had
passed over it quickly. Our crops were gone.
The Earth was black all around. Not the deep
beautiful rich black Earth, fertile for planting, or
the black darkness of the menstrual cave. But
dead black. Killed. Murdered.

My mother's crops were all gone. We would have nothing to eat this winter.

I laughed, cried. Winter. Winter! What would it matter if everyone was dead?

I ran toward the river and up to the menstrual caves. Maybe Mother Lilith had heard my pleas in the night. Maybe my family was safe. Safe.

I ran into darkness. Ran into the walls. Pushed away, my face bloody. Hurried. I heard nothing. They weren't here. They weren't safe.

"Momma?"

"Anna!" I cried. A light appeared. My daughter raised her arms to me. I picked her up and held her tightly. "Momma," she cried. "Momma."

"It's all right," I whispered. "I'm here."

The darkness moved as many came toward me. Lots of women. Some men and children. Safe. Safe.

"Daughter?" Mother Lilith!

"Sister." Sister Lee. Safe.

"Aunt." Pearl. Safe. I sank to my knees and wept with relief.

"Are we all safe?" I finally asked.

Mother Lilith knelt next to me. "No. There wasn't time."

"How did you know?" I asked. "How did you know they were coming?"

"A man came into the city. He was nearly dead. Your warrior. He had escaped them and somehow got to us before they came. Blown here by the breath of the Goddess, he said."

"Has my son returned from the City yet?"

"No," Mother Lilith answered.

"Where is Victor?" I asked. "Is he still here?"

Mother Lilith shook her head. "We brought him here, he was so weak. But when he came to, he left."

"I must find him," I said.

"Momma," Anna said, "don't go."

"It's not safe," Mother Lilith said. "They're still in the city."

"They have burned your fields," I said.

My mother's eyes watered. "We can grow new crops. But many of our friends are dead. I can feel it. We all can."

Anna pulled on my hand. "Please don't go."

I kissed her. "I'll be back."

"Keelie—" my mother started.

"I have to find him." I turned and left the menstrual cave. At least some of us were safe. My child. Mother. Sister. Niece.

My feet crunched over the burned Earth as I hurried toward the city.

The meadow was swept clean of anything living. The fire had eaten all. The trees were black sticks, smoldering still with the fire. And the buildings. They were all gone or burning, flames reaching out of windows to pull more air inside. I could not take it all in. Despite what I had already seen through time. This was home. This was the place: no place like home. It was gone. Father Lee's troops laughed as they watched the flames. There weren't many of them. Had the rest continued on? Bodies lay near the ruins. My community. My friends. I ran toward the burning city Center.

Seph lay on the steps. Grace next to him. They were dead.

I ran.

Kide. A trooper pulling his spear from Kide's back.

Camie. My childhood playmate. Her child smothered in her bosom.

These men laughed at the dead. Laughed at the flames. Ignored me. I was harmless. Everyone was harmless now. This city was home to desolation and ruin.

I hadn't been prepared for this.

Not this.

I ran toward Grand Keelie's house. Her garden. I ran past the gnarled olive tree, into her sanctuary.

She was curled on the ground, a bloody tapestry at her feet.

"No!" I cried. "No!" This couldn't have happened. Couldn't. I had left them all safe and whole. I touched her face. Cool with death.

"Blessed be," I whispered.

I ran out again and down toward my mother's

house. It was gone. Completely destroyed. I wandered through the smoky debris.

"We found nothing of value anywhere," someone called.

I jumped out of the debris. Nothing of value?

I looked toward the voice. Someone reporting to the great Father Lee. He stood on the steps of the burning city Center. Someone else dragged away the bodies of Grace and Seph. I wanted to kill them. I wanted to kill them all.

Father Lee turned his evil head and looked at me.

He smiled.

"My son's wife. How nice to see you again."

The smoke burned my eyes. Drifted in and around the ruins.

"You are a butcher!" I cried.

"And a good one, too," he said. He still smiled.

The smoke eddied around a bent and bloodied figure. Walking through time toward us. Hadn't we played this scene before?

Victor.

Father Lee stopped smiling.

I ran to Victor.

His face was swollen and bruised, his right arm broken and useless at his side. He leaned against me.

"I tried to stop him," he whispered, his breath

323

almost gone. His power spent. "He cannot be stopped."

No. You're wrong. He can be stopped. Someday. Someday.

"We are finished here!" Father Lee called to his lieutenant.

"That's all! You destroy us, destroy our way of life. Our home. And you just say, 'we're finished here'?" I screamed.

Father Lee stopped and turned to me.

"Victor, tell your whore to be quiet or we'll have to kill her, too."

I'm not quite certain what happened next. Another of those moments when time slowed, when I knew if I were only quicker, smarter, something, I could change things. Victor picked up a spear. It seemed to appear from the burned dust. His strength returned momentarily.

"I have seen the future," he said, "and it will end here, today."

He threw the spear with all the strength of a warrior. He had been trained to do this since he was a boy. Time stopped. Everything stopped but the spear. It flew through the smoky air.

Father Lee did not move. He watched Victor. Did not watch the spear. Which fell useless on the steps of the city Center.

Father Lee laughed and started to walk away.

Hart was suddenly on one of the walls of the

city Center. Where had he come from? Thank the Goddess he was safe. Safe.

Father Lee still laughed.

Victor sagged.

Hart stared at Victor. Held a spear in his hand. Saw the enemy. Saw his father the enemy.

I screamed at him. Father Lee laughed.

"Father!" Hart screamed.

Victor looked up. Hart let go of the spear, aimed it at Victor's heart.

I had lived this before. Seen the father kill the son. Seen Victor die. I could not watch it again.

Nothing mattered in that moment except stopping some endless cycle. I didn't think. I just moved. I stepped in front of Victor.

Heard Hart's scream as the spear rammed my chest and pinned my heart to my rib cage.

That was all I knew.

Twenty-eight

••••••••••••••••••••

Wow.
    Coyote licked my face.
Eriskegal slapped it.

Twenty-nine

••••••••••••••••

I opened my eyes. I was sitting, facing Eriskegal. She combed worms out of her hair.

"What the fuck did you do that for? What kind of message is that for young girls?"

"What are you talking about?"

"Stepping in front of that spear. Saving Victor's life. *Stupido.*"

"I wasn't thinking message. I wasn't thinking. I was just tired of it. I'd seen him die before and I hadn't been able to do anything about it. He would have done the same for me."

"You left your children motherless!"

I hung my head. "I know. I know. Leave me alone! I just acted on instinct. Hart didn't know his father had saved most of us."

"So you deemed his life more important than yours?"

"Get off my back, you fucking bitch!" I

screamed. "I just saw the end of paradise and I don't need you to criticize every move I made."

Eriskegal cocked an eyebrow at me. "Not every move, darling. Just that last one."

"So what happened?"

"What do you mean?"

"What happened to Victor and Pearl and Anna and Lilith. Back then."

"Don't you know? You've been to the twentieth century. It just turned out dandy, didn't it?"

"I am fed up with your fucking riddles. I did it. I took that wonderful magical mystery tour through fucking hell—"

"And paradise. It's very important that you don't forget that little detail."

I sighed and leaned back into the chair. "I only wish I hadn't seen the end of it. It was like nothing I could have ever imagined."

"But now you can."

"Now I can what?"

"Imagine it. Envision it. Know it."

"All right," I said. "I get it. I get it."

"Do you?"

I sighed and closed my eyes. Yes, I got it. "The Goddess went underground for five thousand years—or three days, depending upon who's telling the tale," I said. "The God, the father, took over."

Eriskegal nodded. She leaned forward. "So,

you've put all the pieces together, Jigsaw Woman?"

I tried to feel in my body once again what I had come to know: I had to remember those thousands of years before the father—I had to feel all the people who were me, who are my body.

"A temple to what has been and what could be," Eriskegal said.

"It's time for the Goddess to be reborn. To come up out of the underworld."

"And kick some butt!" Eriskegal roared.

"It'll never be the same as it was," I said. "I will never be the same."

"Delving deep does that, doesn't it? You have seen the light. The darkness. Demons cling to you!"

"I'm so exhausted."

Eriskegal shrugged. "It will be an interesting time to watch. Structures will shatter. A kind of Goddess menopause. The women of the world have already started to feel it."

"A jigsaw world."

"Ain't it a puzzle. Are you ready to go into the world again?" she asked as she ate her fingernails.

I nodded. "You know, you've gotten rather sage since last we met. What happened?"

Eriskegal threw her hands up. "Life!" She grinned her rotten grin. "So where to?"

I shrugged. "Back to Pearl. Or forward to Pearl. She needs a mother."

Eriskegal nodded. She had known it all along, of course.

I started to get up. Eriskegal shook her head. "No. Stay there. Just lean forward and you will go where you need to go." She winked. "Until we meet again, darling."

"Not if I see you first."

I leaned forward and reached out. Eriskegal leaned forward and reached out.

My hand touched cool glass. A mirror. I was looking into a mirror.

Eriskegal grinned. I touched my face.

My own grin.

"Why, you clever little bitch," I said.

I looked around for the pegs. They were empty—the corpses gone. I had made the journey. I was Her. Goddess. Alive and awake with stories to jog memories—give hope that all was not lost. We are capable of love. Eternally.

And we were capable of pulling the structures down. Or planting flowers on those structures. Whatever worked.

But now—

I balled my hand into a fist and smashed it against the mirror.

The mirror flew into a million pieces.

"Tata!" we called.

*   *   *

I was looking into another mirror.

Seeing Father Lee's face. Twentieth-century Father Lee in his condo in Florida.

So finally we met alone.

Father Lee pulled at his face, apparently not seeing me, and then went and sat at his desk. It looked out at the ocean. The window was open, and I could hear the soothing sounds of the ocean, the laughter of children playing, clippers opening and closing over hedges. Father Lee looked old.

I hadn't remembered him so old.

Old age had made him look less powerful. No, he just was less powerful. The age of the Father was ending.

A newspaper lay folded on the bed. I sat next to it.

MILLIONAIRE LEE BEAUFORT CHARGED WITH EMBEZZLEMENT, the headline read.

I shook my head. "So you not only stole people's lives and souls, but money as well. How very capitalistic of you." I got up and went to stand close to him. He seemed frail and useless. I was no longer afraid of him.

"I remember every evil nasty cruel thing you ever did. Starting from the beginning. Let me tell you, you daughter-fucker, your reign is over. Your time is over. Time to step down. Time to face the truth. I don't need you anymore. The world doesn't need you any longer."

Father Lee stared out the window for a moment. Then he opened a desk drawer and pulled out a revolver.

"You fucked your children," I said. "You fucked the entire world and you decide to end it all when they threaten to take away your money and put you in jail?"

He turned and faced me. He looked right at me. Saw me.

"You shouldn't have remembered," he said.

My knees started shaking.

"You shouldn't have remembered what I did to you," he said. "And you shouldn't have ever told anyone."

"You stupid fuck! I never did tell anyone. That was the problem. Well, now I'm going to. I'm going to tell everyone everything I remembered. The good, bad, and the bizarre. And most of all: the time before you existed!"

"It's all your fault."

"You're a coward," I said.

He raised the gun to his head.

"You shouldn't have remembered."

"Well, I did. And there's nothing you can do about it. Whether you live or die, that's your choice. I am not responsible for you." I leaned close to him. "I will not die for you."

"You died for Victor."

I stared at him and moved a bit away.

Did he remember it all, too?

"That was a long time ago. I did it because I didn't want him to die for you again. But I'm not doing it now. I'm not dying for you or your son! You were wrong. You were wrong. I was your daughter, your sister, your mother. I was yourself. You shouldn't have fucked with me. You shouldn't have done any of it."

He cocked the hammer and turned the gun toward his face.

I turned, walked out of the room, and slammed the door behind me.

"It's all your fault!" he screamed.

I heard a shot. A pop. A poof. He'd gone and done it. Daddy dearest was dead.

My knees buckled.

The lights went out.

Chirty

....

I opened my eyes to first gold and then black.
The fire crackled. I smelled delicious herbs
and food brewing.

Raven's cottage.

I slowly sat up and threw off the covers.

"Raven?" I called. The raven looked down at
me from the rafters, but no one answered my
call. I was alone.

Outside, snow piled up around the windows.
I sat down again and pulled the blanket up
around me.

I closed my eyes. "It's all your fault," I heard
my father say, heard the gun explode.

I ate stew, drank water, and put more wood
on the fire.

I sat and lay down and slept. I stared at the
fire. I watched the raven.

Watched the snow start to melt.

One day I got up and looked in the mirror. White scars still ringed my neck and thighs.

They would never go away. Victor and Griff had been stupid to promise it. To want it.

Besides, these scars were the least of it.

"Honey," I said to my reflection, "this body and soul has more scars than I can count." I touched my face: Anna. My breasts: Belle. My legs: Lee. They had been and were no more. No, that wasn't true. They were a part of me. All of them. I held the world—the universe—in my body.

I smiled and blew an air kiss at my reflection.

Soon after, I walked out of the woods and got Pearl. Hand in hand we walked back to the cottage.

I held her in my arms for a long time, listened to her dreams and nightmares. Helped her remember.

Grace and Ben visited.

They brought food. The raven watched as they chopped and peeled and boiled. The cottage filled with the aromas of delicious food. Pearl and I sat on the couch watching and listening to the spring birds sing mating songs to each other outside.

There was a knock on the door. Pearl ran to open it. Griffin stood on the threshold.

"Hello, Griffin," I said. I got up and greeted

him. He looked tired and filled with grief. I remembered Lilith had killed herself, unable to find a place for herself in this scattered world. "I'm sorry about Lilith. Please, join us. Pearl, this is my Uncle Griffin."

"Uncle?" Griffin said.

I laughed. "It's a long story. And I'll tell you about it, I promise." Ben and Grace came and welcomed him into the cottage. Ben gave him apple cider.

"How is everyone?" I asked.

"Lilith is dead. But you know that. Hart is in some kind of therapy. Werewolves Anonymous or something."

Everyone laughed. Griffin smiled. I think it was the first time he had smiled in a long while.

"And Victor?"

"He kind of disappeared after his father killed himself."

I sighed. So it had really happened. Father Lee was dead. Felled by his own petard.

"You're going to tell us where you've been all this time," Ben said to me. "Right? We're making all this food in the hopes that you've got a good story."

I laughed. "Yep. The story of the woman who was pieced together like a puzzle. I'm just your ordinary jigsaw woman. A puzzlement to all she meets!"

They laughed again.

Pearl pulled at my hand. "You're silly, Mom!"
I smiled.

"I want to show you something, Pearl. We'll be right back," I said to the others. I grasped Pearl's tiny cool hand in mine, and we walked outside. The raven followed us. Pearl and I walked to a clearing a little away from the house. The raven hopped onto a branch of a nearby oak.

"Daughter Pearl, all that you see is a part of you. The trees, birds, sky, air, and all that is beyond, it's all a part of you. Treat all as you wish to be treated."

I squatted on the ground. Pearl knelt next to me. I dug my fingers into the Earth. "This is the mother. She provides all for us, and she is all of us. Everything. You and me. We create her daily, and she creates us. Can you feel her breath?"

Pearl closed her eyes. She smiled. "The wind!"

I laughed. "Yes. Can you feel her warmth?"

Pearl tilted her head to the sun. She smiled and nodded.

"Can you smell her body?"

Pearl breathed deeply and smiled. "Yes."

"Can you feel her in yourself? The Goddess that is you?"

I watched her close her eyes, settle herself into the soil, smile.

"A little bit," she finally said, just as I had thousands of years ago.

"Dearest Pearl, your body is a gift from the Goddess and the Goddess is a gift to you. No one has a right to touch it without your permission. Your body is yours. Take pleasure in it."

Pearl pressed her hands into the ground. "Momma," she whispered.

A moment later she looked at me. "Momma." She held her arms out to me. I embraced her.

"I love you," I said.

"Me, too," she said.

We got up, dusted ourselves off, and went into the cottage again.

After a sumptuous dinner, we sat around the fireplace together, letting the fire take off the early spring chill. I began the stories, telling them all about Anna and Belle and Lee. And Victor. Helping them re-member.

They all cried. And Pearl curled up on my lap. I wove the tales and felt the pieces falling into place. They cried. Wept.

I told them about the Burning Times. And Victor and Pearl and Anna and Belle and Lee and all of them. More pieces snapped into place. The world began taking shape. Pearl sat up, wide-eyed.

Then I took them back into the world of Mother Lilith and Grand Keelie and Grandmother Belle and Sister Lee, Niece Pearl, Son

Hart, Daughter Anna, friends Ben and Grace and Uncle Griffin. I watched their faces, felt them trying to envision it. Told them of a time when people talked to the trees, animals, rivers, the Earth, and each other. And the more I talked, the more they could envision it. See it. Imagine it.

When Pearl grew tired, I sent them all to bed. They curled up in sleeping bags all over the tiny cottage. I sat at the table and listened to their peaceful slumber and smiled.

Outside, the moon silvered a pathway to her.

I quietly got up and went outside to the clearing where Pearl and I had been earlier.

I breathed the cool air deeply. Crickets welcomed me.

I rubbed the bumps off my arms.

A twig snapped. I turned.

Victor stood in the moonlight.

"Keelie?"

Although he looked better than the last moment I had seen him, before I stepped in front of the spear, he didn't look well. He was bent and thin, his beard ragged.

He had forgotten himself.

"Keelie?"

I held my hand out to him. "Yes, Victor, it's me."

He grasped my hand and pulled me toward him. We embraced. I felt his warmth clear to my toes, felt his electricity, his love. The soul of him that had always been trying to get out. He had been trying to remember himself for such a long while.

I would tell him the stories, too.

We sighed together, trembling, not wanting to let go.

Until finally I did. He stood a little straighter. I ran my hand across his beard.

"You're quite a sight," I said.

He cringed.

"A welcome one," I said. "Go inside. We'll feed you. The others are here, too."

"The others?"

"Griffin. Grace. Ben. Our daughter, Pearl. Go on, it'll be all right."

I watched him go to the open picture window and wait.

Then I raised my hands to the moon. "Blessed be, Momma. The circle is open, but unbroken."

I turned and started back toward the cottage and the people within. I touched my hand to my heart.

"There's no place like home," I whispered. "No place like home."

THE GAIA WEBSTERS
coming from Roc in June

In this wonderful preview of Kim Antieau's *The Gaia Websters*, the healer Gloria finds herself in a desperate situation—the townspeople in her care are falling ill to a mysterious illness, and she must find the cure or else her very life may be in danger . . .

The day was a blur of healings. Over and over. Some people got sick again, some did not. By evening, I could hardly move. I stumbled into the courtyard of my clinic, exhausted beyond anything I could remember. I dropped to the ground and pulled myself up to lean against the palm tree.

Suddenly Primer was there, towering over me like some bent shadow out of a nightmare. "I told you you should have come with me."

"What are you talking about, Primer? Leave me alone. I'm exhausted."

"I said if the governor wanted you, he would get you. You belong to us."

"What?" I wished I could see his face. "Are you saying you had something to do with what's happened here?" I could not move, I was so tired. I had no adrenaline left. I closed my eyes.

"I'm telling you that if you care for these people, you will come with me back to the governor."

My stomach twisted with unfamiliar fear. Where was Cosmo? There. On the porch sleeping. Was this all a dream?

"Will you come?" Primer growled.

Had Primer poisoned the entire town? Killed Cosmo? Just to get me to visit the governor? I had healed Primer's ankle; I should have known he was capable of this.

"Yes. I'll go."

"When?"

"As soon as everyone is well."

Suddenly the numbers and letters flashed in front of me. Someone screamed. I floated away.

I awakened to a starry sky. My body creaked as I sat up. Then I remembered Primer. Had he really been there? I got up and went to Cosmo on the porch. I touched him and he did not move. My heart raced. I put my hands on his head. He was alive, but drugged. Or poisoned. Like the townspeople?

I would kill Primer. No. But I would make certain he made restitution. I was exhausted. I needed rest before I could do anything else. I needed Cosmo. My hands finally felt a connection. After a minute or so, Cosmo yawned and opened his eyes. He whimpered.

I hugged him. "Don't let that man near you again, Cos."

I went inside the clinic with Cosmo, bolted and blocked the door, and fell to sleep again, one hand on Cosmo. I had coyote dreams and awakened late morning to Georgia pounding on the door. Cosmo yelped. I put my hand on his head and gave him a quick healing. He seemed his usual self.

Then I unblocked the door and let Georgia in.

"What's going on?" she asked. "I've never seen this door locked!"

"Primer poisoned Cosmo," I said, "and I think he might be responsible for everyone being sick."

"What?"

I shut the door again, motioned Georgia to a chair, and sat across from her.

"When I came back last night. Primer was here. Cosmo was on the porch out cold. Primer said he'd warned me I should go with him and that if I really cared about you all I'd better go with him now."

"That's incredible. But how could he have made so many of us sick and why? That just keeps you here."

"It was a way of threatening me. 'See what I can do and I'll do worse if you don't come.' "

"I'm not convinced he poisoned us," Georgia said, "but he has, at the very least, used a bad situation to his advantage and he was wrong to threaten you."

"We still need to figure out why everyone is sick."

"Church and Jeri interviewed everyone to gather the information you asked for. They're in the church basement."

"Come on, Cos," I said. "I don't want you out of my sight."

As we started to leave, I noticed a bowl on the porch, empty except for a tiny pool of water in the bottom of it. I picked up the bowl and smelled it. Nothing. I tossed out the water, turned over the bowl, and followed Georgia to the church.

"Doesn't this place give you the creeps?" I asked her as we stepped inside.

"No. Why? I've been coming here my entire life."

"Yeah, but there wasn't a dead man hanging from a cross."

"That is bizarre," she agreed.

We walked downstairs. The place was nearly empty except for Jeri, Church, and Angel. Angel kissed me and handed me a bowl of nuts, seeds, and currants.

Church and Jeri greeted us.

"Good morning," I said as we sat with them.

Cosmo sniffed around behind me.

"What a sweet dog," Angel said. She crouched near him and he stuck his muzzle in her face.

"He's a coyote." I said. "Cosmo."

Church watched their friendly exchange, so unlike his own encounters with Cosmo.

"He's a sucker for a pretty face." I explained.

Georgia told Church. Jeri, and Angel what had happened last night between Primer and myself. Jeri paled.

"We need to hold a public meeting as soon as possible," she said.

"First, we need to get everyone well. What did you figure out?" I asked.

"Approximately eighty percent of the town's population became ill," Jeri said. "Of those eighty percent, sixty percent were reinfected, or got sick again. As far as we can tell, everyone is eating the same food and drinking the same water."

"The soup seemed to help some people," Church said, "but others got sick after eating it."

"Was there any difference? Like where they ate it?"

"Not where they ate it but where it was cooked. The people who ate the soup here generally got better or took longer to get sick again. Those who ate the soup from Millie's all got sick again."

"What's the difference?" I asked.

"The water," Georgia said. "I just remembered the church and a few of the houses have well water while the rest of us get ours from the reservoir."

I thought of the bowl on the clinic porch. Primer must have put poison in the bowl of water and hoped Cosmo would drink it. And in the reservoir.

"All right," Georgia said. "We'll need to make certain everyone gets their water from the church for a while. Also, we'll appoint someone to watch Primer until the town meeting. Gloria, you'll have to heal these people all over again. Are you up to it?"

I hoped so. "Sure," I said.

Jeri and Georgia left. I stayed to finish eating.

"I-I didn't know Primer was like that," Church said. "Threatening you. I thought—I don't know what I thought."

"You thought I was just being stubborn and pigheaded," I said. "Well, I was. I didn't know what he was like either. People sometimes surprise you."

"Do you need anything today?" he asked.

"Strength," I said. "I'm about out."

"I'll pray for you."

"Yeah, you do that."

I spent another day performing almost non-stop healings. By lunch, I was near tears, a rare occurrence for me. Jeri brought me lunch. When I finished, she led me to the next sick person. Cosmo followed me most of the day, but by afternoon, he was completely back to his old self. I hoped he stayed out of Primer's way. Once when I had a momentary breather, I thought of Benjamin and wondered if he had tried to get into town; if not, he was on his way to de Chelly. I had heard Louise Mayhi had her eye on him. She would be at the dance. She was probably ready to have babies and share with him her deepest darkest self. Or maybe she did not have a dark self. Maybe only I did. I placed my hands on the next patient. And the next.

As the day went on, my thought processes seemed to short circuit. Each time I touched a patient to heal, I connected for a moment with their souls, like always. And then disconnected. In my exhaustion, I started to believe each time I touched someone I was connecting with some great cosmic truth, only to have it yanked away when I withdrew my hands. I had no stories to tell, no lines of wisdom, not even nonsense words to babble.

When the last patient left, I was nearly blind with exhaustion. Tears streamed uncontrollably down my cheeks. Then someone—two someones—came to each side of me and led me outside. I noticed it was cold, but that was all. Then I was inside. Warmth. Softness. Cosmo's furry face. Then all blacked away.

Someone touched my hand, and I shattered.

One of the shards mirrored me shattered into a million pieces; another piece mirrored Church.

"Shhhh." A whisper. The glass froze into sand again and the wind blew it all back into the ocean, including all those broken pieces of me.

Still someone held my hand.

My body trembled. I felt as though lightning kept lacing through me, trying to connect heaven and earth.

A kiss awakened me.

Like Sleeping Beauty. Or the woman in the glass coffin. Or the woman who was the glass coffin.

I opened my eyes. My face was awash in tears. My own?

"Hello." Reverend Thomas Church smiled.

"You?"

His fingers squeezed mine. No more shattering.

"Where's Cosmo?" I asked.

Church released my hand as I carefully pushed myself up. I was in bed. The room was dark, like one of the Spanish missions. The refectory.

"Cosmo wanted to take a run," he said. "I left the door open so he could come and go. He doesn't growl at me any more."

"Wonders." I sighed deeply. "I've never treated that many people. I am really tired."

"You've been asleep for a day and a half."

"You're kidding?"

Angel knocked on the open door and then carried in a tray.

"Hi," she said shyly. She kissed my cheek. I felt a momentary shatter, as if I were going to split again, but her lips moved away and I was still whole.

"I'm not hungry," I said. "But thank you."

"They all said you're always hungry," she said.

I smiled. "I guess they were all wrong. But you can leave it. Maybe I'll get hungry again."

She smiled and put the tray on the table next to the bed. She glanced at Church, who was watching me, and then she left us alone.

"Are you going to marry that girl and put her out of her misery, or what?" I asked. I glanced at the food. It blurred into a mass of slop. I turned away.

Church moved the tray out of my sight.

"We talked to Primer," Church said, not answering my question. "Of course, he denied everything. No one else has gotten sick and we've kept a few teams patrolling the river and reservoir. Primer lifted the quarantine and he's leaving town."

"What did he say about me?"

"He said he never threatened you. He denied ever speaking to you that night."

I slowly stood. "I guess I have to go visit the governor."

"But Primer's gone."

"He's unseen. That doesn't mean he's gone. I don't want him coming back and causing more trouble. Is everyone feeling better?"

"Yes."

"Good. I'll get ready to leave soon." I suddenly felt woozy. I dropped down on to the bed again. "Maybe I'll eat a little first. Hey, Rev, is this your bedroom?"

"Yes."

"Very romantic. Where'd you sleep last night?"

"In the bed with you."

I grinned. "Yeah, right. So you do have a sense of humor."

"Apparently." He handed me a bowl of something that looked like gruel.

"Maybe I better go to Millie's cafe," I said. "But don't tell Angel."

Eventually, I made it outside. At Millie's I was treated like a returning hera. Half the town seemed to be packed inside the cafe. I was first given ginger tea. And then apple pie, hot currant bread and butter, pumpkin pie, pinto bean soup, corn on the cob, Cosmo lay at my feet, snapping at the crumbs. I did not have the heart to tell them I was not hungry, so I ate as much as I could.